PRAISE FOR THE CAIT MORGAN MYSTERIES

"In the finest tradition of Agatha Christie . . . Ace brings us the closed-room drama, with a dollop of romantic suspense and historical intrigue." —*Library Journal*

"Touches of Christie or Marsh but with a bouquet of Kinsey Millhone." —*Globe and Mail*

"A sparkling, well-plotted, and quite devious mystery in the cozy tradition." —*Hamilton Spectator*

"Perfect comfort reading. You could call it Agatha Christie set in the modern world, with great dollops of lovingly described food and drink." —CrimeFictionLover.com

THE
Corpse
WITH THE
Platinum
Hair

CATHY ACE

WITHDRAWN

TouchWood
Editions

TouchWood Editions
touchwoodeditions.com

LIBRARY AND ARCHIVES CANADA CATALOGUING IN PUBLICATION
Ace, Cathy, 1960–, author
The corpse with the platinum hair / Cathy Ace.

(A Cait Morgan mystery)
Issued in print and electronic formats.
ISBN 978-1-77151-087-5

I. Title. II. Series: Ace, Cathy, 1960– . Cait Morgan mystery.

PS8601.C41C665 2014   C813'.6   C2014-902762-1

Editor: Frances Thorsen
Copy editor: Grace Yaginuma
Proofreader: Cailey Cavallin
Design: Pete Kohut
Cover image: Kameleon007, istockphoto.com
Author photo: Jeremy Wilson Photography (jeremywilsonphotography.com)

 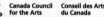

We gratefully acknowledge the financial support for our publishing activities from
the Government of Canada through the Canada Book Fund and the Canada
Council for the Arts, and from the Province of British Columbia through the
British Columbia Arts Council and the Book Publishing Tax Credit.

The interior pages of this book have been printed on 100% post-consumer
recycled paper, processed chlorine free, and printed with vegetable-based inks.

1 2 3 4 5 18 17 16 15 14

PRINTED IN CANADA

Dedicated to the Shirley in my life, my mum

OWNERS' PRIVATE DINING ROOM
TSAR! CASINO
LAS VEGAS

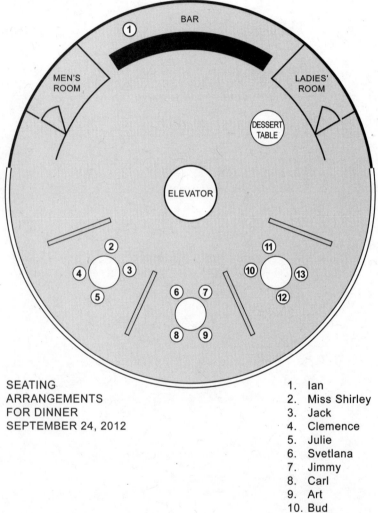

SEATING
ARRANGEMENTS
FOR DINNER
SEPTEMBER 24, 2012

1. Ian
2. Miss Shirley
3. Jack
4. Clemence
5. Julie
6. Svetlana
7. Jimmy
8. Carl
9. Art
10. Bud
11. Cait
12. Tom
13. Tanya

House Lights Down

THE PAST FEW HOURS HAD been an indulgent blend of delicious food, engaging conversation, Bud's wonderful company, and some exciting wines, all in a setting I never dreamed I'd get the chance to visit—the owners' private dining room at the fabulous Tsar! Casino and Hotel on The Strip in Las Vegas. I'd left our table for a moment and had just finished using the washroom's fancy hand dryer, which screamed like a jet engine while threatening to rip the skin from my fingers, when there was a deafening clang. The subtle lighting in the washroom cut out. Luckily, the pulsating neon beyond the floor-to-ceiling glass wall provided some illumination. I pulled open the door to the adjoining restaurant to discover whether it, too, had been plunged into darkness. It had. Even the piped operatic arias that had accompanied our dinner had fallen silent.

A woman called out, "Everybody stay where you are, please. The security system has been activated—the power is off because of it, and we're in a lockdown situation. The emergency lighting will come on in just a few seconds." The authoritative voice belonged to Julie Pool, head of the legal department at the casino, to whom I'd been introduced before dinner.

"I not afraid of dark, I afraid of furniture. Is *moving*." Svetlana Kharlamova's operatic Russian tones had been heard and praised around the world for decades. Now she was simply whining.

"Please, Madame, stay still. The furniture isn't moving, you are. Ms. Pool is correct. If we wait a moment, I'm sure everything will be just fine." Jimmy Green, the Diva Kharlamova's assistant, sounded testy, which was hardly surprising, given the way the woman had been acting toward him all evening.

Everyone in the private dining room heaved a sigh of relief when the backup lighting kicked in.

Everyone except Julie Pool, who screamed, "Oh no . . . Look! Somebody's skewered Miss Shirley to her seat with a silver saber."

Overture

WHAT JULIE POOL HAD SHOUTED sounded so bizarre that a few people smiled, even chuckled, as they followed her gaze, peering toward the seat in question.

As I approached, I knew immediately that this was no laughing matter. I spotted the hilt of a sword rammed against the upholstered back of the chair, its bloodied blade protruding from the front of Miss Shirley's limp body. The entire scene was bathed in the garish colors that flooded into the room from The Strip below. The blade itself reflected the starry, low-voltage emergency lighting.

"I faint!" exclaimed the Russian diva, swooning dramatically and causing all attention to turn from the corpse to her.

"No. No, you don't," replied her assistant as calmly as he could, given that his slight frame was already beginning to buckle under his charge's not inconsiderable bulk as she flailed her arms and moaned operatically. Jimmy steered her to a chair being pushed toward the wobbling couple by our barman for the evening, Ian. He looked flustered, which wasn't surprising. It was, after all, his boss who now sat dead in our midst.

I tried to get a better look at the body, and moved closer. I'm not horribly morbid; it's just that, as a criminal psychologist, I have a professional interest in crime. I was swiftly joined by Bud, whose big, warm hand wrapped itself around mine.

"Can't take you anywhere, can I?" he whispered, sighing as he squeezed my fingers.

I allowed myself a worried smile. "You're not wrong there," I said, and I shook my head in disbelief. "Whither I go, there follow the corpses."

"Is that a saying?" Bud asked, looking puzzled.

I sighed. "No, but it probably should be, given my track record. This time, all I did was leave you for five minutes to pop to the loo. What on earth happened while I was gone?"

"Before I answer that, let's at least make sure the poor woman's dead," said my very significant other, his face etched with concern. "Everyone seems to be fussing around our operatic diva over there, so let's be the ones who pay attention to the real victim, eh? I know from experience that it's possible to sustain such a devastating injury without being killed. The sword might have, somehow, missed every vital organ."

I nodded and looked around for a clean napkin through which Bud could check Miss Shirley's pulse without contaminating the scene. However, as I turned back empty-handed and finally got close enough to the poor woman to be able to look into her face, it was clear that we wouldn't need to check for signs of life. There was surprisingly little blood, but the only sparkle remaining in her glassy eyes was merely a reflection of the Vegas Strip, of which she had been the acknowledged queen. Miss Shirley, the woman who had inherited a fifty-one percent ownership of the world-famous Tsar! at midnight, just fifteen minutes ago, was very definitely dead.

"I think it went straight through her heart," observed Bud. He shook his head, then turned and gently rested his arm on my shoulder. "At least she wouldn't have felt much. Not that that's the point, of course. Terrible." His mouth was set in a thin line. "You okay, Cait?" He looked down at me, concern crinkling the skin at the corners of his eyes.

I smiled—as reassuringly as I could. "I'm fine, Bud." I nodded. "Better than Miss Shirley, in any case," I added wryly.

The deadening whiteness of the emergency lighting caught the silver in Bud's hair and eyebrows in a very fetching way, but their icy illumination gave his rugged features a haggard look.

He squeezed my shoulder as he said flatly, "This isn't going to be pleasant."

"No dessert, for one thing." I decided a wink was in order.

Bud allowed himself an indulgent smile, then shook his head. "Oh, Cait, tonight of all nights. Why tonight?"

I had to agree. "Murder is never a good thing, of course, and I'm so sorry it's spoiled what should have been your birthday celebration."

Bud looked puzzled. "Oh yes. My birthday," he said absentmindedly. *Odd.*

I wondered why he seemed so distracted—other than because he was staring at a corpse.

"Well, that's that," he said, as though he'd made some sort of decision. "We're in for a long night of questions once the cops arrive. Sorry, Cait." He looked . . . wistful. *Very odd.*

Any chance to ask him why he was acting so strangely disappeared as we were accosted by Julie Pool, who noticed us hovering over the body and rushed toward us.

"Stop it! You mustn't touch her. The police will be here any minute. The crime-scene people will want to do their thing. You'd better step away." Her sleek blond chignon sat demurely above the collar of her ice-blue suit, which skimmed her trim figure. Her skirt was far enough above her knee for me to be able to note that her legs were well toned and muscular. This woman was obviously much more familiar with the inside of a gym than I've ever been. Pearls glowed at her slender throat and on her ears, and her light floral perfume smelled expensive. It was almost as though Grace Kelly had been cast as a lawyer. She was a couple of inches taller than me and wore three-inch heels. I straightened my back.

"Please, don't be concerned, Ms. Pool," replied Bud in his calm, professional tones. "I know we haven't been introduced, but Cait here, who I know you met before dinner, tells me you're head of the legal department at this casino?" Julie nodded. "As you know, Cait and I are Tom White's guests tonight. My name's Bud Anderson, and I've been in law enforcement, as a homicide detective among other roles, for decades. I'm retired now, but believe me when I tell you that I know how to treat a crime scene, which this obviously is. You say the relevant agencies are on their way. I'm guessing there's an alarm sounding somewhere right now. Automatic response?"

Again Julie Pool nodded, but now she had a strange look about her. She looked intrigued and superior at the same time. I got the distinct impression that listening, nodding, and taking a backseat were not in her nature, but Bud has a way about him in a time of crisis. All those years on the force might have taken their toll, but they also prepared him to keep a level head in pretty much any circumstance.

"Good," continued Bud. He looked around, paying particular attention to the elevator that sat right in the middle of the room. "Okay, we're in a private dining room at the top of a giant Fabergé egg overlooking the Vegas Strip—"

Julie Pool held up her no-longer-trembling hand to cut across Bud's observations. "Sorry to be pedantic, Mr. Anderson, but it's not a *Fabergé* egg. It's in the *style* of a Fabergé egg. It is an *homage* to the artistic efforts of the Fabergé workshops. No, it is *not* a Fabergé egg, as my fellow legal professionals who work on behalf of that organization have been at pains to point out." She sighed. "And thank you for the introductions, but they are superfluous as I happen to know exactly who you are. In order for anyone to be admitted to the owners' private dining room, they have to be vetted by security. On this occasion they had to refer to me. You raised some interesting red flags on the system when we checked you out." She arched an eyebrow as she spoke, though she didn't use it quite as effectively as I have been known to use mine. "You too, Professor Morgan," she continued, turning her blue-gray eyes toward me. "You have a fascinating background. I can quite understand why you chose to move from the UK to Canada. All those terrible newspaper stories.

It must have been difficult for you." She paused for effect, tilting her head, a knowing smile twitching at her lips.

I understood exactly what she meant. Having been wrongly accused of my ex-boyfriend's murder when I was studying at Cambridge, I'd found it difficult to shake off the press, long after Angus's death made the headlines. When they sense blood in the water, the British tabloids have a well-earned reputation for never giving up the hunt for printable copy. I'd lost all sense of a private life, so I'd jumped at the chance to complete my doctoral work at the University of Vancouver, where I've spent a happy decade or so. I decided to play it cool, because this woman was beginning to irk me.

"You're right, it was difficult. But knowing that I was innocent of the crime of which I was accused made it a little easier. However, since you know about my life back in the UK, you must also be aware that I've gained some very high clearances in Canada and have worked with various law enforcement agencies in British Columbia on cases where they have used my skills as a victim profiler." I didn't phrase it as a question, because I knew it wasn't one.

"Indeed I do. I'm so pleased to see that the two of you are making a go of it as a couple, since the sad loss of your wife, Mr. Anderson." Julie Pool smiled almost sweetly as she spoke, the personification of passive-aggressive taunting.

I could tell by the way his jaw muscles twitched that Bud wasn't impressed by the woman's comments. I hated her for them, but, in typical fashion, Bud continued with his train of thought and spoke as though she hadn't interrupted him at all.

"So we are high above The Strip, your employer has, clearly, been viciously murdered, and we have only one point of access, which is now sealed, due to some sort of lockdown. How do we open up the elevator, so that the emergency services can reach us? Or is there an alternate route they can use?"

The lawyer's face betrayed no emotion as she replied, "There's a staircase, a fire escape, that leads off the men's washroom. It, too, will have been sealed automatically, as a part of the security system being activated, but both access points will open when I reset the system, and we'll get our full electrical power back on too. Alternatively, the fire escape can be opened using another code in the central monitoring office downstairs. It's the new security system that's kicked in—the one we had to install to allow us to get all this stuff on loan from the Hermitage Museum in Saint Petersburg." She gestured toward the various objets d'art and paintings that adorned the shoulder-high privacy panels that partitioned the three tables in the sumptuous room from each other. "It cost a fortune, took forever to get up and running, and there have been no end of bugs. The company we chose to install it was recommended by our head of security, something that nearly cost him his job. It was Miss Shirley's pet project, and a source of great annoyance to her. She said, more than once, that she'd show the people who installed it who was boss. I suspect she'll hold onto their invoice for quite some time before paying them."

She paused, and her expression told me she realized what she'd said. She dropped her eyes for a moment, then rallied. "At least, I suspect that's what Miss Shirley had planned to do. You see, the insurance company wouldn't let us install the artworks here until we could prove there was absolutely no way out with the swag if somebody lifted something. And I mean 'lifted' quite literally—everything here sits on a pressure sensor, even Miss Shirley's own collection of porcelain and gold, so if any item moves, the system kicks in . . . as it has done now. Though what could have moved I don't know." She cast her gaze around the room, giving more attention to the beautiful and priceless antiques that she'd dismissed just a moment ago.

I, too, surveyed the room. I'd already been sitting in it for a few hours, so I'd been able to enjoy much of the magnificent display of

Sèvres porcelain pieces, arranged atop the boxy wooden privacy screens. I'd been delighted to be so close to the magnificent paintings that were hung right on the wooden dividers, and therefore at eye level when we were dining. Delicate still-life studies, sweeping landscapes, and intimate portraits bedecked the room, many by artists whose work sold for hundreds of thousands of dollars.

"Everything seems to be where it should be," said Julie after a couple of moments, "and, as I said, everyone here's been vetted. Other than my husband, you are the only two guests who aren't members of the Tsar! Organization, so I find it difficult to believe there's a thief in our midst. Besides, Miss Shirley's collection is well known, and we've had a huge amount of publicity about the loans from Russia. No one would be stupid enough to buy anything stolen from here, surely?" She shook her head and tutted. "I don't know why I just said that. I must be more flustered than I thought. The one thing I know you can rely on in this world is the stupidity of the people within it."

Choosing to ignore Julie Pool's bleak view of her fellow human beings, I looked toward the round elevator pod in the middle of the dining room and noted that the entire thing was now covered by a cylinder of dark gray metal. It looked as though the tube had descended from the ceiling and locked into place. I reasoned that was likely the cause of the loud clanging I'd heard when the hand dryer had stopped screaming at me in the washroom.

"Obviously, it's just terrible that your boss has been killed . . ." I said, then I took a few seconds to shake my head sadly. I made sure to emphasize the word *boss*, because, childishly, I wanted to give the woman a taste of the medicine she'd just dosed out to Bud. However, I've found that those for whom passive-aggression is natural rarely perceive it when it's directed toward them, so unfortunately my taunt went unnoticed. I pressed on. "What on earth happened while I was away?"

When I'd gone to the ladies' room, the dining room had been

filled with the light from half a dozen glittering gold-and-crystal chandeliers, diners had been chatting festively, and we'd all been enjoying a few bottles of fine Dom Pérignon champagne, which Ian the barman had ceremoniously opened with flourishes of what I suspected was the very Russian saber that had killed Miss Shirley.

Julie Pool sighed heavily and shook her head. "I don't know what happened. I didn't see a thing. There was a crash, a bang, and then the security system kicked in. It all happened so fast. But Mr. Anderson's right, I need to release the elevator quickly, so I'll reset the system. I just have to access the control panel behind the bar, and it'll all be sorted out. They're probably already opening the emergency exit from downstairs as we speak." She nodded curtly and took her leave of us.

"Well, it won't *all* be sorted out," I muttered to Bud, as Julie Pool made her way to the bar. "That poor woman will still be dead."

Bud nodded grimly as we watched the lawyer pull a surprisingly large bunch of keys from her small evening purse and reach above the bar to unlock a mirrored cupboard.

"She's wrong, Cait," said Bud.

"How d'you mean?"

"First there was a bang—almost a pop, really—then, immediately afterward, a cracking noise—not a crash like glass breaking or anything like that. Next there was a huge clang as the metal collar sealed the elevator, then a loud sighing and rumbling. Finally, the power went off." He counted off the list on his fingers. I had more faith in Bud's trained recollection of events than in that of the overly assertive Julie Pool, who regained our attention when she began swearing loudly at an illuminated numbered keypad.

"Maybe you hit the wrong number? You know, like when you misdial on a phone?" Ian was hovering behind the bar next to Julie and speaking to her as though she were a normal human being. I found it hard to imagine she'd ever admit to doing anything incorrectly. Her next remarks, and the vehemence with which she made them, bore out my assumptions.

"I did *not* hit the wrong numbers. I hit all the right numbers, *and* in the right order. It's easy enough, after all. The pads are huge. You'd have to be an idiot to hit the wrong ones. Even Miss Shirley could manage it with her arthritic hands." She glowered at Ian as though it were his fault that her efforts had gone unrewarded.

"What's the matter, Julie, dear? Anything I can help with?" It was Jack Bullock, also a lawyer, who'd introduced himself to me earlier as Julie Pool's husband. He was very gracious when we met, but his just-too-shiny gray suit, his slightly-too-well-styled hair, and the touch of dandruff in his eyebrows had all combined to make me instinctively distrustful of him.

Julie relaxed her shoulders and smiled. It was a genuinely warm smile, from the heart. Looking at the oddly matched couple, it was clear to me that they loved each other very much. She was as elegant as he was sleazy, and her role as a cool corporate litigator was offset by Jack Bullock's grinning presence on thirty-foot-tall billboards that dotted the road from McCarran Airport, announcing that when it came to a DUI or a speeding ticket, if you couldn't get out of it, it was because "You don't know Jack!" *Very tasteful.* Despite these glaring differences, they were clearly besotted with each other.

Julie spoke to her husband in an intimate whisper that my keen ear still managed to catch. "Jack, dear, keep an eye on . . . you know . . . make sure Miss Shirley's body isn't . . . disturbed. I'll do this. I've got three tries. I'll do it more slowly this time."

"Okay," replied Jack, winking affectionately at his wife. "You do that, and I'll stand guard over the old b . . . bird."

"Jack!" admonished his wife, guessing at his first choice of word. "Don't. She wasn't *that* bad. And she's dead." Julie's chin suddenly puckered. "Oh, Jack, *she's dead.*"

Jack gave his wife a hug. "Come on, Julie, love. Keep it together. You do that, I'll do this." For all of his overt greasiness, Jack Bullock seemed to have a cooler head than his spouse in a crisis. He moved to within a foot or so of his wife's late employer to fulfill his assigned duty.

As Jack assumed his position as Guardian of the Corpse, he was joined by the man who'd been sitting opposite Miss Shirley at dinner. Clemence Foy—he'd put a heavy emphasis on the French pronunciation of the "mence" part of his name when he'd introduced himself to me before dinner—was sobbing as he looked down at the dead woman's body and wiped at his tears with a voluminous white handkerchief. The sight made me think of Louis Armstrong.

Clemence was not quite as dark skinned as the trumpet player, but he had the same sort of build and wore a snazzy bow tie—the use of the large linen square enhanced the similarity. Other than his name, I knew nothing about the man. He looked to be about eighty, though his crimped hair was still glisteningly jet black. His surprisingly youthful head of hair aside, he looked tired, almost deflated. I spotted a gaping space between his neck and his worn white collar. I also noted that he was the only person in the room who seemed to be mourning the casino owner, which hinted at a strong connection between the dead woman and this aged man.

I looked back at Julie Pool just in time to see her shake her shoulders and reach out to, once again, punch in the numbers that would reset the security system and allow us to regain access to the outside world. The numbered pads were, indeed, large, and she didn't seem to care that we could all hear the code numbers as she called them out, then punched them in. Each time she punched I heard a beep, signifying that the pad had been properly depressed.

"Zero, nine, two, five, four, two, zero, one, zero, one, zero, zero," she said.

Twelve beeps sounded, then—nothing.

Beginners, Please

THE FEW SECONDS OF EXPECTANT silence that followed Julie Pool's second attempt to reset the security system were followed by uneasy mutterings. I noticed a few concerned faces, but it was, once again, Svetlana Kharlamova who stole the scene.

"I leave now! My voice! My throat. Stress very bad for me!" wailed the satin-swathed diva. I turned my attention away from Julie, who was still swearing at the keypad, to see the Divine Kharlamova, as she'd been referred to in her heyday, push away a glass of water offered by her ever-patient assistant Jimmy, but gleefully accept a flute of champagne offered by Tom White. Clearly feeling he had fulfilled his duties, Tom approached us.

"What's going on, Uncle Bud? What's the delay?"

Bud smiled. "I told you at dinner, Tom, you can drop the 'uncle.' Jack's your uncle; I'm just your uncle's friend."

Tom shrugged. "You've always been more than a friend to Uncle Jack," he said, "especially since his heart attack, and I've always called you 'Uncle Bud.' But if I'm too old for that now, I'll keep doing my best to just call you Bud. Hey, Tanya . . ." Tom motioned for his soon-to-be live-in girlfriend, Tanya Willis, to join us. As she excused herself from the opera singer's clique and approached us, I smiled at this other improbable couple.

At thirty years of age, Tom White might have grown up in the quiet, though beautiful, District of Mission in British Columbia, but he was proving to be a real shooting star in the culinary world, having won a television competition where hopeful chefs are eliminated on a weekly basis. Scooped up by the Tsar!, he was one of the new young guns taking the already world-famous kitchens in Vegas by storm. Six feet tall, with a mass of curly sandy hair, his ruddy cheeks, freckles, and strapping frame were in stark contrast to the pale-skinned, willowy Tanya, who, like me, hovered somewhere between five foot three and five foot four.

At twenty-four, her hair was darker than my own graying locks, but, like mine, it was pulled back into a ponytail. Mine was finished off with a billowing bow of black silk edged with gold thread that matched my bouncy black-and-gold pantsuit—an outfit befitting a very fancy dinner at an exclusive private dining room. Unfortunately, hers was lumped into a grubby scrunchie. A claret-colored blouse, ill-fitting navy skirt, and complete lack of makeup, save a smear of questionable pink lipstick, didn't improve her overall appearance. To top it all she was lugging a huge black purse on her shoulder. Behind her thick rectangular spectacles, the circles under her dark eyes seemed even more pronounced than they had been earlier in the evening. To be fair to her, I reasoned that might just be the effect of the dreadful lighting.

As ill-matched as this couple appeared, Tom had spent most of the evening telling us how happy they were. It seemed they'd recently made a big deal of their nine-month anniversary, with a lavish dinner downstairs at the fabulous Romanoff Room, where Tom was a chef. Tom had regaled us with the less-than-happy tale while we'd joyously savored a delicious main course of skate wing with a merlot and berry reduction sauce, flecked with capers and lemon zest. I'd managed to listen to him even as my taste buds sang with delight at the wonderful flavors. It seemed that Ian, who was a barman at the Romanoff Room when he wasn't on duty in the private dining room, had chosen that particular night to show off his prowess, or lack of it on that occasion, at opening a bottle with a saber, and had ended up drenching poor Tanya with champagne in the process. Tom had laughed heartily when he told us he'd threatened to suck the sleeves of Tanya's blouse dry of champagne as they were driven back to her

place in a cab. Apparently Tanya hadn't been amused. I could understand why. Maybe that's why she hadn't bothered to make an effort
with her appearance for this dinner engagement.

"What's going on?" asked Tanya as she peered in the general
direction of the body. "Why hasn't Julie reset the system yet? It only
takes a moment."

"You sound as though you know what you're talking about," I
replied.

"Miss Shirley took a special interest in you, didn't she, Tanya?"
Tom looked sympathetically at his girlfriend and wrapped his big
bear arm around her. She seemed an insignificant figure beside him,
and almost disappeared into his body as she snuggled against his
chest. Tom looked proud as he added, "Tanya was up here with
Miss Shirley all alone yesterday, weren't you, eh?"

Tanya smiled and poked Tom in the ribs. "Maybe I was, or
maybe I was 'out and about in a boat,' don't you know." They both
smiled as she gently mocked Tom's Canadian accent. I'd gathered
that Tanya had grown up in Henderson, which is just a few miles
from the Vegas Strip where she now worked.

Tom was still smiling, though looking embarrassed at his levity,
when he said, "Don't be coy, Tanya, I know you said it was a secret
between the two of you and I shouldn't mention it, but it can't hurt
now." He dropped his voice even lower, but sounded proud as he
added, "Miss Shirley brought her here all alone, just so she could
have a proper look at the artworks. That was when Miss Shirley
invited Tanya and me to dinner tonight. Of course, I asked if you
two could come, what with today being Uncle Bud's . . . sorry, *Bud's*
birthday. Miss Shirley was delighted about that. I know she meant to
speak to you about you two sharing a birth date after dinner. It was
good of her to announce that when we all sang 'Happy Birthday' to
her at midnight, it was for you too. So we have Tanya to thank for us
being here to enjoy all this."

"Really? Thanks for that, Tanya," said Bud with a wink in the girl's direction.

Tanya shrugged, but Tom blushed and spluttered, "Oh, I didn't mean . . . oh, you all know what I meant." He stopped, lost for words.

"Oh, come on, it's okay," I said in what I hoped was my most reassuring voice. "We were having a very nice evening, up until—this," I said, gesturing toward the body. "But, I have to say, I wouldn't mind if Julie Pool could manage to sort out the blessed security system, so we could start the inevitably lengthy process of dealing with the police. I suppose it'll take hours."

"You talk strangely," said Tanya speaking directly to me. "It's funny. I thought it all through dinner."

"I suppose it's the accent?" I asked. It usually is—there's something about a Welsh accent that intrigues people.

"Yes, it goes up and down, like you're singing," she replied, "but you also use weird words."

"Like what?" I wasn't sure what she meant.

"You say 'police,' not 'cops'; you say 'suppose' instead of 'guess.' It's weird."

Having already spent a few hours with the girl I decided to allow myself a little sarcasm. "Given the circumstances here tonight, I'd say there are more weird things going on in this room than my choice of vocabulary."

"I guess," she replied sulkily.

I'd noticed at dinner that Tanya didn't possess the best interpersonal skills. Over the years I've observed it's not unusual for software programmers like Tanya, who spend more time with computers, crunching code, than with other human beings, to lack such ability. Still, the response seemed odd, even for her. Sulkiness hardly seemed an appropriate response to murder, especially if Miss Shirley had taken a special interest in this intensely bright girl.

Tom had boasted several times at dinner that Tanya had graduated from university before most had even qualified to attend one.

"Listen up, everyone!" It was Julie calling out from the bar. "I have entered what I know are the correct numbers to reset the system. Twice. I've used them before, so I know they work, but they haven't worked this time. I have only three attempts to enter the correct code. If my third attempt fails, we could be in complete lockdown for twelve hours. This will affect us all. I tell you this because I have to decide which numbers to enter for my third and final attempt, and I plan on reversing the two sets of six numbers that Miss Shirley selected as the code. Mr. Sauber . . . Art?" She turned her attention to a short, dapper white-haired man who was still attending to the opera singer. "Did Miss Shirley ever mention a backup code to you?"

The elderly man, to whom I hadn't been introduced, shook his head. "No, she didn't discuss anything like that with me. You'd know more about it than I."

"Just a minute," I shouted at Julie. *I couldn't help myself.* "Are you going to swap the numbers to put her birthday second and the date when the Tsar! opened first, or should you try keeping the overall order and reversing the dates . . . so that they're year, day, month, rather than month, day, year, as they are now?"

"How do you know Miss Shirley's code?" asked Tanya sharply. To be fair, it wasn't only Tanya who was surprised. Julie Pool looked quite put out, and Ian, who'd been hovering at Julie's elbow as she punched in the numbers, looked puzzled.

I sighed as I replied, "Julie didn't make a secret of the numbers. Given that we've only just finished singing 'Happy Birthday' to Miss Shirley, it's fairly safe to assume that her birthday is today, September 25, and she was very open, and delighted, that she was turning seventy. So, zero, nine, two, five, four, two. And the Tsar! officially opened on January 1, 2000, according to the colorful book in our hotel room, so zero, one, zero, one, zero, zero. It was obvious once Julie called out the numbers. So, to repeat my question, do you think, Julie, that Miss Shirley would have swapped the full dates with each other, or reversed the numbers, or just chosen entirely new ones? In which case I'd suggest you consider the birth date of her late husband, or maybe their wedding anniversary, because it's clear she chose dates that were impossible for her to forget."

I glanced at Bud who rolled his eyes away from me, then shook his head, smiling.

"I had to speak up, Bud. She hadn't considered all the options," I hissed.

Art Sauber called out, "I think we should vote on it, because I sure as hell don't want to spend the next twelve hours locked in a room with . . . that." He nodded his head sadly, in the general direction of the body.

Jack Bullock spoke up next. "You should do what *you* think is right, my dear. After all, it's not as though we can reach anyone outside this room to consult with them—I know that you and Miss Shirley had many heated conversations about her never allowing the installation of a landline in here, and the block she insisted be placed on all the cellphone signals and Wi-Fi in this dining room makes that a nonstarter. Though, if Miss Shirley didn't tell you she'd decided to change the codes, and she didn't tell Art, who, after all, owns almost half the place, I can't imagine *who* she'd tell."

Julie listened thoughtfully to her husband. The change in her demeanor signaled to me that she'd made a decision. I'm pretty good at reading people; in fact, it's an important part of my skill set, which I've relied upon on many occasions. The settling of her shoulders, the straightening of her back, and her slightly elevated jawline told me that Julie was ready to act.

"Right. No voting. No phone calls to allow me to check with anyone, and no texts or e-mails either. We're on our own. So here goes . . ." she said resolutely.

This time, everyone listened for the beeps, as Julie muttered aloud the numbers she'd written on a napkin.

After the twelfth beep you could feel the silence.

"Is over? Is done?" asked Svetlana Kharlamova, a dramatic quiver in her voice.

Julie shook her head, as did Tanya.

"No," said Julie. "I'm ... I'm sorry. The code has failed. The whole thing will automatically reboot exactly twelve hours from the time of my last attempt"—she looked at her elegantly expensive watch—"so just before 1:00 PM. There *are* special codes that our security department can use to open just the emergency exit, but this keypad is telling me that three attempts have already been made to do that, down in the main control room, and they have all failed. Miss Shirley must have altered that code as well. Goodness knows what she was thinking. Maybe they'll be able to somehow open the emergency exit from outside before the twelve hours are up. But unless they're able to cut their way through the metal door that will have dropped into place there, we're stuck here. We'll have to make the best of it."

"They *must* open from outside, no? Is emergency exit. This is emergency. Emergency door not open? Is illegal, I think." Svetlana Kharlamova made a good point.

Again Tanya shook her head, though it was Julie who replied. "Miss Shirley must have had some reason to change all the codes. She was the only one who could do it. It's very worrying." I could tell that Julie's legal brain was running through scenarios where lawsuits might rain down upon the Tsar! Organization. Julie looked across the room to Art Sauber. He responded to her questioning glance with a shrug suggesting helplessness and confusion. Julie swallowed hard and continued. "As I said, we'll have to make the best of it. I know these chairs aren't designed for it, but maybe we'll be able to get some sleep ..."

Svetlana Kharlamova leapt from her seat, drew herself to her full height, which was not much taller than me, and swirled her shawl about her shoulders. She dropped her chin and gave everyone in the room, in turn, a penetrating stare. It was like watching Gloria Swanson in *Sunset Boulevard* descend the stairs and demand her close-up, except the Diva Kharlamova was about twice the width of the silent screen star.

"Sleep? You think I sleep? Sleep here? With dead body in room? With *murderer* in room? I not sleep. You sleep. If you die, is not my fault."

After the Diva spoke, it dawned on everyone that what she had said was true. If Miss Shirley had been killed, and she most certainly had been, only one of us could have done it—she'd obviously been killed during the darkness that had befallen the dining room right after it was sealed shut. And we were going to be stuck in the restaurant, together, for the next twelve hours.

I'd been out of the room at the time of the murder, so I hadn't seen anything. My eidetic memory, which I've been able to rely upon when other murders have needed solving, wasn't going to be of any use at all.

Happy birthday, Bud!

Curtain Up

I WATCHED THE EXPRESSIONS ON the faces around the room change as the Diva's dramatic words sank in. I didn't need to look at Bud to know what he was thinking. His thoughts likely mirrored my own.

One of the people in the room had killed Miss Shirley, but who, and why? And how had they managed to do it within such a small time frame, and with so many possible witnesses?

It was as though we were all seeing one another for the first time. A frozen tableau, waiting for a call to action. It came from an unexpected source.

Clemence Foy wiped his face with his giant handkerchief, looked toward Svetlana Kharlamova, and boomed, "You right, ma'am. Gotta be one of us." As he held onto the table in front of him, he looked across it at the corpse, then at the rest of us. He took a deep breath. "Miss Shirley's been my closest friend for over fifty years. She saved my life, and then she helped me build a new one. During all them years she never once complained about hard work, or having to make tough decisions. Some said she was hard-edged and to them I says, 'Yeah, you right,' but she done a lot of what she done to make life better for others, and herself, along the way. There ain't no way anyone like her is gonna come into my life again. She's gone. We can all see that. And she deserves to rest in peace. But as the good Lord is my witness, I call upon her soul to not be quiet until whoever done this terrible thing to her is brought to justice. And if that means that I have to meet 'em in hell 'cause of what I'm praying for right now, then so be it. Whichever one of you done this, you oughta know that the Lord can be mighty vengeful, as well as merciful. And there ain't *nothing* about what you done that deserves His mercy." His deep, gravelly voice cracked with passion.

Having summoned all his strength to speak, Clemence Foy faltered and began to sob once more. My heart went out to the man, and I found myself moving to comfort him. With what little strength he had left, he signaled me to leave him alone. He sat heavily in the seat he'd occupied through dinner, now facing his dead friend's body. He was still the only person in the room so openly lamenting her loss.

Julie Pool hesitantly approached the sobbing figure. She used a soothing tone when she said softly, "Clemence, come along, try to calm yourself. Ian? Bring some water for Clemence, please? Thanks."

As Ian leapt into action, Clemence looked up at Julie and said, "Water ain't gonna solve nothing. An eye for an eye, Miss Pool. That's *it*."

Passing the water from Ian to the elderly man, whose hands were trembling with shock and anger, Julie said, "Come on now, Clemence, you don't want to talk like that . . ."

"Why not, ma'am? Why *not*?" He banged the glass on the table and stared as the spilled water created widening patterns on the tablecloth, not making eye contact with anyone. "What have *you* all lost? A boss? A woman who gave you your first chance, your second, or maybe your last? A woman who took you under her wing and made things better for you when she could? That's what she done for so many people. No, none of you is grievin' for her; *you* all are worrying about yourselves. Like the Russian lady said, Miss Shirley's killer has to be here, in this room. There ain't nowhere else for them to be. They couldn't have killed her till the lights went out, else we'd have seen them do it. After that, there weren't nowhere for them to go."

Jimmy Green, still hovering over the Diva Kharlamova, piped up, "Someone . . . someone might have hidden under the dessert table when it came up from the kitchens below. They could be there now, or hiding in the men's room."

All heads turned toward the dessert table in question. Crisp white linens hung to the floor around the entire circumference of the large circular table. I wasn't the only one assessing the possibility of Jimmy's suggestion. It certainly looked as though there might be enough space beneath the table for someone to hide. Over dinner, Tom had told us that Miss Shirley had been fascinated by a serving system that Catherine the Great had used at her Petit Hermitage private getaway in Saint Petersburg. The widowed Russian queen had installed a platform that ascended bearing tables ready for guests to eat from, without the need for waiters. After the meal, the tables descended beneath a sliding floor, which closed over the space, allowing for totally private meals followed by dancing in the instantly cleared room. Miss Shirley had adopted the same system for one portion of her dining room. The table now bearing the dessert could be raised from, and lowered to, the kitchens below, with a sliding section of floor accommodating its passage.

I thought through what Tom had said, and applied what I knew from my own, somewhat limited, experience of commercial kitchens. Then I asked him, "After the servers removed our dishes following the main course, and set them on that table for it to descend, they left in the elevator. I suspect that means they then somehow made their way to the table in the kitchen, cleared it, and set it with these desserts. Would that have allowed for the table itself to be unattended for very long? What's the security like in the kitchens, Tom? I'm guessing it's not as tight as it is here."

Tom shook his head. "You'd be surprised. Access to the kitchen is very strictly controlled, not least because of all the expensive ingredients we use. Truffles, caviar, and the edible gold leaf they use to decorate some of the cakes and special treats are all small, costly items that would be easy to steal," he replied. "Besides, everyone's in pretty close quarters down there—they prepare and serve the food for the Romanoff Room, which is one floor below the kitchen, as well as this dining room, when it's in use. Here, we use that serving table to bring food up from the kitchen below us. In the Romanoff Room the servers use a pair of short escalators to move between the two floors. It's a great system—no jiggling the food around on the plate, which is perfect for fine dining. As a chef, I've been grateful for that investment on many occasions. We'd notice if a stranger came up into the kitchen that way, or if they used the service elevator we have there that allows for deliveries to be made and garbage to be cleared. We have a much lower turnover of personnel than many places, so everyone in the kitchen, and on the waitstaff, knows each other. I really don't think that it would have been easy for an outsider to sneak unnoticed into the busy kitchen."

Tom paused, and for a moment I thought he'd finished, but he added, almost as an afterthought, "By the way, the platform moves pretty slowly, so the servers would have arrived in the Romanoff Room via this elevator *and* had ample time to use the staff escalator to get back into the kitchen before the table came to rest there. So even if someone did get into the kitchen unobserved, they would have found it very difficult to get under the table, because it is always attended to."

"Someone *could* have hidden in the kitchen for hours, then snuck under the table before it was even set for the first time," pressed Jimmy. He seemed very keen on the idea of a hidden killer, which wasn't surprising, given the only alternative theory.

Bud strode toward the dessert table. "I'll check under the table, then in the men's washroom." He spoke calmly and moved with purpose.

It seemed as though everyone in the room breathed in simultaneously when Bud bent to pull up one edge of the tablecloth. Nothing but six wooden legs and two crosspieces met our anxious gazes. I heard a sigh as everyone exhaled. We all continued to watch as Bud walked toward the end of the bar near where the men's room led off the dining room, its entrance discreetly hidden behind sleek, flame-patterned walnut panels.

"Bud—be careful!" I called. Everyone looked nervous, but no one stirred to join him. Moments dragged by, then he re-emerged shaking his head. "There's backup lighting in there too, but the men's room is empty. And, by the way, I checked the emergency exit in there. It's definitely not opening."

"I was using the hand dryer, which is right inside the door of the ladies' room, when the lights went out," I added. "It was empty when I got there, and no one passed me." As soon as Bud was within hand-holding distance I grabbed him and squeezed all the blood out of his fingers.

"Is no one else here. Is just *us*," announced Svetlana Kharlamova, dropping her voice for effect.

So there we were. One dead body, twelve live ones. No one else to blame. Nowhere to go.

I knew that neither Bud nor I had killed Miss Shirley, but I had to consider everyone else a possible suspect, even Tom, so ten potential killers shared our space. I supposed that every innocent person in the room was making their own similar assessment.

I wondered what the killer was thinking. Unless Julie Pool was the murderer and had purposely messed up at the coded keypad for some reason, then whoever killed Miss Shirley must be surprised to now be trapped in the dining room with their dinner mates. Immediately my mind leapt to the question of what might have been their original plan. They *must* have known that the police would be called, none of us able to leave before being questioned and examined for forensic evidence. So how had they imagined they'd get away with it?

Before I had a chance to pursue that line of thought, Bud

whispered, "I think I'd better step up to the plate. We've got a long night ahead of us, and someone has to take charge. I'm going to give the whole thing some structure. Command and control. Follow my lead?"

I nodded in agreement, and my wonderful Bud became more like his old self than I'd seen him since his wife's tragic death almost seventeen months ago. It warmed my heart. This was the Bud I'd first known—professional, organized, respectful of the living and the dead, and, yes, in command. For most of the past year or so, he'd often been less than sure of himself, indecisive, almost vulnerable, and in need of support. I'd done all I could, and, of course, we'd had many happy times, but it's tough to move on when everything around you reminds you of your dead soul mate. Here, in an isolated private dining room overlooking the Las Vegas Strip, Bud had nothing to remind him of Jan—just a desire to find justice, which I knew had always been his priority in life. I decided I'd do my best to take a backseat and let him "run the case" as he saw fit, as I'd always tried to do when he hired me as a consultant on police cases for which he was responsible. I wondered if I'd be able to manage it. *I like to be in charge.*

Baritone and Chorus

BUD CLEARED HIS THROAT AND in his most precise, professional tone said, "Ladies and gentlemen, we find ourselves in a sad and unenviable position. Miss Shirley has been murdered, and it is highly likely that the person responsible for her demise is here, in our midst."

He paused for just a second at this point, and I did my best to observe and judge the expressions on the faces of those with whom I was about to share the next twelve hours. The eyes of every other person also swept the rest of the group.

Bud pressed on, his voice rich and authoritative. "I know that Ms. Julie Pool here is legal counsel for the Tsar! Organization, and that Mr. Art Sauber, one of the owners, is with us. Of course, I will defer to their presence, but you should all know that I have been in law enforcement for decades. Before I joined the Vancouver Police Department twenty years ago, I put in my time with the RCMP in possibly too many places with Prince or Creek in their name. So I have a broad and deep experience with all sorts of crime. Most recently I headed up the integrated homicide investigation force in British Columbia, before I retired last year. I don't pretend that I can solve this particular crime before we are questioned by your local law enforcement professionals, but I can certainly do my best to ensure that no more laws are broken, and that no other lives are put at risk."

Bud paused and looked across the room toward Julie Pool. "I'm corporate, not criminal," she said gravely, "and I certainly don't want anything else . . . like this . . ."—she nodded in the direction of the corpse—"to happen before we're all able to get out of here. But you're right, Mr. Anderson, I, too, will defer to Art's decision as to how we proceed."

All eyes turned toward Art Sauber. He seemed uncomfortable with being the center of attention. Everything about him exuded one thing—wealth. A good head of white hair for a man I judged to be in his seventies, a slight paunch disguised by an immaculately cut dark suit, a yellow-and-white-striped shirt with a white collar, and a matching yellow silk tie. He sipped the last dregs of brandy from the bowl he held with an ease bred of familiarity.

Carefully placing the empty crystal vessel on the bar, he cleared his throat and spoke, his midrange voice low, but engaging. "I am more than happy to allow someone of your experience in such matters guide us, Mr. Anderson. Though I'm not sure what that might mean under such circumstances. What do you suggest we do for the next twelve hours? How should we ... er ... handle ourselves and the ... um ... situation?" He looked suave, but concerned and confused.

Bud continued, "First of all, it's Bud, please. Secondly, as I am sure you've all worked out, we are, every one of us, both witnesses and suspects in this case. It would be standard operating procedure for the police to question each of us alone, without our having had a chance to confer about what we saw, heard, or did. That means that we shouldn't really talk about any facts pertaining to the specifics of the murder until they arrive."

A throat being cleared dramatically attracted our attention. "I'm Carl Petrosian. My late father, also Miss Shirley's late husband, originally owned the fifty-one percent of the casino she just inherited. Today marks the one-year anniversary of my father's death. And now this ..." He shook his head in what I read as disbelief, rather than sorrow. "I, for one, am quite happy to not talk about this ... circumstance at all, until we're let out of here. In fact, I'm not saying anything more without my lawyer present." The man who had spoken was dressed in a light caramel suit, teamed with a cream-colored silk shirt and a gold tie that was secured with a huge, and I guessed, real, diamond tiepin. His tan was darker than his suit, and his hair was suspiciously brown, given that he looked to be around sixty years old. Unfortunately for him, his teeth matched his creamy shirt, which I noted was unusual for a wealthy American. His light tenor voice delivered his lines in a very matter-of-fact way. "I don't think you should say anything either, Art. We've both probably got the most to gain from Miss Shirley's death, so we'd best be on our guard."

"Why?" asked Bud.

Carl Petrosian opened his mouth as if to answer, then half-smiled and said, "Oh, very clever, Mister Canadian Policeman, but you won't catch me answering any questions like that."

He settled into his chair, pulled a long, fat cigar from a gold tube that sat on the table beside him, then rooted around in his pockets, presumably looking for a cutter and a lighter.

As soon as she spied the cigar, Svetlana Kharlamova pushed herself to her feet, almost knocking her solicitous assistant from his own chair as she did so, and exclaimed, "You cannot do this! You cannot smoke here! My voice. What you are thinking? If there is fire, we cannot escape. Is very dangerous to me. To us all." Her Russian accent somehow added gravitas to her words. I noticed that a look of alarm crept onto a few other faces.

Bud moved toward Carl Petrosian with deliberate steps. "Mr. Petrosian, I think that's a valid point. Given that the emergency exit is locked, we really shouldn't do anything that could either create a fire hazard or impact our air quality. Which raises a good question—does anyone know which systems will be working during our time here?"

"Now that's a question I happen to be able to answer," said Art Sauber. "You can set up an emergency generator to operate as much, or as little, as you want, so long as life and safety systems remain functional. I share Julie's puzzlement and concern that, for some reason, it's been impossible for both us and the central control room to release the emergency exit. That shouldn't happen. However, unless something we also know nothing about has impacted the system's management, we will have air moving, but not chilled; we'll have these emergency lights, but none of the electrical outlets will work; and that's about it. I'm afraid the air's going to get very stale, very quickly."

"Miss Shirley, soon she smell bad," said Svetlana. Her nose wrinkled with disgust as she spoke.

"Don't panic," said Bud calmly. "Just so we all know, a body begins to decay as soon as death occurs, but the rate of decomposition will vary, depending upon many factors. Certainly the ambient temperature is one of those factors, and, yes, when the temperature increases after sunup in the morning, we will find ourselves not only getting warm in here but also, probably, noticing some unpleasant aromas. But on the brighter side, if there is one, when you're in an enclosed space with an increasingly pungent atmosphere, you often don't notice it as much as someone entering the room from the outside. We'll 'get used' to it. That said, I do think it's best if we have a no-smoking policy. For everyone's sake."

I didn't know how many other people in the room were smokers, but I knew that I was desperate for a cigarette myself. Sadly, I had to agree with Bud. We couldn't possibly start to smoke in the room. I silently congratulated myself for pushing a strip of nicotine gum into my evening purse before we'd left our room, and I began to watch for a suitable moment when I could pop one into my mouth. Having thought about it, the need for nicotine was foremost in my mind.

Carl Petrosian gave Bud a sneering grin. "I think you'll find that this is now *my* private dining room, and I can do what I damn well please here."

"What do you mean *your* private dining room?" asked Art Sauber. As he spoke, he raked his hand through his snowy hair. "What makes you think that Miss Shirley left *you* her interests in the Tsar!? She might have left it all to me, making me the outright owner."

Carl shook his head and began, "Miss Shirley more or less told me it would be mine when she was gone . . ." He glanced at Bud and stopped speaking.

"An excellent motive for killing her," observed Bud, somewhat wickedly I thought.

Almost imperceptibly, people edged away from Carl as the smile died on his face. "I didn't mean . . . oh, what the heck . . . everyone knew it anyway. If I don't tell you, then someone else will."

"Exactly," replied Bud quietly. His one word spoke volumes, and I could see concern, panic, uncertainty, and vulnerability on the faces of those who were realizing that others in the room might be planning to tell everything they knew about their companions, in an effort to deflect a cop's interest away from themselves. Bud's body language told me he'd made a decision. "Look, I know that my aim should be to stop us all talking about this evening's events"—his tone was conciliatory—"but my concern is that we might all stew on things, be unable to hold our tongues, and begin to shoot accusations at each other."

"Yeah, you right," crackled Clemence. "Every man for himself." He sucked his teeth, loudly. "Or woman," he added.

"Sadly, yes," replied Bud. "Cait knows all about the psychology of suspicion, don't you? For those of you who weren't introduced to her earlier this evening, this is Professor Cait Morgan. Happily for us, ladies and gentlemen, she is a psychologist who specializes in victim profiling theory at the University of Vancouver. I've had the honor of working with her on many occasions. I believe that her skills will be valuable to us under these worrying circumstances."

"She's also the only person in the room, as far as I know, who's ever been arrested for murdering someone." Julie Pool's unnecessary comment made all heads turn in my direction. I'm pretty sure that Tom and Tanya looked the most shocked, which was understandable. *One up to Julie.*

Julie had taken me by surprise—Bud, too, judging by his expression. Needless to say I was annoyed, but I knew I had to give her comment some context.

"Hello, folks," I said, probably a little too brightly. I took a breath and calmed myself. "As Bud said, I've done quite a bit of work on the psychological dimensions of suspicion. Which is just as well, given the introduction I just received from Julie." I shot a glance in the woman's direction that I hoped would communicate at least a fraction of the irritation I felt. "She's quite right," I continued. "I was once arrested on suspicion of murder. But please understand that I was never charged."

"Who you kill?" asked Svetlana apprehensively.

"I didn't kill anyone." I knew that I sounded defensive, so I took another deep breath before I continued. *Stick to the facts, Cait, just stick to the facts.* "I was *suspected* of killing an ex-boyfriend of mine. We'd had a pretty nasty split, and I should have known better than to allow him back into my home. He was in need of somewhere to stay. I awoke to discover that he had died during the night. His body was sprawled across my bathroom floor. I didn't kill him, and I was completely cleared of any suspicion when the autopsy revealed he'd died from internal bleeding, a result of his spleen having been ruptured. It turned out that he'd been involved in a fight in a bar a few days before, and he'd sustained the injury at that time. No one was ever charged, though there would have been a case for manslaughter, I'm sure. So, as Julie said, I was arrested, but in the UK that doesn't mean anything other than that you're suspected of a crime. His body was found inside my home, and no one else had entered it. So, of course the police suspected me."

"How did you get over it?" asked Art, sounding more interested than alarmed. "I bet those small English villages can be tough on a murder suspect. That is an English accent, right? Or are you Australian?"

I couldn't help but smile. "It's a Welsh accent actually, thanks for asking. And I was living in Cambridge at the time of Angus's death, so a big enough place that I might have been able to go about my business unnoticed. Unfortunately, the newspapers had made rather a meal of my arrest, given that I was a criminologist, so it was more difficult to put it behind me than I had hoped. I was very fortunate to have had the opportunity to move to British Columbia to complete my doctoral work there. If any good can be said to have come out of the situation, it would be that I shifted the focus of my work from criminals to victims."

"Why the change?" asked Julie.

It was immediately clear to me that I wouldn't be able to avoid answering her very direct question, so I decided to answer as briefly as I could. "Angus was a very angry man. During our time together I'd become painfully aware of the fact that he found it impossible to share space with other people without asserting himself, usually by challenging the apparently dominant male. 'Who do you think you are looking at?' would be his opening gambit, and the situation usually deteriorated from there. Because Angus eventually died as the result of a fight in a bar, in other words he became a victim of his own lifestyle, I gravitated toward researching how the life-patterns of victims of crime might have contributed to them becoming a victim in the first place."

"You say is Miss Shirley's fault she dies?" Svetlana was puzzled.

I tried to sigh only inwardly as I replied to what is the most common criticism of my discipline. "My research has shown that while some people lead a life that puts them at higher risk of meeting an unnaturally early death, as Angus did, most victims are not at all to blame for having become one. Unfortunately for them, they become victims despite living their normal, everyday lives. So I spend a fair bit of time using my psychology training to analyze what a person's 'normal' life has been. I don't know what Miss Shirley's 'normal' was. I don't know her life story, or how she came to be who she was. But, in a case like this, there is usually a link between the victim and the killer. Often a close one. Which is why my role as a victimologist means I often work with those who have been close to the victim."

I hoped I'd managed to steer the minds of my audience away from me and back toward the matter in hand. I was pleased when Clemence asked a question that showed he at least was more interested in what I might be able to do to help in this case, than in dwelling on what had happened to me more than a decade ago.

"You reckon you can help us get through this?" he asked. His deep voice was mournful, rather than hopeful.

"I can certainly try. I won't bore you with a big lecture, but I'm sure you can appreciate that anyone whose work involves understanding how a victim might have come to be one will also come into contact with those who cared about the victim. These are the people who are desperate to understand what has happened, and they cannot help but want to lay blame at someone's door. In the search for the truth, the full story, sometimes suspicion might fall upon those they also love, or certainly know, and at a time when their ability to apply a sense of perspective is at its weakest. A look, a hastily hurled insult, even an unspoken one, and grudges can be formed that are likely to last, damaging future relationships. Profiling victims, and working with those who can help to do that, is delicate but important work. We all know that someone here has killed Miss Shirley, so it's natural that we all look at each other with suspicion. In this situation it would be easy for any one of us to succumb to making wild accusations, which none of us would ever forget or be able to easily put aside."

I could tell by people's expressions and shifting body language that I was connecting with some of them. I pressed on. I wanted them to be able to identify with me, to begin to trust me. "Bud and I are like millions of other people—we've come to Las Vegas for a short vacation in a place that's designed for pleasure. In the days since we arrived, we've done what tourists here do—we've been awestruck by the scale and scope of the place, by the attention to detail, the wonderful sights, sounds, and smells of the place. We've giggled at Elvis impersonators strolling along The Strip deep in conversation with a guy in a Transformer getup, or at a girl carrying her giant Hello Kitty costume head under her arm. We've learned, to our cost, that what we visitors might think is a short stroll from one casino to another is, in fact, a considerable hike in heat we're not used to . . . even if it is a 'dry heat.'"

I noticed that Ian and Jimmy smiled as I said that, which was what I needed. "We've really enjoyed our time at the Tsar! Last night's midnight Cossack Parade was quite something. It's a clever idea to pull in the crowds at that time of night for one last hurrah. The troika gliding through the casino carrying that giant piece of amber and all the security guards lined up, dressed in Cossack outfits, were an excellent form of entertainment. Giving out discount coupons for the vodka bar where everything is frozen solid is a clever idea, and fun. But you know what? Bud and I can only see the place as outsiders. You? You all live here. You're the *insiders*. You know what's behind the rhinestones and the neon. Behind the costumes and the makeup. You know the real life of the place. You probably know people who are teachers, bank tellers, dentists, doctors, and those who work in grocery stores and gas stations. We don't. We've only met people whose job it is to provide service and entertainment. Not that they haven't all been fabulous people, but our relationship with them is preset. It's essentially false. Some of you have been here a few months"—I looked at Tom—"and some have always been here"—I nodded at Tanya. "Bud's right when he says that we can't possibly be locked in this room for hours and hours and not be expected to think about what's happened, to try to make sense of it somehow. And I know that if he were able to prevent us from discussing what might well become evidence and testimony, he would. So, given his needs, and using my knowledge, what I propose is that, rather than become anxious and angry, we maybe take some time to talk about how we came to be here. Possibly some of you would even like to talk about how you came to know Miss Shirley, to remember her as she was. It might be a more constructive way of passing the time until we're able to address this terrible thing head on."

I watched the faces around me intently, hoping my suggestion would be acted upon. If I could steer the conversation in the right direction, I could at least take note of, and interpret, how people reacted to the idea of the woman as a person, rather than as a corpse. They might well reveal a glimmer of their true feelings toward her. By inviting them to build a picture of the victim for me, I would try to discern her killer.

Having followed Bud's lead, he now followed mine. He knew enough about my methods to be able to support my cause. "That's a good idea, Cait," he said thoughtfully. "You're right. You and I didn't know Miss Shirley, of course, but I'm guessing she meant something special to every other person in this room. Talking about her would be a respectful way to remember her while we wait." I judged that between us Bud and I had managed to win over the mood of the room. I wondered how each individual would react.

"I have no secrets. My life is open book. I speak," announced Svetlana Kharlamova. "But first, you cover body. Is not good to see Miss Shirley like this. Is not . . . pretty."

We all turned to look again at the body.

"I have some spare tablecloths. They're under the bar, for emergencies, which, I guess, this is," offered Ian. "They're big. We could just, you know, place one, or two, over . . . um . . . Miss Shirley *and* the chair. We wouldn't need to move her . . ." The more he spoke, the more embarrassed he sounded.

"Like a tent? Right there?" asked Tanya Willis, making the idea sound ridiculous.

The barman blushed. "Well, I guess . . ." he stammered.

I looked at Bud, who was clearly thinking through Ian's idea. He shook his head. "I have to advise against that," he said. "This is a crime scene, and we can't compromise any possible evidence."

"If four or five of us place the cloth right over the whole . . . thing . . . it might actually preserve the scene," I said to Bud quietly. "The entire room's a crime scene really, and we'll have to move about within it—we have already—but we could at least secure the immediate surroundings."

Everyone looked at Bud while he gave the matter further consideration. "We'll have to give the seat a wide berth, especially behind it," he said to me, under his breath. "That must be where the killer stood to push in the blade, so there might be something the crime-scene guys could find on the carpet . . ."

Finally, Bud nodded and addressed the room. "Okay, Ian. Let's get those cloths out and see how big they are. Maybe you, Tom, and Carl can give me a hand—you okay with that?" All three men nodded, though Carl Petrosian rolled his eyes as he did so.

Art Sauber caught the look and said, "If Carl doesn't want to do it, I'll help. I owe Miss Shirley a lot more than doing what I can to allow her some privacy at this time."

"Of course I'll help," snapped Carl, rising to his feet. "It's true we didn't always get on, but she was a decent woman, and she made my father happy when he was alive. I guess she wasn't going to warm to a 'stepson' who was just ten years younger than she was. And I *certainly* didn't need another mom."

The decision made, Clemence Foy pushed himself wearily to his feet and the men moved the chairs from around the table where Miss Shirley "sat," then removed the table itself, placing it near the glass wall. An amount of shuffling around and careful footwork followed, until

Bud was finally happy with the outcome. One large tablecloth was all that was needed. Eventually, it rested upon the poor woman's head, the arms of her chair, and, rather alarmingly, the point of the saber.

When they had finished, the men stepped back, and a hush fell over the room. We all took a moment to come to terms with the ghoulish sight. It seemed almost as though this was the first time we'd all acknowledged that Miss Shirley was, in fact, dead.

"So, now is my time to speak?" boomed the Diva Kharlamova, making Tanya Willis jump.

Even Carl Petrosian looked sad as he trudged back toward his seat, but he rallied quickly and said, to no one in particular, "I tell you what, if we're really going to do this . . . this talking thing, I want some of that white chocolate bread pudding, another glass of champagne, and, Ian, bring my cognac to my table, will you? I might not be *allowed* to smoke, but I sure as heck plan on having everything else I want. Miss Shirley's gone—and if ever there was a woman who loved to party . . ." He paused and even looked wistful for a moment. "I say, if we're going to remember her, let's rearrange these tables, get ourselves as comfortable as we can, take what we want by way of dessert, and settle down."

Unbelievably, as Carl uttered the words "white chocolate bread pudding" I felt my saliva glands kick in. *Who'd have thought it?*

"I'm guessing you'll be having some dessert, then," said Bud as though he'd read my mind. Apparently he knows me quite well.

"Maybe just a bit, but I'll help reorganize the room first," I offered.

He smiled indulgently. "It's going to be a long, long night, Cait. Leave the heavy lifting to us strong menfolk"—he winked—"and you grab yourself some of that pudding . . . and some for me too. It looks, and smells, amazing."

He was right, it did—and it would have been a terrible shame to let all the accompanying ice cream melt to nothing, so I followed my nature and hit the dessert table. I wasn't alone, thank goodness.

The Diva Takes Center Stage

WHITE CHOCOLATE ISN'T MY FAVORITE, but any chocolate is better than none, and it's even tastier when it's served with something salty. I allowed myself a few moments to enjoy the contrast between the sticky caramel sauce and the rich, light white chocolate bread pudding studded with golden raisins and topped with excellent handmade vanilla ice cream. Had it not been for the body in the room, it would have been the perfect dessert experience. I worked hard to stop focusing on the exquisite flavors and textures to give my attention to the Diva Svetlana Kharlamova, who was being attended to by Jimmy Green as though he were dressing her for a performance.

She stood at the table where she, Jimmy, Carl, and Art were now placed. Ian, Julie, Jack, and Clemence sat around the second table, while Bud, Tanya, Tom, and I surrounded the final one. We'd pulled the three tables away from the partitions, closer to the central elevator shaft and the dessert table, so the gathering felt snugger.

The Diva eventually appeared to be happy with how Jimmy had rewrapped the highly decorated iridescent blue-green shawl in which she'd been swathed all evening. Finally, she shoved the man away as though he were a mere serf, drew herself up to her full five-four, and regarded us with her imperious look. It was as if she were waiting for her cue, thinking herself into her role, as she prepared to grace us with her legendary voice. The raven-black bun atop her head glistened beneath the starry spotlights, and her gold satin sheath dress was very tight, giving her a cylindrical appearance. As someone whose bathroom scales regularly accuse her of weighing one hundred and eighty pounds, I'm familiar with pretty much every euphemism for "overweight," so I chose to think of her as "Rubenesque," pegging her at two hundred and fifty pounds, or thereabouts. With her shawl now appropriately draped about her torso, she began to speak, her multiple chins quivering as she did so.

"You know me," she said. "I am famous for many years. I am from humble Russian village in south, but I have great gift . . . my voice." She was being dramatic, but I didn't get the impression that she was boasting. Rather, I felt we were seeing her give a performance with which she was comfortable and familiar. "As small child I have big voice. Mama send me to city to sing in street, make money, bring home. I have ten years of age when big man in fur coat say to me, 'You have good voice child, take me to Mama.' We go. Mama and Papa kiss me, man in fur coat take me to school for singers. I sing. They like me. I sing every day. I work hard. I learn Italian, German, and French so I can sing in all languages, but mainly I sing in Russian. I do not play outside, every day I sing. I am very good. I go to Moscow. I sing more. At fifteen, I give recital at Hotel Ukraina to important Communist Party men. I have voice like Adelina Patti, says very old, very important man who sees her in Saint Petersburg when she is there, many years before. Before it is Leningrad, even. I have 'silver' voice, he say. Light, like bells. I work hard to have 'golden' voice, strong like USSR. I sing all best soprano roles in Moscow, in every state. My country loves me. I am *Diva Kharlamova!*"

At this point, Svetlana Kharlamova threw her right arm skyward for effect, disarranging the shawl so carefully placed about her by Jimmy Green, who sat looking up at her with an expression on his face of such awe that she might have been in her prime. I wondered if to him, she still was.

Dropping her voice to a lower register for greater dramatic effect, the Diva continued. "When world change, my country change. Is *perestroika*. I go from Russia for first time. I sing with many companies in many countries. Best singers in world want to perform with me. Greatest maestros want me on stage for them. I make many recordings, I give best roles. Whole world loves me. I sing. I act. I am *still* Diva Kharlamova. But I am not lucky for love. Men are difficult. Want my money, my name. Not understand life of artist. I marry, I divorce. I marry again. I divorce again. Is very sad for me, and not good for voice."

She paused and dropped her head, the skin beneath her chin folding to her chest. She looked up with a pathetic expression. "Now world change again. Skinny singers run and jump on stage." She wrinkled her nose with distaste. "They roll on floor and sing. They climb on scenery and sing. They take off clothes and sing. This *not* opera. Now I not sing opera, I sing here. Miss Shirley bring me here. She beg me to come five years ago. She is big fan. I meet her, we like each other, I come. She give me big apartment in hotel building here. Is just like Seven Sisters, as grand as Hotel Ukraina. She give me Jimmy to help me. I enjoy Las Vegas. People come to Tsar! for beautiful Russian buildings, and art, and food, and *me*. They come to show every night, see Russian ballet, clowns, acrobats . . . and wait for *me* at end of show. The maestro make special arrangement for me to sing great Russian piece, Tatiana's letter song from *Eugene Onegin*. Is always big success. Also, audience always standing after I sing 'Habanera' from *Carmen*—though is not Russian." She looked disappointed. "People here not know many Russian songs. Also I sing 'Kalinka' and men dance in old Russian costumes. Is strange. Is same song I sing in streets when I am child, now I sing here. I stay here three years more, then—how I know? Maybe more. I like Miss Shirley. She have tea with me, many times. She is good woman. I very sad she is dead. I do not kill her. I have contract for Tsar! so I not want her dead. Is not me who kill her."

Having finished her performance, Svetlana Kharlamova nodded her head in gracious thanks for our attention and took her seat. I wasn't surprised that her remembrances of Miss Shirley had, in fact, been her own life story with no more than a mention of the dead woman. Jimmy patted her hand, congratulating her on a job well done. I think she expected us to applaud. We didn't.

Still telling the Diva how well she'd done as she soothed her throat by quaffing champagne, Jimmy Green rose to his feet, looking somewhat flustered. "I'll go next," he said lightly, "though, of course, my life's been nothing like Madame's." He beamed down at Svetlana, who was completely ignoring him. I gave myself a moment to size him up. He was an almost unnoticeable person: average height and build, clean shaven, midbrown hair, wire-rimmed spectacles, and a nondescript, cheap dark suit with a white shirt and a narrow, dark tie. He looked to be in his early thirties and had a way of speaking that suggested he was apologizing for uttering a word. He nodded and hunched his shoulders as he spoke in a manner that suggested humility.

"I'm Jimmy Green, from San Francisco originally. Parents are, *were*, pretty liberal. Dead now." His smile seemed apologetic, rather than sad. "Ma and Joe—that's what I called my father—were young when they had me, so we were all great friends. I say I'm from San Francisco, but we moved around a lot. Ma played guitar and sang, Joe played the flute and sang too. And he played bongos. We lived in a van. I didn't go to school; Ma taught me. We had fun. When I was old enough, I sang too. But I wasn't any good when my voice broke. One day Ma and Joe went off in the van to meet some people, and they never came back. I never really said goodbye to them. They just didn't come back. The Pacific Coast Highway can be a deadly road."

Jimmy's body language told me he was having a difficult time sharing this with us. Clearly, he'd been traumatized by his parents' deaths. I wanted to tell him that I knew how it felt to lose both your parents at the same time, in a road accident. That you can tell yourself that at least they were together when they died ... But I reasoned that what had worked for me might not work for this young man. After all, the matter at hand was Miss Shirley's death, not the loss of parents years ago.

Jimmy continued more quietly, then rallied a little. "I was sixteen when they died. I came to live with Ma's sister here in Vegas. By then it was too late for me to catch up in school, so I didn't graduate. I got a series of jobs working my way up in backstage roles at some of the shows here on The Strip. Well, off-Strip to begin with, you know? I loved the life. Being around performers helped me feel somehow closer to the memory of my parents. I learned fast, and I was good at it. I got to know Miss Shirley when I worked at the theater in the old Sunrise Casino that she owned with Carl's dad before they knocked it down to build this one. I wasn't even twenty back then, just a kid really, but she always had time for me. Seemed interested in what I was doing. I never knew why. I'm not anyone special. She was that way with lots of people. She was very good to me and let me work with the people who designed the theater here, and I worked in it from the time it opened. She knew I'd always been nuts about opera and a huge fan of Diva Kharlamova, as she was herself, so, when Madame said she'd perform here, Miss Shirley asked if I'd like to be her assistant. I was so grateful. It's the best job in the world, Madame."

As he spoke, Jimmy Green beamed with genuine excitement and enthusiasm. I could see the light of a true disciple burn in his eyes. Svetlana was certainly lucky to have him, although, once again, she seemed oblivious to the fact that he was looking at her or even addressing her.

He continued, "I guess I'd just like to add that I certainly didn't kill Miss Shirley, and, for the record, I can't imagine why anyone would want to. She was the most wonderful woman I ever met ... after Madame, of course. Oh, and Ma ... and my aunt. She had time for everyone. She was Vegas through and through, and the best of it. No one better . . ." He finally took his seat and looked over at Svetlana as though hoping to be petted. She continued to ignore him.

Unfortunately, all I'd gleaned from Jimmy Green was that Miss Shirley had been a thoughtful employer, which didn't help much. Once he sat, there was a long pause. Everyone tried to avoid making eye contact with one another. I considered speaking up, to keep the ball rolling, but I was pleased to see that Clemence Foy was waving his handkerchief to gain our attention.

"I'll speak next," he said in his rasping tones, "but I'm gonna sit. Okay with you all?"

Shrugs and nods answered him. I was keen to hear what he would say, having known the victim for so many years.

"Gonna understand me and Miss Shirley? Gotta understand me," he began. "I was born in New Orleans"—he ran the two words together—"and never really went to school. Didn't agree with me. Big family, me the oldest. I guess you'd say we was 'dirt poor,' though I just thought that was how it was for all folks. I come here when I was fifteen. Been here sixty years now. Back then, when I met Miss Shirley, Vegas weren't like it is now." Clemence paused and sipped from a glass of water.

"Times change," chipped in Carl Petrosian. "Casinos get more technical, hotels get bigger. It's progress."

Clemence gave Carl the sort of look usually reserved for a child who's been naughty or rude, but is too young to know better. He shook his head. "That ain't what I mean. I mean the way it was for us blacks back then. Not allowed in the front doors, we weren't. Not allowed to use public accommodations. Less than second-class citizens. Mississippi of the West, they called it, and they wasn't kidding. Made Nat King Cole go 'round back of the Sands to get in to perform. He even had to use a trailer, outside, not a hotel room, till

Mr. Jack Entratter finally let him inside. Only place to hang out in mixed company was the old Moulin Rouge over in Westside. I seen it open, worked there a few months, and I seen it close. Fifty-five was quite a year. Saw all them big stars perform there or just hang out. Rat Pack and all. I even met Miss Sarann at the opening night. She's who owned it later on in the 1990s, for a little while. Tried to open it up again, but couldn't manage it. Fine woman. Weren't till 1960 that Dr. McMillan and Bob Bailey planned an antisegregation march up in front of all them big old marquees. All them men who ran the place behind closed doors sat up and took notice of Mr. Hank Greenspun. He could have made them look real bad in his newspaper and on his TV station. They didn't want no photographs of all of us 'coloreds' walking around with banners in front of their hotels, so they finally let us be bellhops, valets, and work at front desks. Even let blacks who could afford it rent their hotel rooms."

Clemence sucked his teeth and wiped his eyes. He looked, and sounded, sad. "I couldn't have gone if there'd been a protest march when they planned it anyway. Too busy with Miss Shirley. That was when she needed me, not the other way 'round. Tough year for her, 1960. Big year all 'round." I wondered what he meant, because he was clearly referring to something about which he hadn't spoken.

Once again Clemence sipped from his glass, and his eyes misted with remembrance. "We met in '58, me and Miss Shirley. I got beat up, bad, by some young white guys who thought it was funny to kick a black bum when he was down and on the wrong side of town. And I was down. Way down. Hadn't worked out too good for me in Vegas, and there weren't nowhere else for me to go. Miss Shirley found me on the side of a dirt road and she took me in. Smuggled me into her place. Whites only. She didn't have much of anything back then. Waitress in a diner. Nights. Scraping by. Sweet child. She looked after me. We neither of us had no money for doctors, so she just put me in her very own bed till I could walk. Nearly lost an eye. It never did work right after that. Didn't let me have no liquor, neither. And I ain't never touched a drop since then. There's some folks it just ain't good for. She even taught me how to read. 'You must exercise your eyes, Clemence,' she used to say, but we both knew what she was doing. It's because of Miss Shirley that I'm alive, I can read, and write some, and I've had a good life. Better than the one that bum I'd become would've had."

Clemence Foy wiped his face and continued, "Miss Shirley was always a good-looking girl. That's what she was back then, no more than a girl. Met her when she was just sixteen. I was twenty-one. I thought I was all growed up. I guess she knew better. Even when I was back on my feet, all fixed up and holding down a job, we'd go places together, where they'd let us. Where we could afford. Lots of men liked her, and she liked the attention. Natural. Her father died without even knowing she existed. He signed up right after Pearl Harbor and shipped out while him and her mother was just sweethearts. Her mother didn't even know she was pregnant when he left. He was dead before she was born, and her mother out on her ear with a baby to raise. Heidi, her ma was. Heidi Nowak. Named the baby after Shirley Temple, 'cause she was a favorite of hers since she done such a good job of playing Heidi in the movie. Her ma did the best she could, Miss Shirley said, but after the war, her mother married a guy and had some more kids." He smiled. "Funny enough, it were two boys."

I wonder why that remembrance makes him smile so broadly.

Sighing, Clemence continued, "Miss Shirley got kinda sidelined, so she left home and washed up in Vegas. Worked nights in the diner, sometimes days too. Nights off she'd dress up and go to a club. Guys would buy her drinks. She looked a lot older than she was. And when she got back from being away, the end of 1960, she looked a good deal more growed up again. Never told me where she went, but when she come back, she'd lost all the baby weight, and she looked just like Marilyn Monroe. Just eighteen years old, and looked like a real woman. Got the money for some fancy clothes from somewhere and had a fine new hairdo. In fact, she told me that when she saw Mr. Sinatra perform at the Sands in '61, he called out to her in the audience and told her she looked better than Marilyn herself, and that she shouldn't never change. And she didn't. That's why she kept the same style all these years."

That explained a lot. When I'd briefly met Miss Shirley over drinks earlier in the evening, I'd been surprised by her retro style, particularly her bouffant blond hair—classic Marilyn. Women quite often retain a form of dress, a sensibility of styling, that they've established at a time when they feel themselves to be in their prime. In Miss Shirley's case, I'd wondered why a woman who could have easily afforded to wear any designer labels she pleased adhered so strictly to an early 1960s look. I suppose if Frank Sinatra had told any impressionable teenager that she looked more beautiful than a screen goddess she likely would have clung to that. Her prime. Her "best ever look." Before she'd hit twenty.

Clemence cleared his throat and continued. "Anyway, like I said, when she got back she was looking very . . . mature . . . and she got herself a job in another diner, then, pretty quick, she married the guy who owned it. Right there and then, she got me a job. And she done that ever since. Even now." He laughed, making a wheezing sound, pressing his eyes closed. He even smiled like Satchmo. "Now I work in the men's dressing room downstairs, at the Romanoff Room. Swankiest place in town, and I get to be there every day. Makes me laugh that I help men who think it's okay to show up for dinner in two-hundred-dollar shorts understand that they have to wear long pants to eat there."

He shook his head, eyes twinkling, and seemed to notice us all, sitting in the gloom listening to him talk of times gone past, as if for the first time. "You have no idea how angry a man can get when you tell him he gotta wear a bunch of grown-up clothes if he wants to take his lady-wife for a nice dinner. Some of them can get real annoyed. But Miss Shirley likes the way I keep them calm and get them to put on the clothes we keep ready for them down in the men's cloakroom. I organize all the dry-cleaning and laundry every night before I go home, and I check all the items for wear and tear. It's like running a menswear store, only the clothes is just loaned out. After all them years of working men's rooms, it makes a change." He nodded. He'd lived a life I couldn't imagine, and he seemed to bear his lot with grace.

"There's a lot more I could say," he said, "'bout me, and 'bout her. But I'll just say this. There's always been talk in this town that she acted improper to get where she is today. This town do like its gossip. But that ain't true. When that first husband of hers up and died, she worked like a dog to make that diner pay. Then she opened up another one, and another. And when she sold them diners to them guys from out of town and married that no-good singer, she done it for the best of reasons. I think she really loved that crooner, and she wanted to invest in his career. 'Course, he were a handsome devil, too, made all them young girls swoon. She was broken when he just up and disappeared one day. Then it was my turn to help her again. All her money gone, and no home to live in. Couldn't marry, 'cause they wouldn't say he was dead. So what's she gonna do? 'Course she took whatever jobs she could. 'Course she had men friends. And when she finally married that jerk who come in from Tahoe, I knew he was trouble. Told her myself. But they built up a good business together, and she made sure a lot of folks had jobs. Wasn't her fault he run it into the ground. She done the right thing divorcing him. Then there she was, nothing again. Forty, single, and having to work as a dealer. And that's when Mr. Petrosian met her. She dealt him a hand that won him a fortune. She said he could take her out for dinner instead of giving her a tip, and five months later they was married. Quite the couple, they was, right, Carl?"

He looked over at Carl Petrosian, who nodded in agreement but clearly wasn't prepared to comment.

Clemence looked proud as he said, "She was the one who talked Carl's father into buying the Sunrise Casino, just when they was going bust. She worked every department, built everything up, then she and Carl's father decided to knock the old place down to build this place. In less than twenty years they turned a little old gamblin' hall into this, and they made it one of the most famous casinos in the world. She was one heck of a woman, was Miss Shirley, and I loved her as my best friend in the world."

He glanced toward the body of the woman he was mourning, and shook his head sadly. "Like I said earlier, ain't nobody like her gonna come into my life again. And there ain't no way she deserved to go like this."

When Clemence Foy stopped speaking, there was a respectful silence. There was no question about it, Miss Shirley's story was an interesting one. I began to sense the woman's presence grow within the room, and felt even more determined to try to work out who had decided to put an end to her colorful life.

First Intermezzo

AS CLEMENCE WAS SPEAKING I'D noticed that Tom had become distracted, glancing toward the bar frequently as the old man took us back through the years to a Vegas that no longer existed. Tom couldn't need a drink that badly—not unless, like many other chefs, he'd developed a habit of quaffing his ingredients.

Like the rest of us, Tom allowed a moment for Clemence's words to hang in the air, then he cleared his throat and said, "Look, I'm sorry to interrupt, but there's something I must do."

I suspected a call of nature, but was proved wrong.

"It's the caviar," he continued.

I glanced over at the stainless steel unit that sat atop the end of the bar. Three large crystal dishes loaded with glistening black, golden, and gray pearls had been nestled in crushed ice when we'd used mother-of-pearl spoons to help ourselves to the rare treat before dinner. Now most of the ice had disappeared.

"The ice surrounding the caviar is melting," said Tom. "If it gets above forty degrees, we'll have to dump it. I guess there's no power going to the refrigeration unit it's sitting on because it's plugged into an outlet in the floor. I should do something about it."

Ian stood to get a better view of the bar. "Hey, Tom, I'm sorry I didn't think of that. I don't usually get involved with the caviar—they bring it all up from downstairs and I just top up the crushed ice occasionally. I'll see if there's any ice left back there." We watched the young men as they opened hatches beneath the bar, then clattered about a bit. They exchanged a few muttered comments, and both shook their heads.

Tom was still shaking his when he said, "There's no ice back here, and no refrigeration. I suggest we eat the caviar, folks. So long as that's okay with you, Mr. Sauber, Mr. Petrosian?" He'd obviously decided that both men were in charge—a very Canadian approach to dealing with a difficult situation.

Carl and Art nodded. "It'll be quite a feast," said Carl loudly. "Miss Shirley only served the best. There's sure to be a couple of thousand dollars' worth there, flown in fresh from Russia. Dad said she cried when the US banned its import, so they had to go to Russia to eat it. Luckily for Miss Shirley the government changed its mind, so she can get her fix . . . sorry, *could* get her fix here, whenever she wanted. Damn, I just can't get used to thinking of her as gone." He shook his head, then added, "Have at it, folks. Right, Art?"

Art nodded. "Sure, go ahead. Don't know what all the fuss is about, myself. Terrible way they get at the stuff, and it costs a fortune. Just pour salt down your throat, I say."

"Come and get it, then," said Tom. "Bring plates from the dessert table. There's a pile there." I tried my best to not look too eager.

Bud put a hand on my arm. "Hold your horses, Cait, and try to be good?" He smiled warmly.

"I *was* good before dinner. I hardly took any, though it was fabulous to have the chance to try such good beluga, alongside sterlet and osetra. The pearls of that beluga are huge. Didn't you just love it when they burst against the roof of your mouth?"

Bud wrinkled his nose. "Not really my thing, Cait. You know I'm not a fancy eater, and it's quite . . . well, it's very salty, and . . . hey, if you want to load a plate as though it's for me, you go ahead. I'll be your cover for a double portion."

I patted his arm as I rose, then turned to Tom's girlfriend. "How about you, Tanya? Will you have some?"

Tanya made a face as though I'd asked her to drink a vat of acid. "Not likely. You can have mine too, if you want." Her expression had returned to its sulky setting.

"Okay, please yourself," I replied. I tried to keep the edge out of my voice, but it crept through.

As I headed toward the plates and the bar, I felt a spring in my step, which I wouldn't have expected for almost two in the morning.

It seemed as though everybody viewed the caviar announcement as an opportunity to take a break, move about a bit, and reposition themselves. The Diva was giving Jimmy detailed instructions as to how she wanted her plate prepared, Jack and Carl had beaten me to the serving trolley, Julie was standing behind Clemence, bending to speak to him quietly, Bud was trying to engage Tanya in conversation, Tom was helping serve the caviar, and Ian was carrying trays laden with bottles of vodka, small glasses, large glasses, and bottles of sparkling water to each table. Art had placed himself at the end of the bar farthest from the caviar action, and stood with his foot resting comfortably on the rail, sipping a glass of calvados poured from the bottle at his elbow, to which he'd helped himself.

Conversations were muted, but no one seemed to be in deep mourning. I took "Bud's plate" to our table and returned to the bar to fill my own. As I did so, I noticed Clemence making his way to the men's room.

It was clear that we wouldn't be reconvening our joint recollection session for quite a few moments, so I wandered toward the partition closest to the dessert table, to give the porcelain pieces atop it my attention. Julie joined me, a glass of vodka in her hand.

"Cheers," she said as she sipped.

"Cheers," I replied, toasting her with a blini loaded with so much golden sterlet that the mound almost went up my nose as I bit into it. I must have looked surprised and embarrassed because Julie turned away and gazed out through the glass wall.

She sighed, or maybe stifled a smile. "It all looks so beautiful from here," she said almost wistfully. Despite the hour, The Strip was still dazzling, with the giant screens, the constant glittering of the blazing lightbulbs and tubes, the floodlit buildings, and the motion of the traffic still streaming along in multiple stacked lanes.

I managed to mumble my agreement. I was far enough away from the glass wall to not feel the vertigo that usually grips me when I'm looking down from a height. I was able to gaze in all directions and enjoy the view. I allowed myself to do this for a moment as I enjoyed the sensation in my mouth. "We're right at the top of the egg here, aren't we?" I managed to say between mouthfuls, hoping that Julie would run with the topic. Luckily, she did.

"Yes. You've seen the egg from The Strip?"

I nodded.

"It's quite something, right?" she said with some enthusiasm. "The special glass gives it a unique look. Real gold was used in the glass-making process, offering that wonderful finish and a good element of sun reflection. We'll be grateful for that quality when the sun comes up, given that the AC is out."

It was clear to the woman that I was fully involved with eating, so she continued, "The black 'stripe' around the egg's middle is the Babushka Bar. That's where you'd have got off the escalator from the casino and entered the elevator. The black treatment on the glass creates a more 'clubby' atmosphere. Above it is the Romanoff Room. You won't have seen that because security would have used the elevator code for this level. You should see it sometime. It's quite spectacular. Very gold. And red. Very Miss Shirley, and tsarist, of course." She smiled and shook her head gently, clearly thinking of her late employer with genuine affection.

"Above that there's another floor with black glass, right where you'd cut the top off a soft-boiled egg. That's where the kitchen is. Then there's this place, in the bit of the egg that ends up on the plate." She smiled at me, and I did my best to return the expression. The look on her face suggested I might have caviar on my teeth.

"Why's the elevator right in the middle of this room?" I asked, licking my lips. "It seems to be a bit in the way of the best setup for a dining room."

Julie glanced toward the pod. "Oh, that's because they had to hide the machine room outside the glass envelope of the egg somewhere. The shaft runs right through the middle so that all the machinery could be slap bang in the center at the top of the egg and hidden with those four golden, double-headed eagles that look just like a crown on the egg's tip."

I swallowed and looked up. "So what's above us? Between this flat ceiling and the domed roof of the egg?" I couldn't imagine that the cavity really offered a place for an unknown killer to hide, but I thought I should ask.

Julie thoughtfully followed my gaze. "I don't know. Some sort of electrical stuff, I guess. I don't suppose it would have been practical to have this room open right into the top of the egg. I've never really thought about it," she said, a frown furrowing her smooth brow.

"Cait?" It was Bud. He motioned that I should take my seat. Everyone else was back in their allotted places, except Clemence, who was ambling back from the men's room in his shirtsleeves, carrying his jacket. He was swaying a little, quite unsteady on his feet. Julie and I both registered his wobbling arrival at the same moment and headed toward him. I placed my plate on the dessert table as I passed, so I'd have both hands free. We both had our arms out as we met up with him, but he waved us away. Clemence was clearly a man who didn't like to accept help. I noticed a tiny spot of blood on one of his shirtsleeves, which concerned me. Even in the dim light, I could see that his pupils were like tiny pinpricks and his eyes were glassy. He looked disoriented.

"Are you alright, Clemence?" asked Julie, the note of concern in her voice drawing the attention of both Art and Carl.

Clemence looked surprised. "Considering I just lost my oldest friend, I'm doing just fine, ma'am. I hope it doesn't bother you that I've removed my jacket. I'm kinda warm. Now I think I'll sit me down again and listen to how all you other folks knowed Miss Shirley, and what you thought of her. Then maybe I can work out which one of you killed her."

Quartet

"I SURE DIDN'T," SAID TOM and Tanya in unison. They turned to each other and smiled.

"After you," said Tom, nodding at his girlfriend.

Tanya stood so that she could see and address everyone. "I'm not good at speaking in public, so this won't take long." She knotted and unknotted her fingers, then pressed her palms against the table, hunching her shoulders. She took some deep breaths, as though she were about to dive into a pool, and began.

"Tanya Willis, born and raised in Henderson. Dad, Sam. Mom, Maisie. Went to UNLV to study math and computer programming. Graduated 2005. I was seventeen. Got recruited into the Tsar! Organization. Been here ever since. Now I oversee all the computing systems. Biggest job right now is overhauling the loyalty program, which is really exciting. I met Miss Shirley when I was a child. My father worked at the Sunrise, then here for a while. Dad wasn't very lucky with jobs. Miss Shirley's been very nice to me. I'll miss her. I guess I'll carry on working here, whoever takes over." At this point she looked over at Carl and Art. Her body language throughout her short speech had been neutral, if somewhat tense. She sat.

Tom looked surprised. "That's it?" he asked. She nodded. "Oh, come on, Tanya, you need to blow your own trumpet a bit more than that. Listen folks"—he stood, dwarfing his girlfriend, who had sunk back into her seat—"Tanya's brilliant. I mean it. She went to university when she was fifteen." There were a few raised eyebrows around the room. "Yeah, fifteen. I know it wasn't easy for her, 'cause she's told me how tough it was to be accepted and to mix in. But she graduated in just two years, top in everything. See—brilliant!

She's funny and really clever with numbers. She organized all her hours so we can be together when I'm not working—which takes some doing because being head sous-chef in the kitchen downstairs means I work some very long, unsociable hours. And Miss Shirley thought she was brilliant too. Right?" He looked down at the top of Tanya's head.

His girlfriend gave a slight nod, but her expression was blank.

"Yes, she did," Tom continued. "I've been here for ten months or so now. Tanya and I met when I'd been here only six weeks, at the post-Christmas/New Year staff party. Miss Shirley introduced us to each other as the brightest stars she knew in our respective fields. You see, when Chef Michel recruited me to the Romanoff Room, Miss Shirley already knew a lot about me, because of that TV show I was on. She said she liked the way I was always polite to the other competitors and that I always stayed positive. Tanya and I have been together ever since Miss Shirley introduced us." He smiled down at Tanya, who was now looking up at him. She returned his broad, proud grin with a twitch of the corners of her lips, then cast her eyes downward again, the picture of demure coyness. *Odd.*

"And that's us," said Tom. "Without Miss Shirley, we wouldn't be *us*. We've just bought a house out in Henderson, and we'll be moving there once we get the place cleaned up and decorated."

Tom shrugged as he added, "As for why we're here tonight, well, I was delighted to be invited, honored in fact. As I mentioned to some of you earlier on, Miss Shirley invited Tanya and myself to join her here this evening just yesterday. Of course it meant I had to arrange some quick cover for my shift downstairs in the kitchen, but it's been great to be on the receiving end of the food coming out of it while sitting in such lavish surroundings."

Tom bit his lip, then continued, "I'm really very sad that Miss Shirley is dead. Um . . ." He looked around and clearly decided to just say the thing he was unsure about. "She told Tanya that she would have some big news for us, for me, tonight. I was hoping that, when she inherited her late husband's shares at midnight and was finally allowed to make changes to the organization, she would appoint me as executive chef at the Romanoff Room—now that Chef Michel has announced he'd like to take a step back. I . . . of course I'm disappointed that didn't happen, but I'm more sorry that she's dead." Tom looked resigned, rather than heartbroken, which I judged a suitable response to the death of an employer who apparently favored advancing his career.

"I happen to know that's exactly what Miss Shirley had planned," said Julie, as Tom resumed his seat. She stood and smoothed her smart suit. "It's common knowledge in the entire Vegas community that a complex prenuptial agreement was signed when Mr. Petrosian, Carl's father, married Miss Shirley. When he passed, his will stated that Miss Shirley was to inherit his majority holding in the Tsar! Organization if she outlived him and remained single for one year after his death. He wanted a period of stability during that time. Other than normal staff turnover, maintenance, and the completion of the upgrades of this room, which were in hand before his death, nothing was to be changed about Tsar! Mr. Art Sauber, the forty-nine percent owner"—she and Art exchanged formal nods—"has been much more involved with the running of the Tsar! Organization during the past year, and Miss Shirley had become even more hands-on, if that's possible, with all aspects of it during the same period. She was always involved before, of course, in every facet of the business. Indeed, if it hadn't been for some complications because of her previous bankruptcy, which, again, everyone hereabouts knows about, she and her husband, Mr. Petrosian, would have *always* been co-owners of the controlling share. As it was, they felt it better to keep her name off the papers initially. The plan was that after she inherited the fifty-one percent of shares tonight, she would be able to start implementing her own choices regarding the Tsar! and all its interests. I know it's been a lot for Art to handle. As you all know, I head up the legal department here, and there has been a huge amount of paperwork to get sorted since Mr. Petrosian died, so Art and I have been working together. Thank you, Art." Julie nodded graciously in Art's direction, and he smiled back.

Julie continued, "As for how I came to be here at all? It's a story involving chance, which brought me to exactly where I believe I was meant to be. I'm from Maine. I studied at Harvard, was hired by a firm in New York straight out of college, and stayed there until I got involved with a pro bono case for a friend of a friend out in Los Angeles. Being a corporate lawyer I hadn't done much pro bono work until then. I managed to talk my firm into letting me do it, even though it was so far away, because it was such a fascinating case." She paused, gazed around our faces, and said abruptly, "I won't bother you with the intricacies of the case. Suffice it to say I met Jack as a result of it. When Miss Shirley offered me a post here, I took it so I could be close to Jack. I moved here in 1998, and Jack and I were the last couple to be married at the old Sunrise Casino, shortly before its spectacular implosion. I worked with the Tsar! Organization right through the construction period and have been here ever since. It's been fascinating work, and I enjoyed my relationship with Miss Shirley, which became even closer when I was promoted to my current post."

I thought that Julie was about to sit again, but she tilted her head, looked at Tom, and said, "I'd just like to say, Tom, that although Miss Shirley is no longer with us, your promotion is already in the works. I brought a folder full of papers that Miss Shirley had been most insistent she wanted to sign here, tonight, as soon as she was legally able. She only signed one—the document she needed to sign to acknowledge her ownership of the shares. She did it while Ian was swinging the saber to open the champagne bottles. She was going to sign the others after dessert. She didn't. However, I'm sure we'll be able to sort your promotion for you, Tom, because, with the greatest respect, it's not something that ever really needed her specific approval—Chef

Michel has actual executive power regarding the Romanoff Room, so he'll be able to clear your change of status before he moves on."

Tom beamed and squeezed Tanya's hand in excitement. She looked at her boyfriend with relief and crinkled her eyes at him as she affectionately rubbed his big arm.

I saw Carl Petrosian tense as Julie spoke, but rather than say anything, he glanced at Bud and nibbled his lip. Art Sauber frowned.

"So who gets Miss Shirley's shares now that she's gone?" Tom innocently asked. "Mr. Carl or Mr. Art?" It seemed a reasonable enough question. All eyes turned toward Julie. Clearly there was a great deal of interest in the room about the issue of ownership.

Julie sighed and shook her head. "Well, that's the thing, you see. One of the documents she didn't sign was her new will. I know what would have happened to the shares if Miss Shirley had died, or remarried, before the year was up—in other words, before she inherited them. I also know what she planned to do in the new will that she and I worked on. But all of that is moot, because she did inherit the shares, but didn't sign her new will. So her previous will stands."

Again, it wasn't Carl or Art who spoke. It was Tanya, which surprised me. "So, will Carl or Art be the new owner?" she asked. Petulantly, I thought.

The glances passed around the room confirmed that everyone was in a state of anticipation. Julie Pool looked a little uncertain. Her husband stood and put his arm around her waist. He and Julie shared an intimate smile, then she shrugged and shook her head. "I can't say. At least, I don't believe I should say anything more."

Carl Petrosian's dismissive "Huh!" was heard by everyone.

I knew that at some point I'd have to try to find out exactly what Miss Shirley's now-defunct plans had been for the distribution of her wealth after her death, as well as what other papers she'd planned to sign, but hadn't. Both could be important in working out who had a motive to kill her.

Since he was already on his feet, having risen to support his wife, Jack Bullock took the floor as she sat down. "I am guessing you've all had more to do with Julie than with me. I know I haven't represented any of you in court, and that's usually how folks meet me. I've met some of you at corporate events before, but I don't think I've ever had the chance, beyond the confines of our small circle of friends, to tell *our* story. You see, Julie was being very humble when she told you how she came to be here. She actually comes from 'old money.' Her mom and dad threatened to cut her off without a penny if she gave up her promising future with one of New York's finest and oldest law firms to come to Nevada and live with greasy old me."

Jack had a very light voice, bordering on nasal, but he spoke rather well. I couldn't help but wonder if he'd taken acting lessons at some point in his life. Given his chosen profession as a lawyer specializing in getting people out of DUI charges, I suspected that the ability to portray a range of emotions at will in the courthouse would be useful to him. His mannerisms were slightly too well matched to his words, his body language just a little too convincing. As I tried to put aside my snap judgment of him, I couldn't help feeling that we were all being sold a story.

Jack chuckled as he said, "Hey, you all know what I am—and that's what I'll always be. I'm good at it. I don't annoy the authorities too much. I've struck a vein of gold, and I mine it for all it's worth."

He gazed down at his wife as he added, "As Julie said, we met in LA because she was there visiting to help a friend of a friend. At that time I was already living here in Vegas, but I was back in California for a little while, visiting my mom. You see, I'm from LA originally. When Julie and I met it was an immediate attraction, even though we're oil and water. I'm the oily one, of course, and she's the deep water. To be fair, I understood her parents' concerns. Julie could have had her pick of moneyed trust-fund heirs or loaded corporate lawyers, but she chose me, and here we are, fifteen years later, proving them all wrong. We're happier now than we've ever been."

Julie took his hand as he stretched it out to her, and she almost whispered, "That we are. And we can face *anything* together."

I wonder what she means.

"How d'you know Miss Shirley in the first place?" asked Tanya.

Jack smiled. "Funny story. She was the reason I came here from LA in the first place. She was visiting friends in California and happened to walk into the Burbank legal office where I was working at the time. Needed some papers notarized. We ended up having coffee, and she sized me up right away—saw what I could become. She said she knew a guy who ran a practice specializing in DUIs in Vegas and needed an energetic young gun to help out. I liked her from the outset, and I thought it would be worth following up. So I came to stay at the Sunrise, met the guy, we clicked, he offered me a job, and I moved here right away. Stayed at the Sunrise, gratis, until I found a place of my own. Five years later the guy running the practice retired and Jack's your uncle!"

Tom laughed out loud. It was the first time we'd heard such a sound since the discovery of Miss Shirley's body. It drew a few shocked glances.

"Sorry," said Tom, blushing. "It's just that, well, I have an uncle Jack. Sorry. It was inappropriate of me . . ." He wriggled uncomfortably.

"It's my fault," said Jack. "I shouldn't have tried to be flippant. Now's not the time for entertainment. But it's my shtick. Can't help it. Sorry. So, yes, I knew Miss Shirley for years, and as well as anyone can when a woman's the talk of the town you live in and your main reason for communicating directly with her on an ongoing basis is to thank her for all the business she's sending your way. That said, when I met Julie in LA I knew that the Sunrise needed some help in the legal department. For all that Vegas seems like a huge place, especially to visitors, it's really just a small town. People in the same line of work know each other, know what's going on. I knew the guy heading up the legal department at the Sunrise, so I took my chance and dragged Julie to Vegas to meet Miss Shirley, and the rest, as they say, is history. Miss Shirley welcomed her with open arms and offered her the job at the Sunrise on the spot. I think she also convinced Julie's predecessor to retire a bit earlier than he'd planned."

"No she didn't, Jack," snapped Julie. "The Tsar! Organization was much bigger than anything he'd dealt with and the whole thing became even more complex as the years passed. It was more my sort of thing."

Jack smiled indulgently at his wife. "Whatever the reason, Julie became top dog about ten years ago, and we socialized a fair bit with Miss Shirley and her husband, Carl Petrosian Sr. Great company, the pair of them. Miss Shirley didn't do well when he died, but I guess most of you know that. We certainly noticed it. But she didn't take her foot off the gas when it came to the business. As Julie said, she was getting more and more involved, preparing for the formal takeover. I'm guessing that was all for you, Carl, because while her old will named you as inheriting her entire estate, in her new will she added that her next of kin was to inherit the shares in the Tsar!"

"Jack, don't! That's highly confidential information. I shouldn't have told you." Julie Pool shot her husband a dagger-laden glance. It was hard for me to tell if she was more angry at her husband for speaking out of turn, or at herself for having told him something she shouldn't have.

"Oh, come on, Julie. What does it matter now? You must have guessed that you'd be her main beneficiary, Carl, surely?" Jack sounded defensive as he spoke.

All eyes turned toward Carl Petrosian.

"You kill Miss Shirley to get casino?" declaimed Svetlana, horrified.

My money was on everyone thinking much the same thing at that moment: her stepson was the one man in the room with a very real reason to want Miss Shirley dead.

Male Trio

CARL PETROSIAN LEAPT FROM HIS seat. "No one's going to pin this on me. I didn't do it. I could no more have shoved a sword into Miss Shirley's back than I could have into my own father's."

He glanced toward Bud, who shrugged. I'd often observed Bud interviewing suspects, hardly saying a word, just letting them babble on and tie themselves up in knots. I wondered if that was what he was hoping for. Expecting, even.

Carl sounded desperate. "I'm not going to let anyone tell the cops that I had a motive to kill her, because I didn't. I didn't know about her wills. New or old. She never talked to me about the specifics of either one. Just made general hints." He was almost squealing.

"Okay, calm down, Carl," said Art quietly.

"Oh dear," said Julie, sounding distressed. "I shouldn't have discussed any of this with Jack, I know, and he certainly shouldn't have blurted out anything about Miss Shirley's wills. I apologize profusely. It was totally unprofessional of us both." She looked at her husband with shock and disappointment, and Jack looked suitably chastised. Her words interested me, because she seemed to be directing them toward both Art and Carl.

Art Sauber shook his head as he spoke. "Julie, Jack, I really don't think it can make any difference now. Miss Shirley's gone, and I, at least, feel free to speak. As you all know, Carl and Miss Shirley were not blood relatives, and although she married his father, she never formally adopted Carl. He was a little too old for all that." He smiled at Carl, who shrugged and nodded. "Miss Shirley's father died in the 1940s, as we have heard from Clemence, and I know that her mother passed in the late 1970s. Her mother had two boys with her second husband, and they both died in Vietnam. Neither had any children, nor did they marry. Miss Shirley's stepfather passed in 1984. To be fair to Carl, I can confirm what he said: Miss Shirley told me, on many occasions, that she'd decided not to discuss her plans for her estate with Carl, so I think we can all be pretty sure that he didn't know for certain whether or not he was due to inherit—in either of Miss Shirley's wills."

Carl threw Art an almost-grateful glance.

"You see, Carl," Art continued, "during the past year, since your father's death, Miss Shirley and I talked on several occasions about what her inheritance of the majority shareholding in the Tsar! Organization meant. She wondered whether you were the right person to have control over the Tsar! after she'd gone. Of course, neither she nor I imagined that anything . . . like this . . . would happen."

"Very pally of you two," spat Carl as he again leapt from his seat. "How nice that you and she would sit around and discuss the future in such an intimate way. What does your fragrant wife, Joan, think of that? You know, Joan who never, ever comes with you to Vegas. Who stays at your home in Florida, or at the house in Maine, and gives us all a very broad berth. And what did you have to say about me during those secret chats, I wonder?" He sounded childishly spiteful.

Art looked at Carl with what I judged to be an indulgent smile, though his tone was not. "You've never really had a head for business, Carl, so I guess I can't expect you to understand that bequeathing a bunch of stuff, albeit very valuable stuff, differs significantly from bequeathing a controlling interest in a billion-dollar business. Miss Shirley's new will had to allow for that difference."

Carl rolled his eyes and clenched his fists as Art Sauber dismissed him in a sentence. His cheeks grew pink beneath his deep tan as he spoke. "I happen to run a very successful enterprise myself, you know, Art. You do me a great disservice when you say I don't have a head for business." He sounded wounded.

Art sighed and motioned for Carl to sit. "Calm yourself," he said, as Carl grudgingly took his seat. "It's something that your father and I discussed with Miss Shirley before his death. His views and mine weren't that far apart. Miss Shirley took his lead. Look, you're not cut out for running a huge business like this one, Carl. *Your* thing, the thing you're really quite exceptional at, is fixing up cars. You have bought, restored, won awards with, and resold some of the world's most iconic vehicles. Yes, you spend piles of money doing it—but your father, Miss Shirley, and I all agreed you always spend it wisely."

Carl's expression changed to that of a small child being congratulated for an achievement.

Art half-smiled as he continued, "But that's because you understand cars. You know them through and through. You love them. More than people, some would say. I know your ex-wife said it often enough."

Art sighed again and sipped his drink. I could tell he was building up to something. He leaned toward Carl. "Look, Carl, if ever there was a time to be honest, tonight is it. I won't hide the fact that I am amazed to hear from Jack that Miss Shirley left the Tsar! shares to you. I honestly thought she'd leave them to me, allowing me to step up and take full control." He paused for a moment and looked around the room at the rest of us. "Not that I would have killed her for that reason. To be honest, I've always been quite happy to be a minority investor, taking something of a backseat and letting the profits roll in."

He returned his gaze to Carl as he continued, "Of course I expected her to leave you everything else. And that in itself is a lot. The house has to be worth at least five million, even in this market. Just the collection of gold and porcelain in this room is probably worth another couple of million. She was a wealthy woman, Carl, and you're already a wealthy man. I knew she didn't want me to have everything, but, honestly, I find it hard to believe that she left you in charge of the Tsar!"

Carl Petrosian glugged sulkily from his glass of cognac, and Art Sauber drained his calvados, then took his seat. I washed down my final morsel of caviar-covered blini from "Bud's plate" with a swig of room-temperature vodka—something I immediately regretted.

I made a mental note that both Carl and Art had excellent reasons to want Miss Shirley dead, whatever the two of them might say.

"I met Miss Shirley just over a year ago," piped up Ian from his table. We all turned as he broke the awkward silence.

"You're the guy with the cocktail, right?" asked Art.

Ian nodded. "Ian Glass. And, yes, I've heard *all* the jokes about my name, given that I'm a barman," he said as he smiled wanly. "I made a martini for Miss Shirley at a fundraiser for the Center for Performing Arts. She invited me to the Babushka Bar at 9:00 AM the next morning, then said I had an hour to come up with a new signature cocktail for the Tsar! I remember I had to get someone to bring me golden raisins from the kitchen, and she said that was what won her over. Since then the Tsar!Tini has sold and sold. It's the same red as the logo, and there are golden raisins on a little golden saber that lies across the glass, in case you haven't seen it. Vodka-based, of course," he added proudly. "She loved it. She launched it at her birthday party here last year."

Carl stared into his glass as he said, "Of course. I remember that night very well. Dad enjoyed it. It was a great party. Up to a point, of course. She sure knew how to throw one." He drained his glass and looked at it sadly, rolling his unused cigar tube with his free hand.

Ian looked embarrassed as he pressed on. *I wonder why.* "Oh, I'm so sorry. Um . . . anyway, before she hired me, I just knew *of* her. I've been in town just a couple of years. I'm from Seattle. Worked bars there, got some training, and did the cruise ship thing for about five years. Got fed up with the Alaska runs. I'd had enough rain at home. So I moved here. Got here in November 2010, just in time for those terrible floods in December. Ironic. I worked for a company that supplies people for banquets and functions. Did that until Miss Shirley hired me and I became a barman at the Babushka Bar, and now I also work evening shifts at the Romanoff Room. She requested me for this bar when the place is in use. And I was the one who'd go to her house to serve drinks when she was entertaining at home. Like Mr. Carl said, she really knew how to do a dinner, or a party, just right. She was always very good to me. She gave me great opportunities. And great tips. I'm, like, real sorry she's gone."

Ian paused, but he clearly wasn't finished. "Look, I just want to say something else. I know they're going to find my fingerprints all over that sword. But you all saw me use it, right? My prints are bound to be there because I used the sword to uncork all the champagne bottles. I only did it because Miss Shirley herself asked me to. It's a thing I learned working on the ships. She said it sounded like fun. You'll all say you saw me use the sword to do that, right?"

He looked terrified. In terms of a pecking order in the room I guessed he saw himself at the bottom, and he had definitely handled the murder weapon. He had cause to be concerned. Of course, if he was the killer, he had the perfect cover for his prints being there.

But why would a young barman—I put him in his late twenties—want his boss dead? Miss Shirley wasn't being spoken of in anything other than glowing terms. Was everyone lying, or was she really the wonderful, supportive person she was said to be?

"Well, that's just about everyone done," said Art Sauber. "I guess it's my turn now. I met Miss Shirley through her husband, Carl Petrosian Sr., as did little Carl Jr. here."

Carl tutted and splashed more cognac from his bottle.

Art smiled wickedly. "I know you hate the 'junior' thing, Carl," he said, "but I just wanted to use it once, for clarity. You met Miss

Shirley when she and your father had already been together for some time, right?"

Carl nodded. "Yes. He and Mom had been divorced for years by then, and he introduced me to Miss Shirley on one of my rare visits to his house. They were engaged by then. He was very happy with her, and, to be fair, she was a wonderful partner for him—in life and in business. Couldn't have been more different from my mother, who's never happier than when she's baking. The real mystery is why Mom and Dad got together, not why he and Miss Shirley did."

It seemed to me that Carl was being honest in what he said, though his voice was tinged with a grudging tone as he spoke. Given his general personality, that was what made me think he was being truthful.

Art smiled. "I knew your mom and dad from the time I was a kid," he said, "and I think I know why they got together—though I do understand why it didn't work out in the long run. They were a couple from a very early age, but I guess they just grew apart as the years passed and their interests diverged. Let me give this some context for those of you who don't know me at all. When I showed up in Vegas I was just a kid, fresh from Hoboken. It was 1950, and, although no one knew it at the time, Vegas was on the edge of a cliff, getting ready to jump off and become what it is today. Back then, it was still largely undeveloped. A year later they started all the atomic testing out in the desert, a little over fifty miles away. People came to watch the explosions. Strange. Brought a lot of military and tourists into the general area. I remember they used to have Miss Atomic Bomb contests, if you can believe it." Art smiled to himself.

Svetlana looked very puzzled.

Art sighed and said, "Even with a bunch of outsiders coming into the area, a lot of the locals thought that me and my ma and pa were freaks. My classmates, and even a couple of my teachers, told me they couldn't understand a word I said, which made me rebellious. Your mom and dad were five years older than me, Carl, which is a huge difference when you're a kid. But they were both great to me. They took me under their wings and helped me along. Sinatra said that when he was growing up in Hoboken all he ever thought about was how to get out of the place. For me, coming to this place in the middle of nowhere, I felt I'd been taken away from everything I knew, and dumped on the moon. I hated it. To be honest, I'm not sure how I'd have turned out without your mom and dad taking an interest in me. Your dad was a great male role model for me. You see, it turned out that the reason my pa had moved us here from out east was because he'd been hired to do some strong-arm stuff for a bunch of guys whose names ended in vowels. About a year or so after we got here, he got himself locked up, and he disappeared completely when they let him out. Schmuck! Your mom and dad left school as soon as they could, and got married pretty soon after that. It didn't take you long to show up. I got scared when they left the school. I thought they'd ignore me, but, even though your dad was holding down a couple of jobs, they didn't. They even looked after my ma when I got my first job, as a salesman traveling in ladies' shoes."

He looked around the room and grinned. "Carl's mother *and* Miss Shirley always cracked up when I said that. Asked me if it hurt to walk in them . . ." No one smiled. Svetlana looked even more puzzled.

Art shrugged. "Anyway, I did that for almost ten years for a company out of Boston, but it was frustrating work. The people who made the shoes I was trying to sell didn't listen to the feedback I was giving them from the customers. I knew I could do better, but I had to work out how. I took off for a couple of years to visit family in Israel. When I got back here, I had a plan, a new focus, and I put all my money into a small production facility. It took some time, but I guess you all know that Art of Shoes became a real US success story."

Until that point I hadn't connected Art Sauber with Art of Shoes.

I've only been in Canada for ten years or so, but even I've heard of them. Apparently Art was the man who'd shod Middle America for decades. *He must be very rich!*

I didn't try to hide my surprise, and Art spotted it. "Yes, that was me. Luckily for me I listened to Miss Shirley and Carl when they came to me with the idea to invest in Tsar! I sold Art of Shoes in 1997. I was lucky. None of us saw it coming, but, as it turned out, sales of women's shoes from US manufacturers pretty much halved from 1997 to 2000. Can you believe that for timing? Foreign imports wrecked the market for us. But I was out, and I put all my money into this place. Didn't want to run it, mind you. Never interested in that. But I knew, I *believed*, I'd make a mint by backing Carl and Miss Shirley. And I wasn't wrong. My right-hand man at Art of Shoes was my chief financial officer, Stephen Feldblum, and he agreed with me. Now there's a man I've trusted with my life, and I've also trusted him with all my financial decisions. He came on board here during the demo of the old Sunrise and the build of this place, and stayed. You worked with him a lot, didn't you, Julie? Great guy, right? I love him like a brother, like I loved your father, Carl."

Julie smiled. "How's Stephen doing?" she asked. "Living the dream of retirement life?"

"Sure is," replied Art. "Got a nice setup in Florida now, where he works on his tan beside the pool and sees how fast he can smoke his way through his boxes of cigars, while reading book after book on those little electronic things. Deserves it. He's seventy-eight now, but still does a month of volunteering on different projects in Israel every year. Amazing energy for a little whippet of a man. Puts me to shame."

He smiled indulgently. "And that's me, folks. As for me and Miss Shirley? Well, of course I was upset when your mom and dad divorced, Carl, but not really surprised. By then they'd grown into entirely different people. When your father introduced me to Miss Shirley, I knew they were right for each other. By that time I was back east running Art of Shoes and only visited Vegas, and my old friend Carl Sr., on an irregular basis. He was tied up with business here all the time, as was I on the other side of the country. Neither of us had any idea that we'd end up as business partners. Life throws us curveballs when we least expect it. Anyway, when I saw them together, there was no doubt in my mind that they'd make a go of it. I was proud to be 'second-best man,' as your dad called me, on their wedding day. You made a good best man, Carl."

"Yeah, they were real happy that day," recalled Carl. He shook his head wistfully. "Although it was 1984, Miss Shirley still wore a dress that looked as though it was from 1964. All the brides at that time were wearing those giant poufy things, like Princess Di had done a few years earlier, but not Miss Shirley. Looked more like a cross between Marilyn and Jackie O than Princess Di. That pillbox hat with a veil sitting on her big, blond hair, remember?"

Art smiled. "Yes, it was a good day," he replied, "and it allowed me to see that a couple could live together, play together, and work together. What Miss Shirley and your father achieved with the old Sunrise was a real phenomenon, Carl. And I can tell you that I had no doubt I was making the right move by investing in their dream for this place. As I said earlier, it was good timing too. I remember I met you for the first time at their wedding, Clemence, and I seem to recall that you cried that day too." Art smiled warmly at the man, who, throughout everyone's explanations, had remained motionless, except to sip his water.

Clemence nodded now, looking as though he was about to burst into tears again.

"By the way, Clemence," added Art, "there's something I can add to your tale about Miss Shirley's early life. When I bought a house here and began to spend more time in Vegas with Carl and Miss Shirley, we all talked a great deal, as you do over cocktails. You said she left Vegas in 1960, but you didn't know where she went?"

Clemence nodded.

"Well, I can tell you: it was Hollywood. That's when she went blond. Apparently, she'd had a role as an extra in *Ocean's Eleven*, which was shot here in Vegas during January and February 1960. She got the movie bug, it seems, and she took herself off to try to get some roles in Hollywood itself. She never did say who it was she got mixed up with when she was there, but she did mention he had a thing for blondes, and that was why she changed her hair. I have my own ideas about who she meant. So I know *where* she went, but I was never sure why she went exactly *then*. Maybe it was seeing all those big movie stars here in Vegas, and seeing how glamorous their lives were. Or maybe someone offered her some sort of starlet dream. I don't know."

"Hollywood?" said Clemence. "Really? I wonder why she told you and not me." He sounded hurt.

Art spoke quickly. "Well she didn't tell *me*. She told her husband, and he told me. That's the only reason I know." He smiled reassuringly at Clemence. "Did you know she was in that movie?"

Clemence nodded slowly.

"Have you ever spotted her in it?" continued Art.

Again Clemence nodded and smiled.

"I'd love you to point her out to me someday," said Art. "I must have watched it a dozen times or more, but I can't see anyone who looks anything like her, even allowing for the fact that she had dark hair at the time, which she told me herself."

Clemence nodded. "Sure will, Mr. Art, I knows exactly when she's in it. Though you're right, you wouldn't have recognized her. Dark hair, a hat, and a big old coat, covering her babies. It was the next month she gave birth, so she was pretty big then."

Two long seconds of silence followed.

"Miss Shirley was pregnant?" asked an astonished Art Sauber.

Clemence nodded again. "Can't hurt to say now," he said slowly. "I promised not to say, but now she's gone. Twins. Two boys. Ugly as sin itself they was."

Chorus

THE ROOM WAS IMMEDIATELY FILLED with exclamations of surprise.

"You're kidding, surely?" Art voiced the general amazement in the room.

"When did she have them? What happened to them? She never said anything about them to anyone, as far as I know." Carl was up on his feet again and getting red around the neck. Art pulled at his sleeve and encouraged him to sit.

"Why don't you tell us what you know, Clemence," I said calmly. Nodding heads bobbed at each table.

Clemence shook his head sadly. "Come to me in the fall of '59, she did. Cried like a baby herself. Just a girl. She never told me who the father was. But she'd walked out with a gentleman from the Desert Inn a few times. Married. Older. Cash in every pocket. One of them tough guys," he said, squashing his nose sideways with his thumb, making it look as though it was broken. "Don't know what she saw in him. Anyhow, he up and leaves. She's on her own. Says she's just like her own ma. Kept it all hid under her work clothes at the diner for a long time. When she finally showed, she was about two months away. I remember the filming you mentioned, Mr. Art, for the Rat Pack movie. Borrowed a coat and walked across in front of a camera in the crowd, she did. So pleased with herself. Then her final month come, and she was bad. Couldn't stand. Had to rest up proper. Wouldn't let me tell a doctor, nothing. I'm the oldest of nine, so I'd helped with babies afore. My mama had them all at home, with her women friends helping. And that's what we done. I supervised. A girl from the diner helped. Only problem was, there was two of 'em. Didn't expect that.

She was such a small woman I don't know how them babies fit in there. Tiny, they was. All screwed up like wet red paper. Baby monkeys. Ugly. Next month she up and left Vegas. Didn't see her again till late that year when, like I said earlier, she'd lost all the baby weight, had her hair changed, and was dressed real fancy. I never knew *where* she went, don't know why she never told me. Didn't ask. But I knew *why*. Had to find homes for them babies somewhere. Never talked about it after. Never." He let out a rattling sigh, then tears started to flow down his creased cheeks.

Julie Pool was very emotional when she spoke, though she tried to contain herself. "Clemence, are you absolutely sure about this?" Clemence didn't respond. "I'm not sure it would have been possible for her to just spirit away babies, even in those days. There must have been a record of their birth. She'd have had to register them, surely? If she had children it would mean . . ." She looked around, bit her lip thoughtfully, and stopped speaking.

"I guess if they were born small she could have taken them elsewhere and registered them there, under a false name," said Art, thinking aloud. "Joan and I have never been blessed with children, but a friend of hers had a baby at full term and it was so small that it didn't reach normal weight for its age until it was six months old. If Miss Shirley's babies were tiny, as you say Clemence, she could have said they'd been born later, wherever she was. Hollywood, certainly Los Angeles, would fit the bill."

"Why didn't she ever tell Dad?" asked Carl, still looking astonished.

"Maybe she did, Carl," replied Art. "All I can say for sure is it's not something they ever discussed with me."

"But Dad would have told me," squealed Carl.

Art reached over and patted the man on the shoulder. "Not necessarily, Carl. Remember, when they got together, you were a grown man with your own wife, your own life. You and your dad weren't exactly close, on a personal level . . ."

"That wasn't my fault," whimpered Carl, boylike. "He sent me away to school. He wanted me to have the best of everything, and then when I wanted to work with cars, the only thing I ever really wanted to do, he said no, I had to use my fancy education. I'd have done anything for my father. I loved him, admired him. But he made me do things I wasn't any good at—it was *his* fault that I messed up that first business. *His* fault that my marriage fell apart. At least Miss Shirley talked him into letting me try to make a go of it in the car restoration world. You said I'm good at it, and I am. I could have been good at it when I was twenty, not have had to wait forever to finally be good at something."

It seemed that Carl Petrosian was carrying a certain amount of animosity toward his father. But he was yet another person who saw Miss Shirley as a savior—someone who had allowed him a chance to flourish.

When Julie Pool spoke, her voice was calm, but I could tell she was working at it. Her fists were clenched, her knuckles white. She looked betrayed. I suspected that her mind was racing through the possible legal ramifications of Miss Shirley having two secret children. "Clemence, I hate to say this, but if what you say is going to hold any water, you'll need to prove it. Can you?"

Once again our eyes turned toward Clemence, who nodded. "Look in her purse. Photo of her, me, and the two boys. The friend of hers from the diner took it. Borrowed a camera to do it. Miss Shirley was never without that photograph. And I mean *never*. All you gotta do is look in her purse. Over the years she's had a bunch of copies of that photo, so her boys could always be with her. Just look."

Even as he was speaking, I could see eyes darting about, searching out Miss Shirley's purse.

"It wasn't on the table when we moved it," said Ian.

"She had it with her, beside her, when we dined," said Julie. "It was the Tsar! purse—one of her collection of Judith Leiber purses.

You know, it's got crystals set in the logo design. Red, with a big gold Tsar! across it?" Julie began to get annoyed with the blank faces. "You all know our logo, right?" She was losing her patience.

"I don't think they know who Judith Leiber is—they don't know that she designs purses," I suggested.

Julie sighed and shook her head. "Oh, right. Don't worry about that. As Cait said, she's a purse designer. *The* purse designer. All it means is that it's not a little thing made of fabric; it's solid, a metal box with a clip at the top. Opens like a clamshell. About so big." She gestured to indicate a large purse, about ten inches square. I began to work out what such an item must have cost and came up with a huge amount. But I don't own a Vegas casino, so I suppose it's all relative.

"Don't interfere with the body," called Bud, as people began to rise from their chairs and move about.

"Do you think she put it on the floor next to her?" asked Tom, a question largely directed toward me and Bud. "That's what Tanya does with her purse when we're eating."

"It's hardly likely, Tom," I replied. "A custom-made Judith Leiber purse of that size has to be worth about ten thousand dollars. It's the sort of purse you'd have on the table, or at least hanging on a purse hook."

Given the way that everyone's eyes were scanning the room, it was clear that the whereabouts of Miss Shirley's purse was now the main concern, given its possible contents.

"I know where is," said Svetlana Kharlamova, very quietly for her.

Everyone stopped fussing and looked at the Diva.

Jimmy Green shifted uncomfortably in his seat. "Madame found it, tripped over it almost, when Miss Shirley was first discovered to be dead. She's been holding onto it for safekeeping, haven't you, Madame?"

"Yes," replied Svetlana, nodding graciously. "Is here." She waved toward the floor, and Jimmy bent to retrieve the purse from beneath the folds of linen surrounding the table. He reemerged, holding the glittering purse aloft.

"I'll take that, thank you," said Julie Pool quickly, as several hands moved toward Jimmy's prize. "If it contains a photograph of Miss Shirley and her offspring, it'll be a matter for me to deal with." We all knew what she meant, none more so that Carl Petrosian. The contents of that purse could rob him of a lot of money.

Julie stood between the Diva and her assistant as she opened the purse. Her nose wrinkled as she did so, and I could see her give a little sniff and then flinch. *Odd.*

The silence was intense. Julie nodded. "Yes. A blurry photograph of a woman sitting on a bed, holding a baby. It's . . . well, I can't say she looks anything like the Miss Shirley I knew, but I'm sure there are some other photographs of her as a young woman that will allow an identification to be made. She has Miss Shirley's bearing. Beside the bed is a young man holding another baby." She looked over at Clemence. "You?" He nodded. "And you say these are two boys?" Again, Clemence nodded.

"I want to see it," called Carl angrily. "I want to see if it's really her."

Julie shrugged, closed the purse, laid it on the bar, and handed the photograph to Carl. His entire body deflated when he peered at the photo. He passed it to Art, who squinted at it, let out a low whistle, then held it out for everyone to see.

Tanya managed to peer at the photo. "Wow, Clemence. That's Miss Shirley with her son, and you're next to her holding *another* baby," she said quietly.

Art spoke heavily. "You're right, Clemence. That's definitely Miss Shirley. When were the boys born?"

"Finally saw the light on the last day of March 1960. Noisy, they was." He held out his hand for the photograph.

Art looked thoughtful as he passed the photograph to Clemence and said, "So they'd be fifty-two years old. Interesting. Of course, they could have had children themselves by now."

I gazed around the room and did the math.

Art was doing the same thing it seemed. "That means that quite a few people in this room could be either Miss Shirley's offspring or her grandchild. And set to inherit. Sorry, Carl, it looks like you might have to stand in line," he said, without any obvious glee.

"I need to pee, so you'll have to excuse me," said Tanya flatly as she stood. *So inappropriate.* Tom looked shocked, but Tanya's comment hadn't registered with everyone in the room. Most people seemed to be in their own little worlds, thinking through what Clemence had said, and what the photograph meant to them. It was certainly food for thought.

First Intermission

WITH NOT EVEN TANYA'S INCONGRUOUS announcement making it into some personal worlds, I thought I'd take a chance to stand and stretch. I find I have to move every so often or I seize up, and it didn't appear that anyone would mind.

"I can't imagine there's any coffee, Ian," I said, looking at the young man, "but I could do with some more water, and maybe some of that fruit? I can help myself to the fruit, but I don't know where you keep the bottled water. Could you help me out?"

Ian nodded. "Why doesn't everyone come and help themselves to some fruit and cheese?" he called. There were general nods, and people seemed to be less withdrawn.

"Yes, we're all in this together," replied Julie, "so let's have a bit of a clear-up, and then revitalize with some snacks." She stood and began to clear her table. Her husband pitched in, and soon everyone was clearing things up, clattering and busying themselves. All except for the Diva—who was obviously above getting her hands dirty—and Clemence—whom Julie had told, quite firmly, to remain seated.

I was glad of the chance to compare notes with Bud. As we moved about we kept our heads close together and our voices low.

"Jack, a possible son. Ian, Tanya, Jimmy, Tom—all possible grandchildren," I whispered.

Bud shook his head. "Not Tom."

"Yes, Tom stays on the list for now, even though you know his uncle."

"Really, Cait, I don't think . . ."

I sighed. "Okay, we'll talk about Tom later. For now I want to add Julie to the list of suspects too. If Jack is Miss Shirley's son, *he* might not know—but there's a chance that Julie could have found out, and what's his is hers. The only people I can't see having a motive because of this revelation are Svetlana and Clemence."

"Clemence might be in for a big windfall in either of Miss Shirley's wills," suggested Bud.

I shrugged my agreement. "I suppose so. Inheritance doesn't seem like a possible motive for the opera singer, though. And let's be fair, do you think Clemence would have been capable of driving that saber through both the chair *and* Miss Shirley's body? He doesn't look strong enough."

"I had a pretty good look at the chairs while I was moving them about," whispered Bud. "They look substantial, but the backs are mainly foam. That sword has one heck of a point on it and looks to be very sharp."

"It's a *shashka*. A Russian weapon somewhere between a sword and a saber. It's straighter than a saber, with just one very sharp cutting edge, and it's supposed to have a piercingly sharp point. Designed for thrusting *and* slashing. Lethal. As we have seen. There's another one on the wall above the bar. Looking at how it's hung, I'd say it's a partner for the one used by the killer." We both looked up at the glittering saber. Its slicing edge gleamed in the starry lights. "Even with a well-honed blade, and an insubstantial chair, it would have taken more strength, and deftness, than I judge Clemence to have. Everyone else probably could have managed it—and I say that because I reckon I could have done it myself—though I'm not sure about Tanya. She's very slight, and she strikes me as willowy, rather than wiry, under that baggy blouse. Besides, she'd need to possess a good deal more passion than I've seen her display to be able to perform such a vicious act."

"She's got a snappy temper on her, though," observed Bud. I was enjoying the scent of his aftershave and having him so close to me. I'd hoped for a romantic, happy evening, but now I felt as though we were being kept apart by circumstance. "Careful what you say, she's back," whispered Bud.

I didn't need to look around because Tanya was at my elbow almost immediately.

"It *still* could be anyone, except Clemence, I guess," she hissed quietly. Her eyes were ablaze with intrigue. *Might Tanya be one of those people who revel in gossip?* Clearly she'd used her time in the ladies' room to think through the implications of the revelation that Miss Shirley had given birth to twin boys, and had reached the same conclusions as Bud and myself. "I bet Jack Bullock is Miss Shirley's son," she added flatly. "It sounds as though she actively hunted him out. He did grow up in LA, where she abandoned her babies, after all."

"We don't *know* that's where she left them," replied Bud. I flared my nostrils in an attempt to shut him up. I didn't want to involve anyone else in our exchange of ideas. But I was too late. Seeing us deep in conversation with Tanya, Tom ambled over to join us.

"Well, I'm off the hook, at least," said Tom. He sounded quite jovial, considering the circumstances. "You *know* my dad, Bud, and he's certainly not Miss Shirley's son, eh?"

"He's the right age," said Tanya.

Tom looked surprised. "Well, yes. But he's Canadian, not American."

"Children can be moved, Tom. Citizenships changed or acquired," said Tanya quietly.

"Bud knows my grandparents, right?" Tom sounded a little annoyed. "And he knows my dad's brother, as well as my dad."

Bud held up a hand. "Hang on there, Tom. First of all, no, I don't know your grandparents. When I got to know your uncle Jack they were already living in Hundred Mile House, and we were stationed in Vancouver itself."

Tom looked taken aback.

Bud smiled reassuringly. "Don't panic, Tom," he added. "Jack and your dad are so similar to each other in terms of looks, mannerisms, and the tone and timbre of their voices, that they must be brothers, and there's at least ten years between them, so I'm certain that not only are they brothers, but they aren't twins. You're in the clear. Your father couldn't possibly be Miss Shirley's son, so you're not her grandson. I think that, maybe, your girlfriend was having a little joke at your expense?"

Tanya half-smiled. It was hard for even me to read her.

Tom looked at his girlfriend with more than a hint of uncertainty, then brightened. "But, hey, you could be her granddaughter." Tom gently nudged Tanya. "Your dad would have been about the right age, eh? And Miss Shirley was always very good to him."

"Don't talk about my father!" snapped Tanya.

Tom blushed. "Sorry," he mumbled. He looked at Bud, then me, and clearly felt he should explain his girlfriend's comment. "Tanya's dad died, suddenly, a couple of months ago. She still can't talk about him."

Sighing heavily, Tanya said, "Tom's trying to be polite. My father killed himself. Put a gun in his mouth. I dropped in on him, and he was sitting in front of the TV with the top of his head blown off." Her tone was surprisingly devoid of any emotion.

Bud reached out and touched her gently on the shoulder. "I'm sorry to hear that, Tanya. That's got to be tough."

"His life was as tough as his death," she replied enigmatically. "It's not so bad when I don't talk about it." As she looked up at Bud I thought I could see a spark of anger in her eyes.

"Your dad *might* have been Miss Shirley's son. She really liked him, and you, Tanya," said Tom.

As Bud's expression attempted to convey to Tom that he shouldn't pursue the topic, Tanya said thoughtfully, "You're right. She did. But she also helped you, Jimmy, Ian, Carl, and Art. She's even given that awful woman Svetlana a chance to have some more glory days. She took to Julie like she took to you, and it sounds to me as though she gave Jack a career on a plate. She gave to everyone." Somehow she managed to make it sound like an accusation.

Despite her tone, I had to agree with Tanya. I kept my voice low as I spoke. "If everyone who's talked about her is to be believed, it sounds as though Miss Shirley made it her job to advance people's careers. Tell me, did she act that way toward only the people in this room, or did she get herself just as involved in other people's lives?"

"There was the acrobat who broke her leg when she was skiing on vacation," offered Tom, glad to move on to another, more neutral topic. "Miss Shirley gave her a job in her gym, where all the performers in the show here work out and train."

"Miss Shirley owns a gym?" I was surprised.

"Yes, and a gun range," replied Tom.

"A gun range?" Now it was Bud's turn to sound puzzled.

Tom smiled. "Yeah, maybe you've seen the ads on those trucks that drive up and down The Strip? You can go there and shoot all sorts of cool stuff. It's a real tourist trap. Popular with stag parties, even couples. Though we haven't been." He looked a little disappointed.

I'd seen the advertisements he'd mentioned, but I found it hard to see a connection between Uzis, Kalashnikovs, and Miss Shirley.

"Were guns something she was into, then?" I asked, puzzled.

Tom drew closer. "I've heard it said she could shoot a nickel at a hundred paces, just like my uncle Jack, right, Bud?"

Bud smiled. "Yes, he's a really good shot. Used to beat me every year in the divisional shooting competitions. Cups up to here, he has." Bud lifted his arm above his head.

"Oh, come on now, you're pretty good too," I said, trying to cheer him up. "You've got two cups yourself."

Bud smiled. "Yeah, from the two years when I was still in, but

Jack had retired," he said with a chuckle. He added, "How did Miss Shirley come to be such a good shot, do you know?"

Tom shook his head. "No idea. It's just one of those topics that comes up when you're doing prep in the kitchen. Sort of thing employees gossip about, right, Tanya?" Tanya nodded. "But maybe it's all just part of the Legend of Miss Shirley. Mind you, the range is real enough. Making a mint, they say. I wonder who gets that?"

Just as we came full circle and returned to the topic of inheritance, I caught a snippet of conversation between Julie and her husband as they passed with plates full of fruit.

". . . it could be you, Jack. You're the right age. We should find out when we get out of here."

"There's nothing *to* find out, Julie. Mom and Dad would have had plenty of opportunities to tell me I was adopted. They didn't, because I'm not. When we get out of here we'll call Mom and she can tell you for herself. I *am* my mother's son, Julie. The date, the place—they're just coincidences."

"It'd be quite something if all this was yours—ours," Julie added, then they moved out of earshot.

My eyes followed them as they passed our little group, then I caught sight of Carl and Art, who were prowling around each other like kids.

I nudged Bud. "Looks like something might be just about to kick off over there," I warned.

Bud, Tanya, and Tom all turned to look at the men. As soon as Carl put his hands on Art's lapels, Bud said, "Excuse me" and darted toward the men.

Tom made to join them, but I held him back.

"Let Bud sort it out," I said quietly. "He's trained to defuse situations like this. Why don't you gather up some water and fruit for our table? I'd like a quick word with Clemence."

"Sure thing," replied Tom. "How about some cheese to go with the fruit?"

I licked my lips. "Oh yes, please." I glanced at the cheeses on the dessert table. "I can see from here that there's some Époisses—it's one of my favorite cheeses. I can also see some Limburger, Le Nuits d'Or . . . and I think that's Stinking Bishop, the one with the orange rind?"

Tom nodded, smiling. "You like your cheeses really smelly, eh?" I nodded energetically. "Just like Miss Shirley. Bless her." He looked sad. "Okay, I'll make you a plate, and I'll be sure to put some Roquefort on there too," he said. "How about I bring something to the table that'll work well with them? Miss Shirley usually has a bottle of excellent vintage port decanted for these evenings. I'll check with Ian."

I could feel my mouth watering. "Thanks, Tom. That sounds just about perfect. If we don't eat the cheeses they'll stink out the place, and what's a plate of fruit and cheese without some good port to wash it all down?"

"Healthier?" said Tanya.

I decided to let it pass.

Adagio

AS I WALKED TOWARD CLEMENCE, who'd remained seated during our little break, I overheard Jimmy say to the Diva, "No more of *La Gazza Ladra*, Madame, not tonight. Please?" Thanks to the fact that my sister, Siân, loves opera, I knew that the reference was to a work by Rossini. I wondered if "Madame" had been humming while Bud and I tried to have a little tête-à-tête.

I asked Clemence if I could join him, and he agreed. I knew what I wanted to find out, and thought it best to be direct.

"Clemence, I'm guessing you've been Miss Shirley's guest here many times before?"

He nodded.

"So I'm correct in thinking that you're the right person to ask whether anything unusual happened this evening, before Miss Shirley was killed?"

Clemence nibbled a cracker and washed it down with a glug of water. "Besides you and Mr. Bud being here?" he asked, a twinkle in his eyes.

I smiled. "Is it that unusual for 'outside' guests to be invited?"

Again he gave his answer some consideration. I was beginning to get the feeling that nothing would happen quickly if it involved Clemence setting the pace.

"Pretty much. Though Miss Shirley was always tickled to have someone around who shared her birthday. Barbara Walters. Will Smith. Heather Locklear. Michael Douglas. Catherine Zeta-Jones. She's one of you, right?"

"If you mean that Catherine Zeta-Jones is Welsh, then, yes, she is. We're both from Swansea and grew up just a few miles apart, though she began her stage career very early in life. We were in a few Gang Shows together, when we were young."

"Gang shows? *Gang* gang shows?" Clemence looked puzzled.

"No, no actual gangs are involved. It's when Girl Guides and Boy Scouts put on a stage show, to raise funds. I'm getting sidetracked. Do you mean that all those people share Miss Shirley's birth date?"

Clemence nodded. "Be amazed who'll come visit on their birthday when the person askin' 'em is as famous as Miss Shirley. With her own jet to fetch and carry you too."

"All those people have been here? To this restaurant? On Miss Shirley's birthday?"

Clemence winked. "Can't say. Lot of folks been here over the years. Miss Shirley was pleased when Mr. Bud showed up, I know that."

"So, other than an unexpected guest who happened to share her birthday, was anything else unusual?"

I waited patiently for Clemence's considered reply. "Food was the same. Same food every meal, not just birthdays. Caviar, duck, skate wing, the chocolate dessert, smelly cheese. Rich. She knew what she liked, and how she liked it. Never changed." As he spoke, Clemence seemed to be recalling every mouthful, savoring it once again. *I know I was.*

"One thing," he added.

I dragged myself from the happy recollection of balsamic-glazed cherries nuzzling up to tender, delectable duck confit. "Yes?"

"Always sat at the center table, she did. You know, center of the three?" Clemence nodded across the room. His voice was laced with sadness when he spoke again. "Always looking out. Loved The Strip. In her blood. Tonight she sat at the end table. Still looking out. That's different."

I didn't have to look very far to see that Clemence was correct.

Miss Shirley's body was still just outside the edge of the area between the two partitions farthest from the dessert table.

"Did you ask why she'd done that?"

"None of my business. I sits where I'm told to sit," he replied, eventually.

"Nothing else odd?"

I waited.

"That's enough, ain't it?"

"What about Miss Shirley tonight? Did she seem her *normal* self to you?"

I tried to not fidget while I waited for Clemence to answer.

"Playful," he finally replied.

"Playful?" I was surprised.

"Yeah, like she was being a naughty girl. Like when she used to play her jokes."

"Miss Shirley was a practical joker?"

"Not since her husband passed. They'd always be up to something, them two. Like kids, they was. Silly stuff. Made her laugh so loud. Red in the face she'd be with laughing. Took it in turns. One trying to outdo the other. As they got richer, them jokes got . . . you know, kinda complicated. Knocked over a vase, she did, one time. He near had a fit. Expensive, I guess. Ugly thing. Anyhow, she'd gone and had a fake one made by the guys building this place, just so's she could break it. Another time he gets her to come to the hospital sayin' he'd been hit by a car. She shows up all upset, he's sitting there with champagne and a bunch of friends. I was there. Hit him with her purse, she did. Said he was in the right place if she cut him. She nearly did. That day her purse was shaped like some kinda dog. Pointed nose. Sharp."

"So they had fun together?"

"Sure did. Never took nothing or no one for granted. Worked together, played together. Both hard. She ain't been the same this past year. Sad to see her like that."

"How did he die?"

"You don't know?" Clemence looked amazed.

I shook my head. "No one's brought it up."

"Guess not," Clemence replied sadly. "We was here, for Miss Shirley's birthday dinner last year. Then everybody goes back to their big house, to carry on the party there. This time last year it was humid. Unusual. Seems Mr. Carl went for a swim. Found him in the pool. All his clothes on. Miss Shirley thought it was one of his jokes. We all stood there, and she hollered at him. Then she reckoned he'd gone and put a dummy in the pool, made to look just like him. Then we all knew. It was really him, and he was dead. Took it bad, she did. Real bad. Cops said he was liquored up. Dare say he was. But he swam good, did Mr. Carl."

I wondered if the murderer in the room was playing a long game, but I didn't have a chance to think that angle through, because my attention was taken by another kerfuffle between Carl and Art. It seemed that Bud's famous calming technique was being tested. I thanked Clemence for his time and left him sadly and slowly sipping his water.

Con Brio

"YOU! IT WAS YOU!" SHOUTED Art with true venom.

"Me? It wasn't me," squealed Carl. "I wouldn't do that. Why would I do that? It's all going to be mine anyway. Why would I steal from myself? Especially a damn little egg. What the hell do you think I would do with it?"

"That egg is worth well over a million bucks," spat Art. "Bet you could buy a few new cars with that, couldn't you? Market not what it used to be, Carl? Finding it tough to liquidate your assets? Classic cars are expensive toys. Toys people can't afford anymore. I bet the amount you have to shell out in alimony isn't getting any smaller. A handy dandy little piece like that egg could be just what you need right now, without having to wait for Miss Shirley's will to be sorted out."

Bud was pushing against each man's chest as they pressed toward each other. Never a good sign.

Carl laughed in Art's face. "Ha! The witch has found some new fool to bleed dry. Poor guy doesn't know what he's let himself in for by marrying her. At least she's got her fangs out of me. I'm not the one who'll have to fund her little shopping trips anymore. Besides, I wouldn't know how to turn that egg into cash. It's not as though I've got any links with the underworld, unlike some I could mention." Carl thrust his chin toward Art, who drew back, ready to respond.

Bud used his most soothing tones as he said, "Gentlemen, gentlemen, let's keep this classy. Take a breath. Just step back, come on, step back. That's it. We're all adults here, and we're all under considerable pressure. Tonight is a very difficult time for everyone. This is a stressful situation, but we can all learn how to draw upon our inner reserves of patience. There you go, let's just take a little break and get to the bottom of this, eh?"

Carl and Art had stopped puffing out their chests and were backing away from each other. However, they gave the impression of two boxers retiring to their corners for the respite of a damp sponge, rather than men who were prepared to stand down and admit defeat. I decided it was time for me to step up and add my voice to Bud's.

"Bud's right," I began. "It's a tough night all round. Maybe you could tell all of us what's missing, Art? You say something's been misplaced?"

I chose my word carefully, but Art's facial expression spoke volumes.

"Not 'misplaced'—*taken*. There, look." He pointed toward the end partition, beyond Miss Shirley's body. "There was a gold egg, right there in the middle, and it's gone."

We all looked. On top of the partition stood two impressive turquoise Sèvres urns, heavily decorated with handpainted panels. I recalled quite clearly that there'd been an elaborately embossed gold egg sitting between them earlier in the evening. I was pretty close to the partition so I only had to lean over to be able to see that there was an empty little platform poking up from the middle of the wooden structure. It was only about a quarter of an inch high, but it was clearly defined. I suspected it was one of the pressure-sensitive security devices that Julie had referred to earlier.

"See? It's gone," said Art. "And *he* was right next to it." He jabbed his finger toward Carl. "Turn out your pockets, man. Whatever you might think, or say, it's still Miss Shirley's egg until her will, or the courts, officially say different."

"I. Haven't. Got. It." Carl spoke as though Art were deaf.

"I think I should point out that it's not just an egg that's missing," I said, drawing everyone's attention.

"What is it, Cait?" asked Bud sharply.

I pointed toward one of the urns on top of the partition. "This urn should have two handles, like its partner at the other end. I know it must have had both when we got here, because I'd have noticed the lack of symmetry otherwise. Bud, you know I'm good at that sort of thing."

Bud nodded. He's one of the few people who knows about my eidetic memory, and he's also well aware of how obsessive I am about things being either completely different from each other or totally the same. He laughs at me when I minutely readjust the matching vessels holding my parents' ashes, which are placed very precisely at either end of the mantelpiece in my little house on Burnaby Mountain.

Julie approached. "You're right. They're definitely a pair. Or should be. What could have happened to the other handle?"

"Maybe Carl broke it off when he snatched the egg," said Art, glaring at the younger man. Carl sneered back at Art. I half-expected him to poke his tongue out.

I looked down at the carpet on either side of the partition. "Well, however it came off, it must have somehow found its way under there"—I pointed to the tablecloth covering Miss Shirley's body—"because it's nowhere to be seen."

"I don't know about *you* noticing it, ma'am," said Clemence slowly, "but I sure did, and it weren't broken earlier. I was sitting at that table with Miss Shirley and I mentioned how her dress matched them pots. She said how she'd had the woman who makes her dresses match the color. She said it was special."

I jumped right in. *Sometimes I just can't help myself.* "The color is *bleu céleste.* Sèvres developed several unique background colors for King Louis XV, who owned the porcelain factory and moved it to the location near Versailles in 1756. They developed colors that were to his taste. There was this color, a royal blue, a pea green, and a pink called Pompadour, after his mistress. They used the bleu céleste for both the soft-paste and hard-paste porcelains. Of course, they did not produce hard-paste porcelain until the kaolin deposits were found near Limoges in 1768, which is when Sèvres was finally able to catch up with Meissen." I find that, sometimes, facts just pour out of me. On this occasion quite a few eyebrows were raised, Bud's among them.

"Are you an antique dealer on the side?" asked Jack Bullock, a little edge in his voice.

I laughed, maybe a little too loudly. "Oh no, I just read a lot, watch a lot of episodes of *Antiques Roadshow*, the British one, and I . . . tend to retain information, but look," I added, niftily deflecting any further conversation on the topic of my memory, "the urn with the missing handle is also sitting at a different angle."

I stood back a little, allowing everyone to get as near as they could without getting too close to Miss Shirley. "See how the one with two handles is sitting exactly parallel to the top of the partition? But this one's just off. It's turned a little. It's as though something hit the handle that's missing, turned the urn, and took the handle off too. Which means it should be over there somewhere, away from the partition, toward the entrance to the men's room. Can anyone see anything on the floor over there? It would match these other handles, white with gold decoration."

While everyone was hunting about, I leaned in to take a closer look at the partition. "Bud, come and take a look at this," I whispered.

Bud peered at the wooden structure upon which the broken urn sat. "About an eighth of an inch of a little platform," he observed. "Pressure pad, I'm guessing, but it's not fully released like the one underneath where the egg should be. Does anyone know if this would set off the alarm system?" asked Bud, addressing the group.

Julie returned to look at the urn. "Yes, that's enough to put us into lockdown."

"That, or someone taking the egg," added Tanya.

"No, you're wrong, Tanya. No one took the egg before the lockdown," said Carl, ignoring Art's tutting. "Obviously someone has taken it now, because it's not here, but surely we'd have seen someone walk over and take it before the lights went out? They only went out because the anti-theft system was activated, so it *can't* have been the removal of the egg that made the security system kick in. Something else must have tripped it."

"You're talking rubbish! Trying to distract us," shouted Art, immediately inflamed once more. "Come on, turn out your pockets!" He grabbed at Carl. Bud wasn't able to get to the suddenly brawling men, so Jack tried his best to pry them apart, but failed. At least he managed to steer them clear of Miss Shirley's linen-covered corpse. Quite a melee ensued. Arms were flailing, I heard the rip of cloth. Everyone except Svetlana was involved. Shouts and cries filled the room.

The only reason the whole thing didn't get entirely out of hand was because Jack let out a particularly loud shout, then took a nasty tumble against the partition, sending the already damaged urn to the floor. For a moment I thought it would bounce, but it didn't. Even with the cushioning of the carpet, it broke with a sickening crack.

Julie was much less concerned about the urn than with the state of her husband's head, which had hit the partition. She stooped over him, fussing as he assured her that he was fine and didn't have a concussion. The ruckus had brought Svetlana to her feet, as though she were cheering the combatants. Art's pride looked pretty well dented, and one sleeve of Carl's jacket was completely torn off. Bud looked less than his cool self, while Ian brushed himself down and said, "Man, that was something."

Tom hugged Tanya to his side, asking her what she'd thought she was doing, getting into the middle of a group of brawling men.

As Carl tried to tidy himself up, he muttered under his breath, "Damned egg. I haven't got it." He took off what remained of his jacket and threw it at Art. "Here—check the pockets, if you must. There's no egg. Nor here," he said, pulling out his pants' pockets, both of which were empty. "See? No egg. I didn't take it. Not before the lights went out, not since."

Art tossed Carl's jacket back at him and said grumpily, "So who took it? Where is it? I suppose I have to agree that it couldn't have been what made the security system kick in because we'd have seen someone reach to take it. But it's gone somewhere."

"But *would* you have seen someone reach to take it?" I asked. "I wasn't in the room when whatever happened, happened. Maybe you were all chatting and didn't notice someone taking it. I know that when I went to the ladies' room several people were standing about. Miss Shirley had already taken her seat after the toasts and the singing, and there was a natural break in the evening. Maybe you just missed it."

I could see that Carl and Art weren't alone in thinking back to those few moments. I glanced at Bud, who was looking uncertain. Our eyes locked, and I knew he knew what I was thinking. He shrugged. He hadn't wanted to go to the place I was about to lead everyone, but I could tell he was now resigned to the fact. He tilted his head and gave me a reassuring wink.

I nodded back and spoke. "Look, this is something I know Bud wanted to avoid, because he doesn't want to impair the police inquiry, but it's the question that, let's face it, has been inevitable. Where was everybody when the lights went out and Miss Shirley was murdered?"

No one answered. *What a surprise.*

Cadenza

"YOU WANT TO WORK OUT who killed Miss Shirley before the cops get here, don't you?" asked Tanya flatly. "I don't think you can do it. Everyone will just lie. After all, what's to stop us?"

"Nothing," I replied honestly. "You could all choose to lie your faces off. But everybody in this room is a witness to where everyone else was when the lights went out, and that means we might, between us all, catch out a liar. Alternatively, some people might be able to give others a watertight alibi. Two people who were touching each other, holding hands or something like that, for the whole time, and so forth. So it could work either way."

"This is me and Jimmy," said Svetlana. "When lights go out I grab his arm. I let go when Julie screams."

Jimmy glanced down at his now-seated idol. "Madame is correct, as usual," he said. "She had hold of my arm the whole time."

"Then why did you tell her to stop moving around?" I asked.

Jimmy looked puzzled. "I did no such thing." He sounded annoyed.

"Yes, you did. I recall that when I came into the dining room from the washroom, Svetlana was complaining that the furniture was moving. You replied that the furniture wasn't moving, she was."

"I didn't," snapped Jimmy. "Besides, how, or why, would you remember such a thing? It was hours ago."

I sighed. "I remember everything."

"Right," said Jimmy with disbelief.

"It's true," said Bud, taking my lead. "Cait has a very special memory. Some call it photographic, but that doesn't describe it well enough. I've seen her use it time and time again to help with cases.

She's good at it, so if she was around to see, or hear, something, she'll remember it."

Jimmy shifted uncomfortably from one foot to the other, then sat down next to Svetlana. "I don't believe either of you," he said sullenly. "What are you? Like the guy in *Rain Man*?"

I decided to explain a little, but I didn't want to turn into a performing seal. "I'm not quite like that character, though I *can* see and encode objects quickly. So the thing he does with the matches on the floor? I can do that. But unless I give it my full attention, and some real thought, I can't tell you what day of the week it was on July 1, 1867, or anything like that. Though that's a poor example because it was the day Canada was first recognized as a country, and it happened to be a Monday. The point is that we can all recall much more than we think, when we set our minds to it. And that's what I'm asking you to do."

"You haven't been downstairs in the casino counting cards, have you?" asked Art with an enigmatic smile.

I arched my most disdainful eyebrow—which is pretty impactful, even if I do say so myself. "No, I haven't, Art. I don't gamble at all. Though I certainly have no skill when it comes to predicting the roulette wheel or video poker, I promise I haven't been secretly winning at blackjack, rest assured."

"Just like Rain Man if you ask me," muttered Jimmy.

I wanted to direct the attention away from me and back to the matter at hand, so I tried to think of an approach that might work for this man who was clearly an opera aficionado.

"Tell me, Jimmy, how many operas would you say you know well?"

"Why?"

"How many?"

"Depends what you mean by 'well.' I know the stories of most of them, and, of course, the composer, or composers if there have been multiple treatments of a story, like Orpheus. I know the main arias of most of them, and some choruses and recitatives as well. In fact, I can sing along with the right words and notes—in my head, of course—for quite a lot of operas. I listen to them often. They span the ages." He smiled, reminiscing.

"You're recalling some of your favorite moments right now, aren't you?" I knew he was.

"Yes," he smiled wistfully.

"And you, Svetlana. I'm guessing you know many operas?"

"But of course!" she replied indignantly. "I know all operas I sing. I know my part, my fellow artistes' parts, I know orchestra parts. I know many operas, in many languages. If I am not on stage, I not know so well."

I wasn't surprised. I returned my attention to her assistant.

"What about staging, Jimmy? How many different productions have you seen of any given opera? How many do you remember?"

Jimmy gave my questions some thought. "Lots, and all of them." He sounded resigned.

"Jimmy, you asked me why, or how, I could remember something that happened hours ago. You've just told us you remember things you saw many years ago. The expression on your face told me you remember them vividly, and that you'll always be able to recall them. Svetlana has needed to *learn* those operas—the notes, the music, the words, the stage directions, what everyone else is doing on stage at the time. Learning is just encoding, storing, and rehearsing the recall of that information time and time again until you *know* you know it. It's what we expect to happen when we make a conscious effort to learn something. But you know what you do about opera, Jimmy, because it's your interest. Your passion. When you experience opera you give it all your attention. You notice an enormous number of details, simultaneously. Think about those details now. Pick an opera production. Conjure up the costumes, scenery, makeup, hair, lighting, artists' actions, choreography; the orchestration, the voices, the words, the story. And now compare and contrast those recollections with another performance." I gave him a moment. "You can do it. Am I right?"

Jimmy nodded. His expression showed me that he was beginning to accept my arguments about how amazing the human memory can be.

Svetlana quite clearly wanted to be the center of attention, rather than her assistant getting all the limelight, so she piped up, "I am same with opera I see, but do not sing. I do not sing Wagner, but I watch. I know all details, as you say. Is very beautiful. Strong. But his *Ring* at Met this year, with big machine? A sin. Monsieur Lepage should be shot!" I gathered she hadn't been impressed by the controversial production, something about which she and my sister would have disagreed.

"I've always thought I was just enjoying opera," said Jimmy, a plaintive tone coloring his voice. It was as though by understanding what he was doing, he was losing something. I didn't want him to feel that. I wanted him—and everyone else in the room—to understand how the human mind works. How they might be able to recall details of the evening's events that could help to unmask a killer.

I tried to sound sympathetic as I spoke. "I understand that you're *enjoying* it, Jimmy, and long may you do so. I happen not to share your devotion to opera, but I have a sister who does. She'd be beside herself with glee to meet you, Svetlana. She moved from Wales to Perth, in Australia, many years ago, and I know she made the trip to see you perform at the Sydney Opera House not long after she emigrated. She thought you were wonderful. *Madame Butterfly*, I think it was. She spoke about it at length."

The Diva nodded graciously. "Terrible acoustics," was her only damning comment.

"As my sister would agree, watching an opera is a very active process. While you're *enjoying* it, your memory is working hard. You are responding to many stimuli, immersing yourself in the experience. You are encoding everything you're aware of, and many things you're not really paying attention to, including things like the perfume or aftershave of the person you're sitting next to, or how comfortable your body is in your seat. It all becomes a part of the total sensory memory, ready to be unlocked at some point in the future. For example, someone might pass you in the street wearing the same perfume you subliminally encoded as a part of the whole, and *bang!*—you're right back there, in the theater. And you don't know why you've suddenly started humming a certain aria to yourself."

"Is true! This happen to me!" exclaimed Svetlana. "I am in car in London, England, and driver of car smell like old man I meet in Moscow." She lowered her voice as though I was the only one listening, which I wasn't. "I play woman convict in Shostakovich opera *Lady Macbeth of the Mtsensk District*. I am young. *Very* young. He help me with my career. I do not know name of smell. For me is ... difficult smell. He give me pretty things. I *like* pretty things. Smell can bring good memory, or bad. Ah ... life is hard, then we die. But I have my voice."

I allowed Svetlana to dwell on her youthful indiscretions, and continued, now addressing the group more widely. I was determined to make my point. "We don't always know that we're encoding, or what makes us recall things. We're very rarely aware that we are automatically comparing a current experience with previous experiences or attitudes. It's the process that makes us 'feel' a place is homey, or not. We're assessing multiple stimuli and gauging them against what we already 'know.' Ever bought a home, Jimmy?"

Jimmy looked surprised to be called back from his reverie. He shook his head.

"Well look, when you went hunting for somewhere to rent, did you pick a place that 'felt right'?"

He nodded.

"Since you moved in, has it always still felt that way?"

Jimmy smiled sadly. "No. It didn't feel at all the same when I moved in. I thought the woman who rented it to me had changed something, so I called her. She said the day I viewed it she'd been making toast just before I arrived, and burned it. She had worried it would put me off. I didn't even notice it at the time . . . or I didn't know I had. I don't know why burnt toast would make me feel like I was home, safe. But I believe it did. I don't remember Ma burning toast in the van that often, but maybe she did, and that's what it was. I do remember we used to go somewhere when I was very small that was bright, noisy, and smelled of toast and grease. I have no idea where it was, or whether I went there once or many times. But I do remember it smelled like that."

"You see, Jimmy? That's what I mean. As humans we don't knowingly encode all the stimuli around us. We can't. We have to selectively give our attention to certain things and 'ignore' others, or we'd stretch our poor brains to the point where they couldn't cope. Right now I'm choosing to ignore the unpleasant odor of the warming remnants of caviar and cheese and so forth, the flashing of the giant screen across the road, and the fact that someone in this room is very angry."

"How you know someone is angry?" snapped Svetlana. "This is this Rain Man also?"

"No, Svetlana, it's nothing to do with Rain Man, nor is it anything to do with Spider-Man . . . I have no 'spidey-senses'"—the Russian opera singer looked confused, but I let it pass because I just didn't have the time, or the will, to explain Spider-Man to her—"but I know that anger changes our body chemistry. Most of us are familiar with the idea that pheromone production plays a role in attraction. It's the same sort of thing. Think a dog can't smell your fear? Think again. Their powerful sense of smell, combined with the change in a person's bodily chemical excretions when they are afraid, means dogs *can* smell fear at a great distance. If you are, somehow, able to act with confidence, or bravado, for long enough, you might be able to fool your body into changing back to its normal chemical balance, and that's when the dog can no longer smell fear."

"You smell us all to find murderer?" Svetlana guffawed.

I allowed a smile to curl my lips, but I didn't let it reach my eyes. "No, but I *can* sniff out a liar, and I think you were less than truthful with me when you said you and Jimmy were in physical contact for the entire time the lights were out."

"Why did you think that the furniture was moving?" asked Bud, right on cue.

As Svetlana fussily rearranged her wrap, her nostrils flared with anger. She tossed her head and addressed Bud. "I feel table move. Table touch me here." She indicated her midsection.

"And that's when you cried out?" Bud spoke sharply.

"Yes. Is dark. I am afraid. Table moving like séance. I think now is Miss Shirley's ghost leaving when she is killed. I *feel* her being killed."

Jimmy sighed. "Okay, it was *then* that Madame let go of me. She stopped clutching my arm, but the lights came on just a few seconds later. I know she was sitting next to me the whole time. She could not have killed Miss Shirley."

"Ah, my Jimmy," said Svetlana, beaming.

"Did you feel the table move, Jimmy?" Bud was still using a clipped, professional tone.

Jimmy shook his head. "No, not personally. But I wasn't touching the table then. I'd pushed my seat back from the table to stretch my legs. I was . . . I was thinking about dessert. I could smell the chocolate, and my stomach was growling, even though we'd not long finished the main course."

"You see," I said quietly, trying to be just as professional as Bud, "you recalled some things you didn't know you had encoded. That's really useful."

Bud spotted his next cue and jumped right in. "Folks, I know it's late, and I know we're tired, but if we're going down this road, we need to give our attention to the moments immediately before the lights went out, during which they were out, and immediately after they came back on. If we can do that I'm sure we can work out where everyone was at the critical moment."

"Now? I could really do with just putting my feet up and being quiet," said Ian. "I started my shift at Babushka Bar at ten this morning, so a very long time ago, and I didn't get a break at all before I opened up the bar here ahead of dinner, so I'm beat. Just so you all know, I was behind the bar, in my usual spot, the whole time."

"No, you weren't, Ian. You're misremembering," said Art. "I was at the bar pouring myself a drink. You were at the dessert table before the lights went out."

"Was I?" Ian looked puzzled.

"Yes, you were," added Julie. "Jack and I were standing over there near the window wall having a chat, and I saw you standing behind the desserts, wiping off the saber with a cloth."

"Oh yeah, you're right," said Ian, sounding surprised. "It was wet with champagne. I didn't want it to spoil the silver . . ." He glanced toward Miss Shirley's corpse and shuddered.

"Where did you put the shashka after you wiped it?" I asked.

Ian gave my question some thought. He looked uncertain when he replied, "On the bar, then I walked around to rehang it. Or, I guess, I meant to. I'm pretty sure I'd put it down before the lights went out . . ."

"You must have, unless you were the one who used it to kill Miss Shirley," said Carl, finally deciding to get in on the act.

Ian blushed and nodded. "Yes, right. Of course I'd put it down, but I think I was still standing between the bar and the dessert table."

"So anyone wanting to get to the blade would have had to pass you?" I asked. Now we were getting somewhere.

Ian sighed heavily and rubbed his head. "I dunno. I'm confused. I guess it would be easier if we all just went to the places we were when the lights went out, after all." He got up from his seat with obvious reluctance and moved to the end of the room farthest from Miss Shirley, between the bar and the dessert table. "I was here," he said loudly, "and I was heading this way, so I probably got, I dunno, about this far." He walked all the way to the end of the bar nearest the ladies' room, where there was an entry point to his workspace. "What about the rest of you?"

Julie Pool got up. As she straightened her jacket and skirt, she spoke brightly. "Come on, Jack. We might as well get this over with." She began to move toward the window, pausing when she noticed that her husband wasn't rising. "Are you alright, Jack? How's your head, dear? You look a bit off color. Do you feel up to doing this?"

I looked at her husband too. He was still in the seat his wife had forced him into after she'd helped him up from where he'd fallen on the floor. He certainly appeared pale, and beads of sweat glistened on his brow.

Jack Bullock sounded weak when he replied. "I'll be fine, dear. I think I have a pretty thick skull, but you're right, I'm not a hundred percent. Still, I guess moving around a bit won't hurt." He got up to join his wife, then paused. "Should we clear this broken urn, before it gets ground into the carpet?" He looked down at the remains of the porcelain pot.

I spoke up, spotting a way I could confer with Bud. "I tell you what, Bud and I will clear that away, if you can all go back to the points as close as possible to where you think you were when the lights went out. Maybe we could move at least two of these tables back to their exact original positions. Of course, we can't interfere with the body, so let's put the third just approximately where it was, and be careful to work around . . . Miss Shirley." I only just managed to stop myself saying "it," rather than "Miss Shirley." "It" is not a good word to use when referring to the corpse of a loved one.

Second Intermezzo

I MADE SURE THAT EVERYONE gave the once-precious urn a wide berth as they moved to take their places, while Bud grabbed a tablecloth from behind the bar. As he and I bent to gather the shards of porcelain and lay them on the linen, we managed a whispered exchange.

"I'm not too keen on this line of investigation, Cait," he opened. "The cops here will be livid. Probably with me, given my background. We're giving the killer a great opportunity to get their story straight before we're all formally interviewed."

I nodded. "I know, Bud, but we have to manage this process, because people will talk about it anyway. If I can get people to focus on what they can recall of everyone's actions at the vital time, it might give us some insight into what really happened. If they can stand where they were, see the room again as it was, or as close to it as possible, then they might recall something that will help us work out who could have been able to get at the saber and Miss Shirley. The logistics will help, but, to be honest, I really want to consider *motives* for the murder. There's a lot that's come to light on that score already. Miss Shirley had twin boys, so there's a question of inheritance. That's certainly one avenue, but there could be other reasons. Petrosian is an Armenian name, and this is a Russian-themed casino—so there could be some sort of organized crime connection. Maybe Svetlana's been a traveling Russian mobster all these years, with opera singing as her cover?" I managed a wan smile, which Bud returned. "There's the disappearing egg . . . so maybe plain old theft is at the bottom of this, and Miss Shirley got in the way somehow—possibly quite literally. By the way, did you know that Carl Petrosian Sr. was found dead in his swimming pool a year ago, fully clothed?"

Bud's shocked and concerned expression showed me he hadn't learned that fact.

I kept my head down as I continued, "Sounds as though pretty much everyone here tonight could have been at the Petrosian house that night, though Clemence wasn't clear about that. Of course, tonight might be an entirely separate issue. Maybe Carl Sr. just had too much to drink and fell into the water. We don't know. Clemence told me the cops said he was drunk, and I'm sure he'd have mentioned it if there'd been any sort of investigation other than what would be carried out in the case of an accidental drowning."

Bud nodded his agreement. "Why so much animosity between Art and Carl, do you think? They were pretty tough to handle. Once the issue of the stolen egg came up, Art was all over Carl. You have a take on that?"

"Testosterone, and a billion-dollar business on the line?"

"I'd have thought that Art was a bit too old for testosterone to play much of a part, but they clearly have a relationship that's got some barbs in it. Could you find a way to get them to talk a bit more about themselves, Cait? You're good at that, in this sort of informal setting. It's not like I can point shiny lights in their faces and sweat it out of them, eh?"

"If only." I smiled. "But for now we might at least be able to pin down who was where, when. I'll try to get everyone to use my memory techniques to draw out the truth on that score, for a start. We might find out something useful. Is there anything *you've* remembered that could help?"

Bud shook his head. "I stayed at our table after you left, but Tom and Tanya got up and moved away. As you know, I was facing the window wall, not the bar, and I had my back toward Miss Shirley's position."

"Where did Tom and Tanya go?"

"I don't know, Cait, sorry. I was mesmerized by the lights outside, just letting the whole thing wash over me. I was just thinking about . . . stuff. They were behind me somewhere, near the bar, I believe."

"And you're sure you heard a pop first, *then* a crash, then the metal collar clang down around the elevator shaft, and then the power went out? In that order?"

"Certain. Though, like I said, it wasn't a real crash."

"Okay, I'll go with that. I am aware that this is a risky undertaking, Bud, but we're stuck in here for hours yet, and this is all bound to come up at some point. We might as well manage it the best we can. Okay?"

Bud nodded. "You lead on this. I know I possess special cop powers"—he winked—"but this is the time for a gentler hand than mine. You take the lead, I'll back you up. You're good at directing a room full of suspects, Cait." He smiled. My heart and my head agreed that I was the luckiest woman in the world to be with Bud Anderson.

"Aw shucks! You know what to say to a girl to make her feel real special," I hammed. I was so distracted by Bud's warm smile and glinting blue eyes that I wasn't paying as much attention to my task as I should have been, and I managed to slice the pad below my left thumb with a particularly sharp-edged piece of porcelain. "Ouch!" My cry drew some attention around the room, but not much. "Ow— that hurts."

"Oh Lord! What have you done to yourself now?" Bud didn't sound annoyed. He seemed unsurprised that I'd managed to injure myself. He shook his head as he said, "You go wash that, and I'll find a clean napkin to bind it. Unless you've got a few dozen Band-Aids in that purse of yours, like you usually do?"

I shook my head and licked the blood off my hand, which was probably a stupid thing to do, but I did it anyway. "No, it's just my evening purse—too small for anything but the barest of necessities, like all evening purses. I wonder why Miss Shirley had such a large purse with her this evening? The red didn't work with her turquoise dress at all. Odd choice."

"Cait, stop it. Go get that cut washed, then I'll bind it. After that we can get everyone to explain where they were at the moment of the crime, *then* you can give fashion notes, right? Priorities, Cait. Procedure. Go."

"Yessir!" I pushed myself up from my squatting position with some difficulty, and more than a few groans—*it's amazing how quickly I seize up these days*—and set off for the washroom.

On the way I passed Tom and Tanya having a heated debate at the bar about which of them was standing exactly where at the time of the murder, and Jimmy Green trying to pacify Svetlana, who was whining, "... just a *little* one, Jimmy ..." I suspected I knew what she was talking about, and, indeed, as I rounded the privacy screen designed to shield the diners from the door of the washroom, I noticed Jimmy moving toward the decanter of port with a small glass in his hand.

When I came out of the ladies' room with a freshly washed, but still bleeding, hand, I paused for a moment. I was struck by a strange sense of déjà vu. Well, *almost*. Something wasn't right. In fact, it hadn't been right the first time around—I just hadn't realized it until this chance to see people "in place" for a second time.

When I'd emerged from the washroom earlier in the night, when the dining room was without any light save that which shone in from The Strip, I'd been aware of shapes moving—silhouettes against the backdrop of the myriad colors outside. Of course, the room looked different now, under the deadening low-energy emergency lighting. This time faces were washed out, people were looking haggard or just plain disheveled. Bud and Art had removed their jackets, joining Clemence and Carl in shirtsleeves. Julie's perfect hairdo was threatening to come apart. Svetlana's wrap had been so overused it was looking like a wrung-out rag, Jimmy's dark suit revealed how cheap it was by being so badly creased, and Tanya looked as though all the blood had drained from her face. As I noticed her pallor, I realized that I hadn't even looked at myself in the mirror in the washroom, and I was quite glad I hadn't, because I could imagine I was in just as sorry a state. My bleeding hand aside, I knew I must, by now, have eaten off all my lipstick, and that my hair was probably poking out of its ponytail somewhere. It usually tries to escape after a few hours of confinement.

"Got it!" I said aloud. Almost immediately Bud was at my side, wrapping my injured hand in a large, fresh white linen napkin.

"*What* have you got?" he asked as he expertly wound the cloth around my bleeding flesh, creating pressure as he did so, and tied a sound knot. "There!" He looked pleased with his work. "That should help stop the oozing and keep it clean. Okay?" I nodded. "Now—tell me, what have you 'got'?"

"It was really helpful for me to enter this room again from the washroom. This is pretty much exactly where I was standing when the lights came on. I knew there was something nagging at me about the room when I first saw it, and the scene this time, but I couldn't put my finger on it. Now I know what it is."

Bud looked around. "Well," he said thoughtfully, "quite a lot is different now. The table that was in front of Miss Shirley is in a necessarily different position, the urn and the egg are missing, there's a tablecloth covering the corpse, which will give a very different spatial sense. In fact that whole section, between the two last partitions, has changed a lot. Folks have moved two of the tables back to their original places so people can show the exact spots they were in, but because we can't move the table where Miss Shirley was sitting, Clemence just took the seat he'd have been in if the table were where it was originally placed. But we can't get too close to the body. You know what I mean?"

I nodded. "I know all that, but that's not what I mean. Look at the room, Bud. Look at the two tables back in their original places . . . now look at the position of Miss Shirley's body."

Bud looked. He shook his head. "Okay, I'm not seeing what you're seeing, which is annoying, so just tell me."

"Miss Shirley's body, and therefore her chair, are beyond the partitions by a good foot. She's positioned much closer in to the center of the room than anyone else's seat. Why was her chair so far from her table, or why was her table so far out of alignment with the others?"

Bud looked again. "Yes, I see what you mean. Jimmy's sitting at the middle table, his chair is pushed back so he can stretch his legs, but he's still not poking out beyond the edges of the partitions. Either Miss Shirley was sitting two feet away from her table, or the table was two feet farther toward the middle of the room than the other two tables. But why?"

"*Exactly.* Before it all happened, just before I left for the washroom, I saw Ian hold Miss Shirley's chair for her to sit, after all the toasts and the singing of 'Happy Birthday.' Just give me a moment . . . let me do my thing—I'll narrate."

Bud glanced around. "Okay, no one's looking. You go ahead."

I closed my eyes to the point where everything goes fuzzy and hummed to myself, which is, for some reason, what I need to do to be able to recall past events. I conjured up the moment I wanted, and I was off . . .

"I am standing beside our table, between it and the bar, looking down toward you, Bud. I look up and can see across the room to where Miss Shirley is being helped with her chair by Ian. He moves back from her chair. Miss Shirley's chair is drawn up to her table. The table is not out of line with the others; it's in exactly the same relative position. She's looking up at Ian, turning her body to face him, toward me. She's smiling. She's thanking him. She's seated within the partitions, not poking out into the room like she is now. She has her large red purse on the table to her left. Ian leaves her and walks toward the dessert table, toward me. Miss Shirley is opening her purse and moving it to her lap. I am tucking my seat out of the way at our table, and now I am looking down, placing my napkin beside my cutlery.

Tom and Tanya are still seated. Tanya is . . . nervous, squirmy. Tom is holding her hand, stroking it. She picks up her water and drinks. I am turning toward the ladies' washroom. I have my purse in my hand. I step out ahead of Ian. He smells of . . . alcohol. I can see that the sleeve of his red satin Cossack shirt is stained with something dark. It's wet. I think it's champagne. He spilled some when he was opening the bottles. Now I walk silently across the thick carpet, I can feel its pile yield beneath my tread. I round the privacy screen, and I enter the washroom. The door swooshes as it closes."

I opened my eyes. "It's not much, but at least I can say with certainty that Miss Shirley's table wasn't out of line with the others. So, in order for her seat to be where it is now, she must have moved her chair away from the table by a couple of feet. Did you see anyone help her do that?"

Bud shook his head. "I didn't see anything, Cait. I was in my own little world. Pretty useless observer, for a cop. But I wasn't being a cop at that precise moment. I was enjoying a wonderful dinner with you, and looking forward to the moment you returned from the bathroom."

I smiled. "Miss me that much?"

Bud patted my good hand. "Yes, but that's not why I was looking forward to your return. I had a special reason. But that's irrelevant now. Now we have to do this, and do it well. Are you up to it, Professor Morgan?" As he spoke, an expression clouded his face that I found impossible to read. It was complex. I decided to let it pass, because I knew I had some serious work to do.

"I certainly am, Officer. Everyone seems to be in place. I'll try to find out what I can about Miss Shirley shuffling her chair around, and dig up some more clues about possible motives for murder *and* theft. They might be linked, they might not. Hopefully, we'll find out."

I turned my attention to our fellow guests. "Everyone in place?" There were nods all round. "Okay then, let's begin . . ."

Da Capo

JULIE WAS THE FIRST TO speak. "Jack and I were standing right here, from several minutes before the security system kicked in until the lights finally came up. I know we were this close to the glass wall, and standing right in this spot, because this is pretty much the only place where you can see all the way to the beam shining from the point of the Luxor pyramid. I recall that I was talking to Jack about how incredible it is that it can be seen from the space station. So I was here, facing this way, and Jack was just to the side of me, where he is now. After Miss Shirley signed what should have been the first document of several, she asked me to give her a few moments to attend to the others, and to leave the folder containing the other documents. I left her to it and moved away to join Jack, who was already standing here. Right, dear?"

Jack Bullock looked unsteady on his feet as he replied weakly, "Yes, yes, that's right. I'd been sitting next to Miss Shirley, so I got up and walked over here, out of the way, when Julie brought the papers. Julie wanted to sit beside her. Clemence remained seated, opposite Miss Shirley, with his back to us as we are now. Right, Clemence?"

Clemence nodded. "Yessir. I only get up when I really needs to, these days. I weren't in the way of nothin' nor no one, so I stayed put."

"Were you looking at Miss Shirley when she signed the papers, or were you looking around the room?" I asked.

Clemence considered his reply. "I weren't looking about. Don't believe she had my full attention, though. No one was payin' me no mind. Dinner was rich. I was thinking 'bout what I'd eaten. Might have closed my eyes for a moment. I do sometimes. They needs a rest now and then."

I wondered if Clemence might have nodded off for a moment or two.

"So, Julie and Jack were there at the glass wall, and Clemence was there at the table. Does anyone remember anything that might suggest that what I've just said is incorrect?" It seemed the most polite way to ask if anyone thought that Julie, Jack, or Clemence were lying.

Everyone shook their heads. That was that.

Before I had a chance to turn my attention to anyone else, Jack said, "If it's okay with everyone, I wouldn't mind taking a seat now."

"What's wrong, Jack?" Julie sounded anxious. She peered at her husband, her face showing her concern very clearly. "Tell me, what's wrong? You don't look good. You're sweating even more now. Come on—sit down and have some water."

There was no question that the room was much warmer now than it had been when we'd arrived at 9:00 PM. Many long hours had passed since then, most of them without the benefit of air-conditioning. But Jack Bullock was sweating more than anyone else. That was clear.

"Some water would be good," he said. Jack stumbled as he tried to sit. Bud rushed to his aid.

Once he'd helped the swaying man to a chair, Bud held his hand in front of Jack's face. "Follow my finger with your eyes."

Jack did his best to do as Bud had asked.

"Are you feeling nauseous?" asked Bud. Jack half-nodded. "Tired? Listless?"

"I'm exhausted," replied Jack, gladly accepting a tumbler of water from Julie. He smiled weakly at his wife. "I'll be alright, dear, don't worry."

"You might have suffered a concussion when you hit your head," said Bud, concern lacing his tone. "Look into my eyes a moment," he added. "How does your vision seem to you? Can you focus as you can usually?"

"I guess my vision's a bit fuzzy," replied Jack.

"Headache?"

"Pounding."

Bud looked even more concerned. "Look, given our circumstances, there's not much we can do, except keep you quiet and hydrated. You should get yourself checked out as soon as we're out of here. You can't mess around with a concussion . . ."

"What if it's more serious? People die all the time after hitting their heads," said Tanya as she and Tom left their places at the bar and joined us at the other side of the room.

"Tanya, don't say that!" remonstrated Tom.

Jack returned the glass of water to his wife and said weakly, "Don't panic, Julie. I love you very much, but you do fuss sometimes. I'm fine. Just need to sleep . . ." Jack would have fallen off his seat if Bud hadn't caught him. He helped the incapacitated man reach the floor without hitting his head again.

Bud arranged him on his side, in the recovery position, and told everyone to stand back. "I need something to make him a little more comfortable. Bring me some wet cloths, and you might as well bring some sort of receptacle, in case he vomits." I noticed that Carl and Art were the first to move—they threw dreadful glances at each other, obviously mindful that it was their fracas that had caused Jack to hit his head in the first place.

Everyone had crowded toward Jack, despite Bud's instructions to do the exact opposite. Julie Pool was dissolving with panic. The restrained professional woman had completely disappeared, to be replaced by a sobbing wife, terrified that her husband was in a critical condition.

"Help him! Please help him! Can't you do anything? Look, he's unconscious—completely out of it. That can't be good. To bang your head and lose consciousness—it must be bad. Oh, please, do *something*!"

She was closest to Bud, but her pleas were directed at everyone in the room.

Bud's voice was low and commanding as he said, "Cait, can you take care of Julie, please? Maybe a brandy? I need some space here. Come on, folks, give me some space!" Bud finally used his most forceful tone, and the huddled group slowly shuffled back.

I pushed through the throng to grab Julie and pull her away from her husband. I sat her down and shouted at Ian, "Could you bring some brandy for Julie, please? And maybe some water." He didn't hang about and dashed to the bar.

I tried to calm the poor woman, but she was thoroughly distraught. The brandy was waved away, but she sipped the water between sobs. "Oh, Jack, my darling Jack. Please be alright . . ."

"Cait—right, leave Julie, help me here, now!" I'd never heard Bud use that tone before. He was full of anger, but it wasn't directed toward me. "I need to get him on his back, start CPR. He's not breathing . . ."

The next quarter of an hour or so was a blur, as Bud tried to breathe life into Jack, and pumped his chest. Julie wailed as Tanya tried to calm her; Art and Carl stood to one side of the main group, swearing and cursing at each other. Everyone else looked horrified, nervous, or full of dread.

When it was clear that Bud was completely exhausted I offered to take over, but he shook his head.

"He's gone. I'm so sorry, Julie, I did my best . . ."

The howling, screaming noise that left Julie Pool's body was barely human. It sent chills through us all. When she finally drew breath, there was complete silence.

Jack Bullock lay dead on the floor, just feet from Miss Shirley's corpse.

"What happened, Uncle Bud?" asked Tom plaintively. He looked like a very large little boy.

Bud stood up, shaking his head. "I have no idea. I've never seen anything like that happen so quickly. He went so fast. I thought I'd done all the right things. Maybe a blood clot? I just don't know. His brain couldn't have swelled that fast. I've seen dozens of concussions. Nothing like this. I'm so terribly sorry I couldn't save him, Julie. So very sorry."

Bud moved toward Julie to comfort her, but she leaped out of her chair, pushing Tanya out of the way, and threw herself at Carl Petrosian. "This is your fault! You did this!" She hit him on the chest with both of her fists, pummeling him as he tried to back across the room. "You and Art. If you hadn't fought, Jack wouldn't have tried to break it up. He wouldn't have fallen and hit his head. He wouldn't be . . . oh my God—Jack!" She turned from Carl and hurled herself onto her husband's body, sobbing and stroking his face.

I moved to pull her away, but Bud held me close. "Let her hold him, Cait."

I stepped back.

As Julie held her husband's corpse to her shuddering bosom, his body rolled over and the back of his jacket pulled up. There was a pattern of red dots on his shirt, just above his belt. I nudged Bud and whispered, "What's that on his back? Is it blood?"

Bud squinted at Jack's body, keeping his distance. "It looks like it. Can't be anything I did. And I don't think he could have cut himself when he fell. Couldn't have fallen onto the broken urn—it didn't fall until after he was down."

"So why's there blood on his back?" I asked.

"I don't know, Cait. I just don't know."

"It reminds me of something . . ." I gave myself a moment, trying to shut out the sounds of the room and recall what the spots on Jack's back reminded me of . . . then I got it.

"Bud, I need to have a quiet word with someone for a moment."

Bud's smile was tired, as was his nod. "I didn't think he'd hit his head that hard," he said, his voice conveying confusion and defeat. My heart felt his pain, but I didn't believe that it was a crack to the head that had killed Jack Bullock. Before I said anything to Bud, I wanted to confirm my suspicions. Only then might I be able to convince Bud that he couldn't have helped Jack more than he had. I decided to use a direct approach and speak to the person I believed had originally been in possession of the weapon that had likely drawn Jack's blood and led to his untimely death.

Duet

THE MOOD IN THE ROOM was somber, to say the least. Julie's sobbing was heartrending. Tanya did her best to console the poor woman. Tom lingered beside the pair of them. Ian, Carl, and Art were standing several feet away, looking uncomfortable and confused. Svetlana was seeking comfort from Jimmy. Bud was clearly beating himself up over his inability to save Jack Bullock. At least there was something I could do about that.

I moved across the room as unobtrusively as possible and sat beside Clemence, who was sipping water and wiping his face with his giant handkerchief.

"Clemence, when you came out of the men's room earlier on, I noticed a spot of blood on your shirtsleeve. There."

The elderly man pulled at his shirt to see the mark.

"Clemence, are you a diabetic?"

"Yes, ma'am," he replied. "Found out about six months ago."

"So I'm guessing you've been put on a special diet, which would explain your recent weight loss."

Clemence looked puzzled. "Yes, but how d'you know I lost weight? We only met tonight."

"Your collar. It's very loose on you, which means your neck is smaller than it once was. Do you inject insulin?"

"Sure do. Don't like it. Not very steady handed."

"Syringe or pen?"

"Pen. Easier than keepin' everything in a fridge all the time. Costs more, 'course, but Miss Shirley made sure I could afford it. Here—" He turned to his jacket, which hung on the back of his chair. He felt around all the pockets, then searched his pants' pockets. He looked concerned. "Don't know where it's gone to. Little bag I carry. Got my pens, my drops, and my pills in it. Always have two insulin pens, in case I mess up with one. Had them earlier. Used one right after dinner. New pens. Full. First dose."

"How much insulin is in each one, Clemence?"

"A lot." I waited while Clemence gave the matter due consideration. "Yep, a lot."

I tried a slightly different approach. "How long would a pen last?"

"Month."

That *was* a lot of insulin, and he'd had two pens. "Is it possible to inject the entire contents of a pen in one go?" I suspected I knew the answer.

"Can't do it. Dose is controlled. You don't want to overdose. Dangerous," said Clemence. As he spoke, I could sense he was beginning to follow my train of thought. He sucked his teeth. "My insulin kill him?" asked Clemence quietly. He was sharp.

"I don't know. It might have done. Can we keep this between ourselves for now?"

The man nodded slowly. "Sure thing."

"Thanks." I got up and began to move toward Bud. I stopped and turned back. "Clemence, when will you be due to use more insulin?"

The man looked at his watch and did some mental calculations. "I guess pretty soon. I test when I get up in the morning, and we're getting to 'bout that time."

The dread I felt made me swallow hard. If Clemence didn't have access to his insulin, because it had all been pumped into Jack's body, he ran the risk of suffering from ketoacidosis. The expression on Clemence's face showed me he understood this too.

"I ain't got no insulin till we get outta here? That's bad, ma'am. Bad. Ain't like when you got too much insulin in you, when you can eat or drink to try to balance your blood. No insulin is no insulin. Ain't nothing but insulin any good for you then."

I looked at my watch. It was nearly 6:00 AM. A long time to go before outside help arrived. "Do you use small doses, so that you'll be okay for quite some time?"

Clemence made a chewing motion as he thought. "I balanced myself right after dinner. It was a real rich, heavy dinner, as you know. You ate it too. Lotta bad stuff in it for me. For everyone, I guess. Usually after a meal like that my morning readings are off, so I do what I needs to do. Ain't nothing I can do about it without the insulin." He looked up at me with rheumy eyes, his entire expression conveying deep concern. "Maybe you could find it? I could really do with it."

"Do you happen to know if anyone else here is diabetic?"

Again, Clemence chewed air as he thought. "Nope. Not unless they's keeping it a secret. I know I sure don't. Why would I care who knows about that? But maybe some folks don't like others to know 'bout their health. Dumb, though. If they have a problem at least folks'll know what might be wrong with them if they know's they're diabetic."

I had options. I could tell everyone my suspicions, alerting the killer to the fact that I knew how they'd murdered Jack—because that's what had happened, I was sure of it. Alternatively, I could say that Clemence had misplaced his insulin, and ask everyone to look for his pens. This would also tip off the killer to the fact that I'd worked out what they'd done, but at least it would mean that the guilty party would have to look as though they were making an effort to hunt down Clemence's insulin. Maybe then I could spot something out of the ordinary?

I did my best to hide my concern as I spoke to the worried-looking man. "Clemence, keep drinking water, try to keep as calm, and as still, as possible. I need to talk to Bud, but I promise I'll do my best to find any insulin that's in this room."

"I'll just be making a visit to the washroom, ma'am," he replied, looking more tired and deflated than I'd seen him look since I'd met him, which wasn't surprising.

"You need help?" He didn't appear totally steady on his feet.

Clemence gave me a huge grin. "You offering?" He winked wickedly.

It was good to see him retain a sense of playfulness. "You be good, young man," I quipped.

"Always was, so the ladies said," he jested as he moved slowly toward the men's room.

I wondered how long it would be before he began to experience the effects of being without his insulin. If he was very lucky, I'd be able to help. If not . . . I couldn't think of that. I had to talk to Bud.

Another Duet

BUD WAS STARING OUT THROUGH the glass wall at The Strip below. I wondered what he was thinking. His expression suggested he was still dwelling on his inability to save Jack Bullock's life.

"Bud, I need to talk to you in private," I whispered.

He turned and looked around the room. "Over at the far end of the bar?" he asked quietly.

I nodded, and we weaved our way between chairs, people, bodies, and tables.

"I still can't believe what happened to Jack," said Bud softly as we managed to get away from everyone else. "I've never seen that happen so fast. A concussion doesn't usually—"

"I don't think it was a concussion," I hissed.

Bud's puzzled expression spoke volumes. "What do you mean?"

I knew that what I was about to tell him had serious implications, in more ways than one, so I reached out with my bound and bloodied hand and held his arm affectionately as I began to speak. "The symptoms of concussion are very similar to those of hypoglycemia. Confusion, clumsiness, headache, nausea, fainting, possible coma, and then, as we saw, death. It's very much the same for both conditions."

"Hypoglycemia?" Bud sounded, and looked, stunned at the thought. "I dealt with a couple of cases like that back in my uniformed days. Diabetics get it, don't they? Not enough sugar. Was Jack diabetic? Are you saying that was all he needed? A cookie, or some fruit juice? I could have *saved* him? Why didn't his wife say something . . . ?" Bud was confused, angry. His whispered voice was about an octave higher than usual.

"Bud, stop, my love, stop. Wait, and I'll tell you what I think—"

"Cait! You're saying it was just hypoglycemia?" Bud grabbed onto both of my forearms, his face contorted with anguish.

"You couldn't have helped him, Bud. *Listen!* Jack wasn't a diabetic, but Clemence is, and two fully charged insulin pens he was carrying with him have gone missing. I think that someone deliberately injected Jack with a massive overdose of insulin. So massive that a bit of sugar or carbs wouldn't have been enough to save him. You *couldn't* have saved him. No one could have. He was as good as dead as soon as he was injected."

Bud let go of my arms and rubbed his face with both hands. He raked his fingers through his hair, scratching at his scalp. Bud only does that when he's under great stress.

"You're telling me you believe someone stole Clemence's insulin pens and injected the insulin into Jack?" I caught the anger in his voice even though he was whispering.

I nodded.

"There must be some sort of limiting device on those pens, or people would be overdosing all the time?"

Again, I nodded. "You'd need to inject the target several times to get a fatal dose of the hormone into them."

This time Bud ran just one hand through his hair. "Surely Jack would have felt that? Wouldn't he have cried out? I mean, you'd feel being injected several times, right?"

I nodded. "I believe it was done to him when he was trying to stop the fight between Carl and Art. There was mayhem at the time. Jack might well have felt pressure, several times, he might even have felt a sharpness and cried out, but I doubt we'd have heard him above the cacophony at the time. That pattern of tiny blood spots we saw on his shirt?" Bud nodded. "I think that the killer took the pens, set them to their highest dose, and used them on Jack. He wore a double-vented jacket, with a flap, not like yours, which has a single split. It wouldn't have been too difficult for someone to reach his lower back. His jacket flap would have hidden the blood from view. If he felt any soreness he might have thought it was from the fight, or his fall."

Bud looked thoughtful. His expression gradually changed from disbelief to acceptance. "Whoever is doing this, we've got to stop them, Cait. Someone in this room is a desperate killer," he said, voicing my own thoughts.

"I know. Two people have been killed in ways that demand an ability to think fast, seizing upon situations that present themselves unexpectedly, and to take action under the possible scrutiny of a room full of people, without being seen. It's . . . very unusual, and more than a little frightening. Especially for Clemence."

"Clemence?"

"He has no insulin left. He'll need it very soon. Otherwise, he could develop ketoacidosis, which can be deadly. And he knows it."

We both automatically glanced toward Clemence's seat, but he wasn't there. Bud looked alarmed again.

"Don't panic, Bud, he's gone to the loo. He'll probably have to go quite often. Thirst and the inevitable aftereffects of quenching it are a couple of the symptoms of ketoacidosis. They go hand in hand with increasing confusion, tiredness, weakness, a fruity scent on the breath, and, eventually, coma and possible death. But, unlike with hypoglycemia, we can't even *try* to help him—the only thing that can possibly help him is insulin. So, Bud Anderson, you and I have to make a big decision . . ."

"Which is?"

"If someone stole Clemence's insulin pens, there might be a chance that they didn't use both of them, or not *all* of both of them. So there might be some insulin here, in this room somewhere. Clemence isn't aware of anyone else being diabetic, so finding his own supply, if any remains, is our best bet. I could announce that

Clemence has misplaced his pens, but that might tip our hand. The killer might realize we've worked out how they killed Jack Bullock. My question to you is—do you think that matters?"

Bud pinched the bridge of his nose, then rubbed both eyes as he gave the matter some thought. "You and I think alike, Cait. It's our strength in terms of our relationship, but it can be a weakness when it comes to an investigation. Because we both come at a problem the same way, we run the risk of missing things. We've always had to be careful not to do that, and we need to work through this carefully. My best assessment is that the most likely upshot of us spinning a yarn about Clemence losing his insulin is that we let the murderer know that we've worked out how they killed Jack, as you said, and put ourselves in possible danger. Maybe the killer did what they did because they thought that Jack was onto them for the killing of Miss Shirley, and we don't want to put ourselves in the firing line. Whoever this person is, they are not averse to taking huge risks, so I don't think they'd balk at killing either of us if they felt they had to and could come up with a way of doing it. But if we are completely open and announce the way we believe that Jack was killed, and that we all need to try to find any insulin that might be left in the room, we stand the best chance of finding a possible lifesaving dose of medication for Clemence, while simultaneously removing the murderer's need to kill us . . . because everyone would know. Do you agree with that summary?"

"Yes, I agree with you. But . . ."

"I might have guessed there was a 'but' coming," responded Bud, almost smiling.

I pressed on. "*But* if we tell everyone right off the bat that we believe Jack was murdered, how do you think that might impact Julie? She's distraught enough thinking it was an accident. I'm leaning toward just asking folks to look for Clemence's misplaced insulin, then I can observe how people look for it. It could be a telling process. Other than that, I don't have any other points to make, except that I'd feel a lot better if we had some idea why Miss Shirley and Jack Bullock were killed. I certainly think their deaths are connected, but possibly not in the way you just mentioned. I have my own theory."

"Inheritance?"

"Precisely," I replied. "Miss Shirley seems to have lived a colorful life, and what we've been told about her by everyone here paints her as a caring, hardworking woman. I'm sure she had many opportunities to make enemies over the years, but the facts seem to suggest she was a woman who helped, rather than hindered, people's careers. My thinking is that Jack Bullock was a prime candidate for being her estranged son. I heard him protesting to his wife that it was impossible. But what if the killer also thought he might be her son, and that it was just too big a risk to take?"

"Could be," said Bud thoughtfully.

"Which means one thing."

Bud nodded.

I drew even closer to him as I whispered, "No other man here is the right age to be one of Miss Shirley's sons, so that leaves us with grandchildren. The killer might be someone who knows they are, or at least believes themselves to be, Miss Shirley's grandchild. That points to Tanya, Jimmy, or Ian."

Bud nodded. "I agree. Tanya, Ian, and Jimmy. We know a little about each of them. But not enough."

"Right. However, that assumes that the motive for the murder is the inheritance of the shares in the casino. If it's a general inheritance issue instead, then everyone, Tom included, is still in the frame. Which isn't really helpful. So we need to find out what was in the existing will versus what would have been in the new one. That would be something concrete that could help us eliminate several suspects. I know she wasn't prepared to break her client's confidence earlier on, but do you think you might be able to get Julie to tell us the full facts now? It does seem as though Jack spilled the main points, so maybe after all that's happened she'll be more likely to talk."

Bud nodded. "I've dealt with some difficult situations over the years when I've had to question people who've lost a loved one. I don't want Julie Pool to think that someone deliberately killed her husband—I agree with you, I don't believe we need to subject her to that thought right now—but I do think I could take her aside and try to get what I can out of her about the two different wills. If I do that, could you come up with something about Clemence losing his insulin, and get folks to hunt about for it? It's not as good as everyone being searched, but it might turn up something useful."

I reached up and kissed Bud on the cheek, lingering for two seconds longer than a peck. He smelled so good. I could feel the skin on my drying lips pull taut as I smiled at him and spoke. "I'll keep it as low-key as I can, but we have to do it. It could save Clemence's life. I'll also take myself off to do a proper recollection of where people were standing when I came out of the ladies' room the first time, when everything was dark, compared with when I came out the second time, when everyone *said* they were in their original places. There's still something nagging at me about those two setups that isn't right. And I don't just mean Miss Shirley's odd position. You take Julie to one side and find out what you can about Miss Shirley's intentions, past and present, for the disposal of her estate. Good luck, my love."

"You too," replied Bud, returning my kiss. "None of this is good, so let's get going."

I popped a fresh piece of nicotine gum into my mouth and chewed hard. I wondered if two at a time might work better, but I knew I had to ration it. We still had hours ahead of us.

Chorus

I HADN'T NOTICED THAT THE sun was rising. When I looked out, trying to decide exactly how to frame the topic of Clemence's insulin, it was already illuminating the peaks in the west with a bright, buttery light. Miles beyond The Strip, I could see the mountains rise up from the plain in a stark, unyielding statement that whatever man might do to a landscape, it's ultimately nature that dominates. Closer to the casino, the neon lights of The Strip were now overwhelmed by the daylight, and, as I looked down, I could see tiny humans jogging along the streets, making the most of the shade cast by the towering hotels. A skateboarder shot along the sidewalk, a dog on a leash running beside him, something that would be impossible to do in just a few hours' time, because by then the throngs would be out in force. Las Vegas was a city waking up, rubbing its eyes, and deciding which glittering, rhinestone-encrusted outfit it would wear for the day. It made me think of the mask of normality that the killer in our midst must be wearing.

I turned to face my current reality. I knew that as the sun moved overhead, the glass-clad egg we were in would heat up even more. It wasn't going to be pleasant. With the temperature outside likely to soar to maybe ninety or a hundred degrees, our claustrophobic quarters were likely to become quite unpleasant.

I called for people's attention and began my little performance. "When Clemence took his jacket off some hours ago, he misplaced the bag he always has with him that holds his insulin pens. It's very important for him that we find those pens. Clemence, could you describe the bag, please, so everyone can have a hunt about for it?"

"Sure," said Clemence. "It's red. Red leather with a gold zipper.

Long. Like a fancy pencil case some rich kid might have, I guess. Miss Shirley gave it to me 'cause I could never find my pens. Now I can't find the bag."

I was glad that Clemence stopped when he did.

"When did you last have it, Clemence?" asked Art.

"After dinner. Used it then. Ain't seen it since," replied Clemence.

I managed a relatively bright smile as I spoke. "Maybe folks could check the floor, the men's and ladies' rooms, behind the bar, under chairs, and so forth? Thanks." I really wanted to be an observer, but I knew I'd have to participate in some way.

"Why ladies' room?" asked Svetlana, puzzled.

"We should just check everywhere," I replied, panicking a little. *Silly of me, how could Clemence have left it there?*

Carl called out, "Looking for a red leather case on a red carpet? That's a nightmare."

"Let's divide up the room, and each search one particular area," suggested Tom.

"Good idea," said Ian. "Let's pretend the room is a clock and divide it up by segments. Then we can all start at the center and work out, or the other way around."

"We'll have to steer clear of the area around Miss Shirley's body," I said, probably unnecessarily.

"Should we move Jack's body?" asked Jimmy in respectful tones.

"What's the point?" asked Carl. "We'll just work around it. *Him.* It's the same general area as Miss Shirley's body, so let's just avoid that part of the room altogether." Carl seemed to be appropriately uncomfortable when referring to the corpses in our midst.

We spent a few moments dividing up the room, and then we began to tackle our allotted portions.

As people searched, I watched closely. *That's annoying— everyone seems to be completely focused on their tasks.*

"You want me search behind bar?" said Svetlana imperiously.

"Clemence not go behind bar. Bag not there. My throat. I not search behind bar."

It was interesting to note how Svetlana managed to use her throat, and its undoubted sensitivity, as a convenient way to avoid doing anything she didn't want to do. I suspected she'd always used it that way, throughout her stellar career. *It's amazing what stars can get away with, which we mere mortals have to endure.*

There was always the chance that whoever had taken the bag had tossed it behind the bar, so I said, "Maybe I could give you a hand back there, when I've finished here," knowing that Svetlana wouldn't be the most reliable searcher in any case.

"I could help as well," suggested Jimmy, flying to his idol's aid. "My section's a pretty easy one to check—in fact, I'm almost done. Nothing here. Let me check behind that section of the bar, Madame."

It only took a matter of fifteen minutes or so before everyone agreed that we'd searched the whole place and there was no sign of Clemence's little bag. The only areas we hadn't searched were those around Miss Shirley's corpse, under Jack's body, and right where Bud and Julie were sitting, deep in conversation. I could see that Bud was fully engaged with the still-sobbing woman, so I knew I had to step up. Clemence's health was at stake—extraordinary measures were in order.

"Jimmy, Ian, Tom, I need you three to help me. You too, Carl, if you please." Four male faces turned toward me and showed a similar expression—apprehension.

"If each of you could stand at a corner of the cloth covering Miss Shirley's body, keeping your feet well back, and reach forward and lift the cloth so I can see underneath, that would be most helpful." Grunts and shufflings aside, the men undertook their task silently. I lay down on the floor to peer underneath the raised cloth as quickly as possible, and without their having to lift it too high. I was hoping to see a small red leather bag on the floor, but I didn't. What I did catch sight of was a large, soiled handkerchief, made of pink silk, piled on the floor beneath Miss Shirley's chair. I hadn't noticed it when we'd first seen her body, but I reasoned that I'd probably been at the wrong angle—upright, rather than prone.

"Does anyone know if Miss Shirley owned a pink silk handkerchief?"

I looked up at the faces surrounding me. Every one displayed bafflement. As I lay there, I smelled something unusual. I sniffed. Chemicals. Maybe carpet-cleaning solution? It smelled oilier than I'd have expected. I wriggled forward, toward Miss Shirley's chair. I didn't want to get too close, but I could tell that the smell got stronger as I got closer. I knew that at this distance my reading glasses wouldn't help me focus on the handkerchief any better anyway, so I settled on squinting. I could just make out that the stains on it seemed to make the cloth almost transparent. Maybe they were the source of the oily smell? It was puzzling. I desperately wanted to reach out and grab the cloth, but I didn't want to disturb what might turn out to be a valuable clue to the killer's identity, which the cops, when they finally arrived, would need to see in situ.

"What on earth are you doing down there?" asked Bud as he approached. He held out his hand for me to pull myself up. Luckily he's quite strong.

I brushed myself off and said, "Thanks for your help, gentlemen." Carl, Jimmy, Ian, and Tom gently released the edges of the cloth. As they wandered off, I addressed Bud. "I was seeing if Clemence's little bag had somehow found its way under the cloth. It hasn't. Oh, and the handle from the urn isn't there either."

I could tell from Bud's expression that he'd completely forgotten about the urn that was now in pieces, wrapped in a cloth, and tucked into a bin behind the bar.

"This night is nuts," said Ian, drawing everyone's attention. He'd settled himself on a bar stool and was leaning heavily on the bar itself.

"It's like one of your operas." He nodded in Svetlana's direction.

"Is right," whispered Svetlana, peering over her shoulders, a look of terror on her face. "But I hope is not opera. In opera sometimes everybody die. Especially leading lady. Soprano dies often. I am soprano, I know. I die very often in operas. Of course, first I sing beautiful aria, then I die."

"So don't sing. Anything. *At all*," said Carl. "Maybe we'll all be safe then. From the killer, and from your singing. Though, frankly, it doesn't feel like any of us are safe. I wonder who's next."

The Diva shot Carl a disdainful look, and Jimmy's expression toward the man left me in no doubt that given half a chance he'd have swatted Carl for making such a derogatory comment about his idol.

Art snapped, "If you don't shut up, Carl, I'll make you. Do you even know what the word 'inappropriate' means?"

"But he's right," said Tanya. "We still don't know who killed Miss Shirley, or who took the egg. Now Jack's dead, though I'd say that's your fault, Carl, and yours, Art, for fighting in the first place." Both men looked shocked and reddened. "Maybe there's someone here who wants us all dead, for some reason. We just don't know." Her tone seemed to convey resignation tinged with annoyance.

Tom gathered Tanya in his arms. "Come on, Tanya, don't say that. Of course there's something . . . amiss. But I cannot believe that I'm looking at someone, here in this room, right now, who wants to kill me."

Tanya looked up at her boyfriend. "Not you, silly. No one could want you dead. But the rest of us? Who knows?"

"Who knows, indeed," said Art quietly.

"On that cheery note I'm going for a 'nature break'—so long as no one thinks that's inappropriate!" snapped Carl.

"Glorified used car salesman," hissed Art to no one in particular, as Carl headed toward the men's room. If Carl heard him, he chose not to rise to the bait.

132

"Is good time for breakfast," said Svetlana loudly. "We have food now, yes?"

The rest of us were taken by surprise. "I don't think there *is* any food, Svetlana," I replied.

"Is always food when needed," she replied and hoisted herself from her seat. "Jimmy, come, we make good meal for everyone, yes?"

"Sure," replied Jimmy, as confused as the rest of us.

I indicated to Bud that I, too, was going to use the washroom, and I headed off to find some peace and quiet where I could recollect earlier events. I caught Svetlana humming as she directed Jimmy. I couldn't imagine what sort of "meal" she was going to produce, but I knew I was hungry, so I didn't really care.

Just as I reached the washroom door, Bud caught me by the arm.

"Cait, I guess you're off to do your memory thing, but I need you to do your thinking thing too. Julie told me that the only major difference between Miss Shirley's old, existing will and the new one she didn't sign is the introduction of a clause that says, 'To be read after opening the letter I have given to my lawyer for safekeeping.'"

"Good job, Bud. I'm glad she chose to open up to you about it. So, has Julie got the letter with her, here? What does it say?"

Bud shook his head. "That's just it. Miss Shirley didn't give Julie a letter. She didn't give her anything. Julie said they worked through the clauses of the new will one at a time. Miss Shirley made a minor amendment to the amount of money she left to Art, and she listed a few extra items she wanted to leave to Svetlana, a silver Romanoff tea urn among them. Carl gets the bulk of her estate in both wills, but there's that additional clause in the new will saying that the shares in the Tsar! Casino are to go to Miss Shirley's 'next of kin.' She left money to Tanya, Ian, Jimmy, Clemence, Julie, and Jack in both wills, with no differences between the two. She also made bequests to a good number of charities, and to quite a few people who aren't among our group. She didn't leave anything to Tom in either document. What it all means is that pretty much everyone is in the same position whether the new will was signed or the old will stands. The only significant difference is the clause about the shares, and the reference to a letter, of which Julie has no knowledge."

"Do you believe that Julie is telling the truth?" It was a critical question.

Bud nodded. "Yes, Cait, I do. Of course she's overwhelmed right now, but she seemed to pull herself together enough to cogently answer my questions about the letter, and what was in those two wills. I know you're a better natural reader of people than me, but I've got a good few years' experience myself, and that's my considered professional opinion."

I nodded. I trusted Bud's instincts.

He continued, "That letter could have major implications for someone in the room, if it contains information about who Miss Shirley's 'next of kin' might be. I'm more certain than ever that the motive for the poor woman's murder was tied to someone here being Miss Shirley's child or grandchild. As for Jack's murder? Well, that confirms to me that someone's got their eyes on the ultimate prize of owning this casino, because Jack was the only real candidate in the room when it comes to being one of Miss Shirley's sons."

I gave Bud's information some thought. "I'm pretty certain, too, that we're down to Tanya, Ian, and Jimmy as the possible killer—the only people in this room who could be Miss Shirley's grandchild. I'll give them special consideration when I'm recollecting this evening's events," I replied. "By the way, how's Julie doing?"

Bud shook his head. "As badly as you'd expect. She's having a little chat with Clemence now. It seems their misery and loss is being shared. Go on—do it, Cait—see if you can recall anything that helps."

I nodded. It was a huge responsibility, but I pushed open the door to the ladies' room, allowing it to swoosh closed behind me, then I locked myself in one of the two stalls, took the only seat available, screwed up my eyes, and started to hum . . .

Reprise

I AM EMERGING INTO A darkened dining room. Luckily, before it cut out, the lighting in the washroom was very dim, much dimmer than the blazing chandeliers in the dining room, so my eyes are better acclimatized to the darkness when I enter the main dining room than maybe those of the people who were sitting in there when the lights went out.

Immediately I smell sweetness, chocolate, and I also smell... alcohol and... Bud's aftershave. Bud held my hand at dinner, and his scent has ingrained itself into my skin, even though I've just washed my hands. I take only a few steps into the room. I am in front of the privacy screen, near the end of the bar. I hear the rustle of fabric. It's Ian.

How do I know this?

He smells of alcohol—the spilled champagne—and I know that what I am hearing is satin. He's the only one in the room wearing satin that would move like that—his Cossack shirt. Svetlana's dress is too tightly bound around her body. The cloth rubs against itself as he moves, making a very distinctive sound. I know he's very close to me, though I am not looking at him.

I am looking toward the glass wall of the egg. The diamond-shaped glass panels are edged in black against the glowing colors of the neon outside. I know that from the outside, the panels look like they're outlined in tiny white lights, twinkling like diamonds against the reflective gold of the glass.

It's odd to be inside the egg.

The topmost part of the window wall appears darker, because it's against the sky, which, although not black, is more subdued than the pulsating Strip.

I stay where I am. I do not feel as though I am in danger. There's been some sort of power problem. I wonder what the loud clanging was. A figure darts across my line of vision.

I must concentrate. What exactly do I see?

I see a crouching figure. I cannot tell if it is a man or a woman, all I see is a silhouette. It moves toward me.

I go back to the beginning of this scene in my mind.

Am I certain that the figure is really between the tables and the outer glass wall?

Yes. It is close to the glass wall, I am sure of this. I am also certain that the silhouette doesn't have Svetlana's distinctive hairdo of a rounded bun atop her head. *It isn't Svetlana.*

"Everybody stay where you are, please. The security system has been activated—we're in a lockdown. The emergency lighting will come on in just a few seconds." Julie Pool is speaking. I turn my head toward her voice. I see Julie's silhouette plainly. I even catch the side of her face washed with red and gold light.

So it wasn't her who darted across my field of vision.

Julie has her arms raised to get people's attention, as though they can see her. I realize that everyone *can* see her—she's clearly visible, backlit against the glass wall. Beside her is a male figure, her husband, Jack. To me they are visible only from the waist up, as there are partitions and people blocking my view.

At this moment, unless someone was standing up, in the path of the light coming from The Strip, I would not have been able to see them.

"I not afraid of dark, I afraid of furniture. Is moving." Svetlana Kharlamova speaks. No, she whines. She sounds like a small, irritating child.

She has annoyed me all evening. Although I know my sister would probably surrender a limb to meet the woman, Svetlana's laugh has drilled away at me throughout dinner. Launching it for no apparent reason, her laugh is always "Ha Ha Ha," or else a short descending scale, just like "Adele's Laughing Song" in *Die Fledermaus*. My mum sang that at the Clydach Operatic Society in the late 1960s. I haven't thought of it for years. I sat on a wide windowsill at the Mond Hall, watching my mother play her part of a maid in disguise at a masked ball, wearing an elaborate pink satin costume. She sang beautifully.

I drag myself back from Wales, to focus on a Russian diva in a Las Vegas dining room. *How odd it feels. Unreal, almost.*

"Please, Madame, stay still. The furniture isn't moving, you are. Ms. Pool is correct. If we wait a moment, I'm sure everything will be just fine." Jimmy Green has way too much patience with the woman. I must rerun that segment again.

Did I see or hear anything that suggests "moving furniture"? No.

The air in front of me moves. I definitely feel it.

Is it Ian? No. He's still to my right.

I smell . . . soap. Yes, I smell soap in the whooshing air.

Is it the smell of my own hands? No.

The lights come on. Though they are really quite dim, they seem bright for a moment.

Now I must concentrate very hard and compare what I see at this moment with the way people arranged themselves for the restaging of the time of the murder.

On both occasions Julie and Jack are standing in exactly the same spots—beyond Miss Shirley's table, between the table and the glass wall. Clemence is seated opposite Miss Shirley. The first time he is leaning forward on his cupped hands, which are supporting his head, his elbows on the table. The second time, because the table has been moved, he is sitting upright in his seat.

At the moment the lights come on, Bud is still sitting at our table, exactly where he was, how he was, when I left. Tom and Tanya have left the table. They are standing at the bar, to my right. Tom is farthest from me, Tanya is nearer me. They are close to the middle of the bar. However, when they retook their places, they reversed their positions—with Tom closer to me.

Maybe that was what had jarred me? No, there's something else.

When the lights come up, Tanya is standing with her back to me, and her huge purse is on her shoulder. When the scene is reset, not only is she on the other side of Tom, but she doesn't have her purse.

Why does she have her purse the first time, but not the second? Why is she in a different position?

At the center table, Svetlana has her back to the bar, as does Jimmy. They are seated next to each other. The two seats opposite them are empty. Art is standing at the far end of the bar, near the men's room, and Carl is standing beyond the partition farthest from me.

Why is he there?

He's quite close to Miss Shirley's body. During our reenactment Art is once again standing at the bar, though closer to the center now, and Carl is sitting at the center table.

That's not right—why has Carl changed spots?

Ian is in front of the bar, between me and Tom and Tanya. When the lights come on, he continues to move to the rear of the bar. The second time he's just hovering.

Maybe understandable?

Shall I take Ian's word for it that he placed the shashka on the bar? If so, anyone who wanted to use the sword to kill Miss Shirley would have had to first retrieve it from there, unless it was Ian himself who used it. Ian was at the correct side of the room to have easy access to the blade, and Miss Shirley's back. He might have been the person who caused the air to move.

No—he definitely smelled of alcohol, not soap. The person who passed me smelled of soap.

He was very quick to point out that his fingerprints would be on the murder weapon, and he's just the right age to potentially be a grandson of Miss Shirley's. He told us about his upbringing in Seattle, but there's no reason why a boy adopted in LA in the 1960s couldn't have grown up and moved to the Pacific Northwest to raise a family. Ian's father might never have spoken to his son about his antecedents, if he'd even known about them himself. Sometimes people lie to their children. So, yes, Ian could be Miss Shirley's grandson, and he had access to the weapon, *and* he's lived in Vegas for long enough that he might have had a chance to somehow find out about his true identity.

I need to find out exactly why Ian came to Vegas, other than that it's maybe a good place to find work as a barman.

I am keeping Ian on my list of possible killers.

Next I turn my thoughts to Jimmy. He's using Svetlana, and the way she was grabbing him, as his alibi.

Would the Diva have noticed his not being there? Yes.

Would she have commented upon it? Possibly not.

Jimmy could have got up, run around the tables, picked up the sword at the bar, thrust it into Miss Shirley's back, then pushed past Svetlana, causing her to cry out about moving furniture. But that would mean both he and Svetlana lied about him being at the table and her holding onto him when the lights went out. *Could they be covering for each other?*

His might have been the figure I saw run in silhouette, but he'd have been between me and the tables, and I'm really pretty sure that the figure was between the tables and the wall. Also, he would have passed me only on his way to pick up the saber from the bar, because he would have just darted from Miss Shirley's table back to his own seat at the next table. He wouldn't have come back along the bar.

Jimmy could be Miss Shirley's grandson—he's the right age and was raised in a traveling van by parents who hailed from San

Francisco, just a stone's throw from LA. Maybe the place he used to visit that smelled of toast and grease was his grandmother's diner here in Vegas. Jimmy could have found out his true identity during his time in Vegas—he said he stayed because he found work here, but it seems that his artistic tastes are more refined than one might be able to indulge in Vegas. *Why didn't he gravitate toward New York?*

I'm definitely keeping him on my list of possibles.

Now Tanya.

I focus on her. I try to push aside my natural dislike of the girl. Bud's always telling me I'm too judgmental, though I try to convince him that all I'm doing is reading a myriad of cues and clues to allow myself to decide how I feel about someone. Tanya's not blessed with good social skills. I like Tom. I think Tom deserves better. I mustn't let this color my assessment of the girl.

Tanya could have grabbed the shashka, stuck it into Miss Shirley, and returned to her place at the bar unnoticed.

Would she have had the strength to deliver the deadly thrust?

I'm on the fence about that one because I'm not sure how strong she is, or how much force it would take to do that with what was, admittedly, a very sharp blade. Bud said it wouldn't take much effort. I suppose if I could do it, Tanya could have. So, yes, she could have killed Miss Shirley.

Could she be Miss Shirley's granddaughter? Yes. She's the right age. Her father was a local, bringing her up in Henderson.

Did her father know who his mother was? I don't know about that.

Her father recently killed himself. *I wonder why?*

Tanya's lived in the area her whole life; she might have discovered her father's true identity and her own. So, yes, I cannot discount Tanya as a possible suspect.

Why did she have her big purse with her at the bar? Habit?

There are two more things I must focus on . . . the urn and the egg.

Okay, the urn. I can see it as the lights come up. It has moved, twisted on its axis, and the handle is definitely missing. Also, the golden egg is still in its place atop the partition. I am certain of these two things.

Did I notice when the egg disappeared?

I allow the evening to play through, and I am sure I did not see it being taken.

I finally settle myself to think through the fight scene that surrounded Carl and Art. I take another deep breath and screw up my eyes one more time.

I can see Art shake his fist at Carl, and Carl push out his chest at Art. Bud is between the two men, one hand on each man's chest. They calm down. Bud moves to be closer to me, and we talk. Suddenly, Carl and Art fly at each other. Okay, now I have to try to think things through very clearly.

Who is where, when?

Carl is close to where Clemence is sitting. Clemence shies away as Carl is almost pushed into his chair. I can see Clemence's jacket is still on the back of his seat. Jack rushes to pull the two men apart. Julie wades in, helping Jack pull on Art, who is swinging at Carl. Tanya is being held back by Tom, but she pulls away and starts to move around the back of Clemence's chair toward the melee. Ian is with her.

I give my attention, momentarily, to Bud, so I do not see exactly what happens next. But when I look back, I see that Julie is now pushing Carl away from Art. Art has hold of Carl's sleeve. As Julie pushes Carl, the sleeve begins to rip away from the rest of the jacket—I hear it and see it. As this happens, Carl begins to stagger back. Art also begins to stagger backward. Tanya is behind Art, beside Jack, and has her arm linked through Jack's—she seems to be trying to pull him sideways.

Ian is in front of Art, though Art and Carl are still connected by the jacket sleeve, and Ian is trying to catch Art as he falls back. Jimmy hasn't entered the fight, though he's very close by, since Svetlana is on her feet, almost cheering the action.

Finally, Carl's sleeve rips off. Art falls back, knocking Jack, who tumbles against the partition. I hear Jack's head make contact with the hollow wooden structure. I wince as I hear it. The urn falls from the top of the partition and bounces with a dull thud onto the carpet, then splits asunder.

Tanya and Jimmy help Jack to his feet, brushing bits of urn from his jacket. Jack puts his hand in the small of his back and arches it, like a cat, in both directions, then moves his head from side to side. Julie is rubbing his head, checking for blood, a lump, anything. They move away from the throng.

What have I seen?

I haven't seen anyone pump Jack full of insulin, though Tanya, Jimmy, and even Julie would all have had the opportunity to do so. Though maybe only Tanya and Ian would have had a real chance to take the little red pharmaceutical bag from Clemence's pocket during the flight.

I have seen the whole thing in flashes because I was giving my attention to the main fight, the Diva, and Bud. I am annoyed with myself that I didn't keep staring at the fight the entire time.

I was just about to return to Bud in the dining room, but stopped myself before pushing open the door of the stall where I had been sitting. *There's something else I want to recall.*

I think back, once again, to my first glimpse of the seat in which Miss Shirley's body is sitting.

The lights have just come on, I'm as far away from her as I can be, and I am looking at her dead body, in profile, sitting in her seat. I don't know that she's dead at this point, but why didn't I notice the hilt of the sword poking out of the back of her chair? I think back . . .

Ah—it's not where my attention is drawn.

My attention is drawn to her feet . . . As the overhead lights come on, a glint catches my eye—it's the light reflecting off the thousands of red crystals with which Miss Shirley's purse is covered. Her purse is on the floor, between her chair and the partition. The base of the purse is facing me. It glitters in the lights. There is no pink silk handkerchief on the floor. I can see right through the legs of Miss Shirley's chair. I see the legs of the chair, I see the woman's legs, and I see the purse—but nothing pink.

How did Svetlana end up with Miss Shirley's purse when she didn't get that close to the body? Where did the pink silk handkerchief come from?

"Cait? You done in there?" Bud knocked on the heavy outer door, pushing it open a little.

"Coming," I called back. "Out in a minute."

"Okay, but don't be long. You'll want to see this."

"Right-o." I was afraid to ask what had happened. Surely things couldn't get any worse?

Medley for Two

I ENTERED THE DINING ROOM with trepidation. What had Bud meant? *What* would I want to see? Then I saw it. The dessert table had been transformed. Gone was the unappealing heap of picked-over cheese, fruit, and white chocolate bread pudding. Even the puddle of what had once been ice cream had been cleared away. Instead there was an appetizing spread of neatly sliced pudding, fruit rearranged on a plate, chocolates wrapped in foil, jugs of water, bread rolls, biscuits, crackers, cookies, and a dozen or so cans of soda.

"Where did you find all this?" I asked.

Svetlana beamed. "Is my idea. Food is better when looks good. We clear, we choose best fruit—is still good. Ian have mints for after dinner behind bar, and I have candy in purse, I share." She glowed with pride. I suspected that sharing was not something she did often, or naturally. "Tanya have candy in purse, she share also. Water from tap is cool. No bottles left. Cans from refrigerator—not cold, but not hot. Is good, yes?"

"You've done a great job, Madame," said Jimmy, his smile so wide it threatened to split his face.

Bud called out, "I think we should all eat and drink what we can. It's been a very long night, and we still have"—he looked at his watch—"four more hours before help can reach us."

"I know it sounds odd," said Ian, "but we have some crème de menthe behind the bar. In case someone wants to, you know, kinda use it as a gargle, to have a minty flavor, without the chocolate." He noticed the appalled expressions on everyone's faces. "Well, I thought it might work. We don't have coffee or tea, but we do have cola, and the chocolates might help. Sugar instead of caffeine. I can't remember the last time I started a day without coffee. Like Svetlana said, the sodas are only a little below room temperature. The water from the tap is good, though—I tried it. I let it run, and it's really quite refreshing. I guess that'll have to do instead of coffee. Will everyone help themselves?"

We all nodded. I whispered to Bud, "I'll see if Julie wants anything, and we have to keep an eye on Clemence ... by the way, where is he?"

"He went to the men's room a few minutes ago," replied Bud quietly. "How about I see to Julie? She and I have built a sort of—rapport. I'm not sure it was of any comfort to her, but I was able to talk about losing Jan."

I felt a sad smile crease my face. Jan's death would always be a part of our life together. There was no getting away from it. If it hadn't been for Jan being murdered, Bud and I would still be work colleagues, nothing more. Whenever I thought about her death, I experienced a very complex, worrying set of mixed emotions. I did my best to set them aside as Bud continued to whisper.

"Because I was able to talk to her from the point of view of someone whose spouse has been killed, I think she was able to cope with my questions a lot better. She still thinks he died because he hit his head. So, listen, you sort yourself out. I can't quite bring myself to eat small squares of cold bread pudding, so I'll just grab a few after-dinner mints and some water."

I felt my expression brighten. "I'm glad it was such a huge pudding. Just as well Miss Shirley called for such a substantial birthday dessert. It'll be fine cold. Better than nothing. And I'll keep an eye open for Clemence when he comes back, so you can focus on Julie."

Bud started across the room toward where Julie was sleeping before I could tell him about my recollections. I caught up with him when he was quite close to her and pulled at his arm.

"I'm surprised she can sleep," I noted softly.

"Different people take shock, grief, different ways," replied Bud. "But you're right—I hadn't realized she was asleep. I don't think I could just drop off, sitting on the floor with my back propped up against the wall like that. I won't disturb her. I'll let her sleep for a while. What did you want?"

I looked around to make sure no one was listening before I spoke. "I've done my recollecting thing, as you asked, sir"—Bud almost managed a chuckle—"and I've come to some conclusions. If we're working on the assumption that it has to be Ian, Jimmy, or Tanya who killed Miss Shirley because they know themselves to be her grandchild, then any one of them could have accessed the shashka, killed her, and been back in their position when the lights went up. My main concern is that, whoever did it, it was an incredibly audacious and risky way to kill someone. To act like that, on the spur of the moment, when the lights went off, is incredible to me. Also, I've recalled that Miss Shirley's purse was on the floor when she died, but the pink silk handkerchief was not under her chair. *And* that Tanya and Ian both had the opportunity during the fight to get to Clemence's bag containing his insulin pens, as well as that she or Jimmy could have injected the insulin into Jack's back while he was struggling with Art and Carl. I don't see how Jimmy could have got hold of Clemence's insulin at that particular moment, but he might have been able to get to it sometime earlier in the evening."

"Well done, Cait. That's really useful. Anything else?"

"I want to find out more about Tanya's father, and her upbringing, but I don't want to ask her. I thought I'd pump Tom about it, okay?"

Bud shrugged and nodded.

"I'm also curious about why she had her big old purse with her when she left our table after dinner, but not when everyone took up their places again later on. Oh, and I need you to try to find out why Carl was standing near Miss Shirley's body when the lights went up, but chose to seat himself at his table when we reset. Can you do that?"

"You're saying that everyone was in their correct places when we reconstructed the scene except Carl?"

I nodded. "Pretty well, yes. Tanya and Tom had swapped places at the bar, but I'll tackle that one with Tom. I'll grab something to eat and get him away from Tanya. Could you check out the Carl thing? Or maybe pop to the men's room to make sure that Clemence is alright first?"

Bud nodded. "Clemence first, then Carl." He looked at his watch again. "They should be here in less than four hours. I just hope that Clemence can cope without his meds for that long. He's clearly not a well man in any case, and I know there's nothing we can do to help him. If only we could find those insulin pens. They must be *somewhere*. Whoever killed Miss Shirley and Jack has one hell of an evil streak running through them, Cait. All those years I was working homicides, there was one thing I was very aware of—there's always an alternative to killing someone. Always." His voice was still low, but angry.

I hugged Bud. It was all I could do. As I held him close I whispered, "Bud, this person is driven. Focused on their task. I believe they had a plan all along and took advantage of the circumstances to get Miss Shirley out of the way—" As I spoke, a thought occurred to me. "Though there is another possibility." I pulled back from Bud, my mind racing.

Bud's expression changed from anger to hope. "What is it, Cait?"

"What if the killer *knew* the security system would be forced into lockdown, and that the lights would go out? What if they planned the whole thing that way, so they knew there'd be a sword handy, that Miss Shirley would be where she was, and that they'd have the cover of darkness? Right at the outset I wondered how anyone could think they would get away with it. You know, hope to get out of the room without being interviewed by the cops? Maybe they didn't. Maybe their plan hinged upon the cops arriving right after Miss Shirley's death. The variable they didn't expect was Miss Shirley changing the security codes. That's the only reason we're still here. If those codes had remained unchanged, we'd have been out of here and down at police headquarters, all being questioned and examined forensically, within an hour of Miss Shirley's death."

The more I thought about it, the more this new idea made more sense than someone simply acting on the spur of the moment.

I kept talking it through, which helps my thought process a great deal. "Maybe Miss Shirley's murder was carefully planned. It has all the hallmarks of a bold killer taking advantage of circumstance, but it might not have been. It's the subsequent action of Jack's murder with Clemence's insulin that's the improvisation. Even if the killer knew they were Miss Shirley's grandchild, they might not have known that Clemence was aware of their father's existence. It's only thanks to him, and that photo that Miss Shirley always carried, that we even know about that fact—oh! The photo from Miss Shirley's purse! Where is it?"

Bud looked puzzled. "I don't know, Cait. I've kind of lost track of it. Maybe Clemence still has it?"

I looked around. "And her purse. Where's Miss Shirley's red purse gone? It's not on the bar where Julie put it earlier."

Bud glanced toward the bar, then the men's room. "Let me go see how Clemence is doing, then I'll help you gather all the bits and pieces that are clues, or possible clues, together in one spot. Meanwhile, how about you talk to Tom about Tanya?"

"Okay, you go and see to Clemence. We'll reconvene as soon as we can, right?"

We both winked, rather than kissing, and headed off in opposite directions.

Deceptive Cadence

I ONLY HAD TO MOVE a few yards to be beside Tom, grab his elbow, and steer him away from the dessert table. I did it quite roughly because I was tired and had little patience remaining. He didn't seem to mind. He'd been picking through the collection of apples, tangerines, and bananas on the table.

"Can we have a few words, away from Tanya?" I asked quietly.

"Sure." Tom shrugged and looked around. "I can't see her anywhere. I think she's—you know, in the ladies' room."

I couldn't see her either, which was good. I didn't waste any time. "Tom, I need you to know that Bud and I are doing our best to work through all this. I also have to be honest and say that Tanya is one of our main suspects."

Tom looked aghast. "Tanya?" He said it quite loudly, then noticed that he'd drawn the attention of people in the room. He stepped closer to me. "Tanya? How can you say that? What do you mean? She wouldn't kill Miss Shirley. She couldn't do it. She's very placid by nature. Honestly. I know her really well. She just wouldn't do it."

"Let's move a little farther aside, Tom, and talk over here," I suggested. We stood closer to the glass wall—as close as my creeping vertigo would allow. "We've all heard that Miss Shirley had two sons, and Tanya is just the right age to be a possible granddaughter. So, let's not beat about the bush—tell me what you know about Tanya's father. She said he recently killed himself."

Tom, quite rightly, looked rather taken aback by my abrupt questioning of him. I apologized before he had a chance to speak. Somewhat mollified he said, "Tanya's had a pretty tough life, and she's handled it all with patience and hard work. I think it's unfair of you to believe she could kill someone, so, okay, I'll tell you all I know about her and her family to prove it. Her father? Waste of space. She's better off without him in her life. She doted on him, and with no cause. On the occasions I met him, he struck me as one of those people who—oh, you know, they act as though the world owes them a living. I wouldn't say that to Tanya, of course, but the guy was just one of life's losers."

"Can you be more specific?" I hoped he could be.

Tom nodded. "You and Bud came to Vegas to have a good time. It's a great city to do that. Loads of my friends come to visit, and they love it. It's like there's something in the air. An expectation that people bring with them that they're going to have a wonderful, crazy time, and they do. But for some, it's the worst place in the world. They don't have a 'flutter.' They have a sickness that sometimes kicks in when they visit, then it goes away when they go home. But if they live here, it's a condition they can't escape. Tanya's dad was a gambler. He had it bad. He'd have bet on anything, and often did, but mainly he played poker. He was awful at it. He'd lose a pile, then, amazingly, he'd show up at home with a bunch of money, from somewhere or other. When he won, he'd shower her with useless gifts she didn't want or need. When he lost, she'd help him hide from the guys who'd be looking for him—telling them he wasn't home, she hadn't seen him. All while she was still just a kid. I suspect that was the life her mom got sick of, and that's why she up and left."

"Have you ever met, or did she ever mention, grandparents? Specifically her father's parents." I was curious.

Tom shuffled from one foot to the other. "No, we haven't talked about either her mother's parents or her father's. Then again, I don't think I've talked about everyone in my family to her, either. You don't always, as a couple, do you, eh? Her mother hasn't been in the picture for years. Took off when Tanya was thirteen. I can understand that the woman might have had enough of her loser gambler husband, but can you imagine a mother walking out on her kid? Awful. Tanya never talks about her, which is understandable. Before he . . . died, Tanya used to talk a lot about her dad. The worst of it was, he was a dealer, so he never escaped the atmosphere. Worked at the old Sunrise, when it was here, then came back when they opened Tsar! It was especially tough when Tanya went to university. She would have liked to have gone to MIT—she had the chance. But she stayed here, went to UNLV instead. Got a scholarship, but it was really difficult for a while. She was only fifteen. Brilliant girl. So clever. Then her dad got fired. I think, to be honest, that Miss Shirley had saved him a few times, but they finally had evidence of him doing something pretty bad at the tables, so he was out."

"Did Tanya do well at university? Make *any* friends?"

"No friends to speak of. She did well academically—top of her class, even though she was only seventeen. When she graduated, she got a job here, right away. She's worked her way up really fast. Cait, I know Miss Shirley liked her and trusted her. She was great with Tanya after her dad killed himself. Tanya's never really talked about it since he died, but I got the impression that he'd finally got into a situation he just couldn't see his way out of. They were about to take the house, the car was already gone. Tanya's had her own little place since she turned eighteen, but now we'll have a proper home. White picket fence, the lot. And kids. We want a real family. That's the sort of person Tanya is. She just wants a normal life. She had no reason to kill Miss Shirley. She liked Miss Shirley."

"Why do you think Miss Shirley took Tanya under her wing to such an extent?"

Tom gave his answer some thought. "Tanya first met Miss Shirley when she was very young. They used to have family days for the people who worked at the old Sunrise, and her dad always took her along, of course." Tom smiled. "I've seen photos of Tanya back then. When her mother was around she dressed her like she was a little doll. Frilly dresses, little socks, big specs. She looked cute. I guess she just won over Miss Shirley's heart. But I don't think Tanya had much contact with Miss Shirley until she started working here. Well, of course, Miss Shirley presented Tanya with her scholarship money, but that was it."

"Why would Miss Shirley present a scholarship to Tanya?"

"It was the first year of a new scholarship Miss Shirley funded at UNLV. It was for the best university entrance qualifications for a child of an employee of the Tsar! Organization. Tanya won it just before her dad got fired. Lucky, really, eh?"

I nodded. I could see a pattern emerging. Tanya's dad had been supported by Miss Shirley through difficult times—she'd offered him employment until there'd been evidence of misdeeds she couldn't ignore or overrule. Maybe she'd even helped him clear his debts over the years. A big lump sum had found its way to Tanya just when she'd needed it, and since her father's death, Miss Shirley had allowed Tanya to lean on her even more. Miss Shirley had even taken an interest in Tom. Though, on that count, it seemed as though Miss Shirley had taken a very hands-on approach toward many people's careers. It sounded to me as though Tanya's late father might well have been Miss Shirley's son. I wondered if he'd known that Miss Shirley was his mother. Of course, there was a chance that I was seeing a pattern where none existed.

"How does Tanya feel about Miss Shirley, Tom? Do you two ever talk about that?"

Tom sighed. "Not that this means anything, but it's funny you should ask that. Tanya's been . . . different since her dad killed himself. Bound to be, right? That's a tough thing to take. But she's been very . . . um . . . stoic about it all. She hardly cried at all during the first few weeks after it happened. Maybe it was shock, I don't know.

She just sorted everything out and made sure everything was taken care of. But a couple of weeks after we emptied all her dad's stuff out of his house, before they repossessed it, she became . . . cold. That's it. *Cold.* She started crying at night. Not when she was over at my place, but when we were at hers. When I've been over at her place during the past couple of weeks, she's gotten up in the middle of the night and gone off into the kitchen to cry. I tried to console her once, but she lashed out at me. Cold. Hard. Angry. Not like her at all. She's gone kind of flat. But I don't know why. Other than her dad dying, you know? And when it comes to Miss Shirley, she's been very off about her. Criticizing her to me, which is also odd for Tanya."

"Do you think that Miss Shirley said or did something to Tanya that made her change?"

Tom shook his head. "Tanya's never been good at talking about things, but I think she'd have told me that. Though I have no idea how she's *really* coping with her father's death. But that doesn't mean she'd kill." I was beginning to get a picture of Tanya that squared more with my own instinctive assessment of the girl. She was definitely hiding something, at least a part of her true self, from us all. Tom included. I asked my final questions.

"I know this is going to sound a bit odd, Tom, but why does Tanya have such an enormous handbag with her this evening?"

Tom looked puzzled. "Has she?" He clearly hadn't noticed.

"Yes, she does. Big black thing. It doesn't really go with her outfit."

Tom shrugged. "Sorry, I have no idea. It's not really my sort of thing, choosing a handbag. It's just a thing women have. Tanya usually dumps hers on the floor out of the way whenever she has the chance, that's all I know."

I smiled, and Tom smiled back—good, he was back onside— then I asked, "Why did you two swap places at the bar when everyone restaged the positions they were in when the lights came on?"

"*Thank you!*" exclaimed Tom. "I'll tell Tanya you said that. I told her we were the other way around, but she wouldn't have it. I was sure I'd been the one standing closer to Miss Shirley when the lights came up. Tanya insisted *she* was. Does it matter? Maybe it does . . . hey, look, if you think she killed the poor woman, which I'm sure she didn't, wouldn't she be more likely to insist she was farther away from her, rather than closer to her?"

"You make a good point, Tom. Thanks." I leaned in and added, "I really appreciate you being so open and honest. It's been most helpful."

"I knew you'd see it couldn't possibly be her," replied Tom, smiling.

If only he knew I am thinking the exact opposite.

As we moved back toward the dessert table, I looked around for Bud, anxious to share my theory, but I couldn't see him. *Where can he be?*

When Bud's voice rang out from behind the privacy screen near the men's room, his tone was urgent, commanding. "I need some help in here, please. Guys—quick as you can. Clemence has passed out. I need to make him more comfortable in the main room."

All the men rushed forward, just as Julie emerged from the ladies' room, screaming and covered in blood.

"It's . . . it's . . . I only went in there to . . . she's dead! I tried to save her . . . she's dead!"

Confusion reigned. No one knew where to turn. I ran across the room, pushed past Julie, and threw open the door to the ladies' room. Tanya's body lay sprawled on the floor, her blood oozing onto the tiles. The handle of a corkscrew protruded from the back of her neck. Her face was contorted, her eyes staring. I reached to feel for a pulse. There wasn't one. Beside her lay her giant purse, some of its contents spilling onto the floor. I knew she was beyond help, so I pulled the door open again to attend to Julie. She was still standing right outside the door, the streaks of blood on her face in stark contrast to the pallor of her skin.

"Oh my God!" she said, then she threw up.

Second Intermission

AS I LEFT THE LADIES' room on this occasion, I already knew that Bud had his hands full with Clemence, so I took control.

"First things first, no one enters this ladies' room again. Svetlana—" I looked over at the Diva, who was standing near the dessert table, a silver cake slicer in one hand, a plate in the other, frozen in a motion that would never be completed. "We ladies will be using the men's room from now on."

Svetlana nodded, dumb for once.

I continued, "Ian? Ian!" Ian's head popped out of the men's room. "Could you come here, please, Ian? I need you. The other guys can help Bud."

Ian was beside me in a moment. His face paled as he saw the blood on Julie's face and the vomit at her feet.

Julie was holding her belly and moaning. "I'm so sorry, Tom. I'm so sorry. I couldn't save her."

Tom was standing in the middle of the room, completely immobile. He looked utterly helpless, and his chin puckered as he croaked, "That's Tanya's blood on Julie? Julie said Tanya's dead. Cait? Is Tanya dead?"

I had to think quickly. I tried not to bark as I said, "Ian, quick, grab a chair for Tom before he falls."

Ian managed to get Tom onto a bar stool and propped against the bar before he hit the carpet. Tom held his forehead, and big tears started to roll down his ruddy, freckled cheeks. When he spoke again, it was as though he were in a daze. "That's Tanya's blood, right?" he whispered, looking at Julie's stained suit. "She can't be dead. Tanya can't be dead. She's okay really, right?" He wasn't speaking to me, he was speaking to himself.

I turned my attention to Julie, who was swaying and still holding her tummy. I was afraid she might faint. "Ian, can you give me a hand with Julie too, please?"

Ian took a chair to Julie so she could sit down where she'd been standing. I knew that Bud should see her as she was, before she got cleaned up, because there was obviously the question of whether Julie was telling the truth about trying to save Tanya.

Art, Carl, and Jimmy emerged from the men's room carrying Clemence between them, with Bud giving directions. They laid the unconscious body of the elderly man down on the floor, against the privacy screen, just a few feet from the two corpses in the dining room.

Once Clemence had been arranged according to Bud's instructions, Art rushed to Julie's side, trying to calm her.

Svetlana sat down in a chair with its back right against the glass wall. She faced the room. She looked defiant and beckoned to Jimmy to join her, which he did.

Ian and I cleaned up the mess Julie had made on the carpet. I can cope with blood. I don't have a problem with it. But vomit? I could feel myself gag as Ian and I did our best to get it all up. The only way I managed it, without adding my own contribution, was to keep telling myself it had to be done. The room was now very warm, and the last thing we needed was for this smell to begin to mix with the aromas of the warm, spoiled caviar and the now more-than-stinky cheeses, not to mention the creeping sickliness that was beginning to crawl from beneath the tablecloth covering Miss Shirley's body.

I tried to breathe through my mouth. We kept at it, and, finally, after running through two entire rolls of paper towels, Ian and I realized we'd made a pretty good job of it.

When we were done, I felt utterly exhausted and on the verge of tears. Both my hands were filthy—and the binding on my injured one even more so, it seemed. None of me was in good shape, but my hands definitely needed attention.

"I'm using the sink in the men's room," I said as I swept into the facility that mirrored the ladies'. Well, it didn't mirror it exactly—the ladies' room didn't have a urinal—but they were comparable in terms of the richness of their decor. A look in the mirror as I washed up told a sorrier tale than I'd expected. Half my hair had escaped its band and bow, my lipstick and blush had disappeared, I had raccoon eyes, and there was a big smear of blood on my cheek. I didn't bother to rebind the cut on my hand, which seemed to have closed up pretty well, so I was able to use two wet hands to plaster my hair back into a ponytail. Luckily I could feel the hairspray I'd applied the night before turn to glue as I did so. It would have to do. I'd completely lost track of my little evening clutch purse with my lipstick in it—but who would reapply lipstick at a time like this anyway? I just wiped the blood from my face and left it at that.

Emerging from the men's room was quite a change, and it gave me a very different perspective on the dining room. I stopped for a moment to take in the scene—not so much the people, but the space itself. This part of the room felt much more open than at the other end of the bar. I reasoned that this was because there was no dessert table here. No one seemed to be paying any attention to me, so I walked a few steps to be beside Miss Shirley's body, and I squatted down, getting almost the same view of the room that the woman herself would have had before she was killed. As I did so I realized that not only was Miss Shirley's seat a good foot beyond the outer edge of the partition, but she also wasn't aligned the right way to have been facing her table. Her chair was turned a little away from where the table would have been, toward the partition itself. *Odd.*

As I looked at the partition, and saw the empty space where the golden egg should have been, I sighed with exasperation. Even when I'd thought I'd worked out how Tanya could have killed Miss Shirley, and how the urn had been involved, I'd still been confused about the egg . . . and the pink silk handkerchief . . . and the glittering red purse.

But, there, I'd been wrong about Tanya—after all, she was lying dead in the ladies' room, and I found it difficult to believe there were two killers in our midst—so maybe what I really needed to do was start all over again.

Could Julie Pool have wanted Miss Shirley, her own husband, *and* Tanya dead? Would a woman be able to calmly kill her own spouse, and her employer, but then throw up after killing someone she merely worked with?

I was confused. I wondered if I should try my wakeful dreaming technique. There were enough clues, bodies, and problems to be sorted out that allowing them to try to tell their own story while I was in a half-trance might work. In fact, I realized I was so addled, it might be the only way to tackle the whole murderous mess.

But first there was something concrete I had to sort out.

I walked around the outer edge of the room, past the huddled Svetlana and Jimmy, to the ladies' room. As I stood outside, I grappled with my conscience about disturbing a crime scene, but decided I needed a good look at what had happened to Tanya. Glancing around the dining room I could see that everyone was still engrossed in their own interactions, so I stepped into the ladies' room one more time.

The corkscrew in Tanya's neck told me that someone with great strength had killed her. It would have taken great force to ram it in as it had been. Force, or fury. The excellent soundproofing of the washroom meant that no one outside would have heard a cry. Once again the killer had audaciously taken advantage of a tiny window of opportunity, and had used a weapon that was to hand. I turned my attention toward Tanya's purse. A bottle of pills had rolled out. I also caught sight of a dark green, lumpy wallet and something metallic. I bent down to get a closer look. It was, unmistakably, the muzzle of a gun!

I nipped into the dining room, grabbed an unused napkin from the dessert table, went right back into the ladies', and used the napkin to pull the gun from Tanya's purse. Then I grabbed the shoulder strap of the purse itself, swung it over my arm, and dropped the gun, wrapped in the napkin, inside. It was the only way I could think of to hide the weapon—my tiny little purse, which I'd spotted on the table where I'd sat for dinner, didn't stand a chance of accommodating it.

The discovery of the gun puzzled and panicked me. I knew for a fact that just at the entrance to the elevator in the Babushka Bar, we'd all had to go through a very ornate archway that, for all its decoration, was clearly a metal detector. How on earth had Tanya managed to smuggle a gun into the private dining room? And why would she? Besides, if she had a gun, why didn't she shoot her attacker? And who *was* her attacker? Would Julie really have had enough strength to ram a corkscrew into Tanya's neck?

Damn and blast! The girl lying dead at my feet had been my prime suspect. I'd obviously got the whole thing wrong. *Everything.*

Miss Shirley, Jack Bullock, Tanya Willis. Who would want them all dead? Who could have found three opportunities to kill unseen?

I needed a break. My brain needed a break. I had to start again, fresh.

I walked out into the dining room with Tanya's purse hanging from my shoulder, my mind whirling, my heart pounding. There I saw Tom, sobbing like a child, being comforted by Bud, who clearly felt he could do no more for Clemence. The elderly gentleman's unconscious body was still lying against the privacy screen outside the men's room. He looked almost disturbingly peaceful.

Julie sat close to the bar staring into space, muttering to herself, clearly in shock. Art and Carl were at her side. Jimmy was trying to calm the Diva, who looked surprisingly neat and tidy, considering what we'd all been through. Ian was moving things around behind the bar, seemingly without purpose.

"Cait?" It was Bud. He'd left his seat beside Tom and was now right next to me. I realized I was standing in the middle of the room with what I suspected was a weird look on my face. "You alright, Cait?"

"No, I am not alright, Bud." I didn't shout, but I was close to it. "I could be worse, I suppose, but I am far from alright. *This* isn't alright.

It's all very, very bad. I have to sit quietly and work it out. I can do it. I know I can." I didn't know who I was pleading with, but that was certainly what anyone listening would have heard in my voice.

"Please stop killer before everyone dead," said Svetlana. She was still sitting in her chair, her back to the glass wall, but now she was holding her knees, looking terrified. "I very afraid. Now I sit here. Nobody come near me. Except Jimmy. Jimmy okay, I think. This is safe. I very, very afraid," she whimpered. Jimmy patted her arm, looking deeply concerned.

"We're all afraid," said Art. For the first time since we'd been introduced, I was truly aware of Art's age. He looked much more frail and disheveled than he had when we'd all been celebrating Miss Shirley's inheritance.

"You're not kidding," added Carl, who seemed more angry than defeated. "Someone in this room is completely nuts. Stark. Raving. Mad. Gotta be. Who the hell would do all this otherwise? And *how* are they doing it? I think Svetlana's got a point. I'm not leaving this space, where everyone can see everyone else, till the cops come out of that elevator. I don't care if my bladder bursts—I'm staying right here."

"I have good idea," said Svetlana, nodding. "I sit here. I not move. Police here soon. I must trust American police. I sit very quiet." Given her size, she couldn't have made herself any smaller.

"Do you think there's someone here who wants everyone dead, Uncle Bud?" asked Tom through his sobs.

"I'm not sure what to think," replied Bud. He squeezed my arm and looked apologetically torn as he took his leave of me to return to his young charge.

I knew that Tom's anguish and grief trumped my frustration, and inwardly praised Bud for his compassion for the poor young man, who he held close to him, their two bodies gently rocking back and forth.

I looked at my watch. Still three hours to share a room with someone who'd already killed three times and might still end up with Clemence's death at their feet. Three hours can be a very long time indeed.

Nonet

I WALKED OVER TO WHERE Bud had rejoined Tom and whispered, "Bud, I'm sorry to do this, but we need to talk, in private. Now." I sounded as deflated and confused as I felt, but I knew I had to tell him about the gun.

Bud looked up at me from the seat he was occupying next to Tom, who was red eyed and nosed, and still crying bitterly. Bud shrugged helplessly. "I can't leave Tom, not like this," he mouthed.

"You go, Uncle Bud. It's nice that you're here, but none of us can really do anything until the cops get here. I . . . are you sure she's dead? *Really sure?*"

I touched Tom's shoulder and bent my head to his. "I'm sorry, Tom. There's no doubt at all. I saw her. Checked for a pulse. She's really dead."

"I'll never love anyone like I loved Tanya," said Tom through his sobs. Then he stopped and looked at Bud and me. "How'd you do it, Uncle Bud? When Jan was killed . . . after Jan was killed . . . how did you start again? I mean, you're with Cait now. How did you *do* that? How *could* you?"

Bud blew out his cheeks, gave me a sad smile, and held Tom's hand as he said, "When you lose a person you love, you're right, Tom, you think you'll never love again. But what I hope you're able to realize— and I know it might take some time—is that love can be found where and when you least expect it, and that it can be real more than once in a lifetime. Cait knows I'll never love anyone like I loved Jan, but I don't think she'd want to be loved like I loved Jan. She wants to be loved as I love her, which is different. Not less. Not more. Just different."

Tom's expression didn't change.

Bud realized that people could overhear what he'd meant to be a very intimate conversation. "We'll talk about it properly when you're ready, Tom. Promise."

"Love's a funny thing," said Jimmy. "Love can make you do things you never thought you'd do. I was all set to head off for a job in New York before Madame came along. Now I'll never leave her, not as long as she'll have me by her side."

Svetlana pulled her hand away from Jimmy. "Do not speak of love this way. You cannot love me. You love men, not women. I am woman. *Real* woman."

"What?" snapped Jimmy. "You think I'm gay?"

Svetlana nodded her head sharply.

"I'm not gay!" Jimmy sounded astonished, rather than offended. "I'm straight. Yes, I've got a lot of gay friends, but—come on, because of the world I've always worked in, the theater, every other person I know is gay. But I happen to be straight."

"Yes?" said Svetlana disbelievingly.

"Yes," said Jimmy.

"You never have girlfriend," said Svetlana quietly.

Jimmy stood very upright, towering over the woman. "Do you honestly think I'd put up with what you dole out to me on a daily basis just because I think you have a wonderful voice? *Had* a wonderful voice I should say, because, let's be honest, it's not what it once was. And I don't mean that to be cruel, I just need you to realize that, for once, I'm going to be *totally* honest with you. I love you, Svetlana. Can't you see that? I love you as a man loves a woman. Okay, I idolized you at first, but . . . oh, Svetlana, if these past hours have shown us anything, it's that life can be horribly brief—I'm sorry, Tom—and I'm not going to go on like this. Either you accept my feelings for you, or you can find someone else to be your assistant. After this is over, we'll be together as a couple, or I'm out of here. So there. Think on that, Svetlana Kharlamova. Think on that."

The Diva's mask slipped for a moment, and I saw her as an aging woman, frightened of spending the rest of her life unadored and unloved. Her terror of being murdered might have subsided momentarily, but it had been replaced by the vision of a lonely future. I wondered how she would react to Jimmy's declaration of his feelings for her when she'd had a chance to process what he'd said.

"Stray dogs," said Carl. It took us all by surprise. "Miss Shirley loved stray dogs. You know, human ones. Like me. I wasn't doing anything with my life, and she kick-started me into my business with cars."

"I wasn't a stray dog," said Julie Pool quietly. "I was a princess, and Jack was my prince. That's it for me. You're young, Tom, you'll love again. But for me? Jack was it. He's gone. I'm as good as dead myself. There's nothing left for me. It's over." Her tone was flat. Bitter. She wasn't being dramatic, just stating her feelings, simply.

No one spoke for a moment.

"I need to use the washroom," said Julie. Art helped her to her feet. "I'm fine, Art. You've always been very kind to me, thank you. It hasn't gone unnoticed. Jack and I always enjoyed your visits from Florida. It's been fun working with you more closely, more often, this past year. It's been quite a year, hasn't it?"

Art seemed puzzled by Julie's line of conversation, but played along. "It certainly has, and we have a lot of work ahead of us. If we're going to open up in Macau, we'll have to put our noses to the grindstone. At my age it'll be a lot of work, but we're a good team."

"Macau?" snapped Carl. "Miss Shirley was dead set against expanding over there. And if I get her shares I will be too. It's too much of a stretch. We'd need a bunch more investors. Times are still tough here. It's hardly the right moment to invest a bundle over there—"

"Now, now, boys," said Julie weakly as she teetered across the room toward the men's room. "There'll be plenty of opportunities for you to have all the arguments you want, and all the *fights* you want, when you finally find out who gets those shares. So maybe you could wait until then. Besides, some of those papers Miss Shirley was going to sign tonight make it quite clear she wasn't as opposed to the idea of expanding into Macau as she might have led you to believe, Carl. She didn't get where she was without being able to keep a secret or two. Tonight has shown all of us that, only too clearly. Your father always complimented her on her great poker face." Julie disappeared behind the privacy screen as she shot this parting comment toward Carl, who pouted in her general direction.

"Can I say something, please?" It was Ian, still standing behind his bar. I wondered if he saw it as a way to remain safe, or if he was the killer and he was using it as a vantage point.

"What is it, Ian?" Bud replied.

"I feel I have to say this. The corkscrew Julie said was used to . . . you know?" Bud nodded. "Well, it might be mine. I left mine on the bar, and it's not here now. And . . . you know . . . like the saber, it'll have my fingerprints on it. I just wanted to say, once again, that I didn't kill anyone. Even though I have handled . . . um . . . both murder weapons. Sorry."

Could this young man really be a ruthless killer? Was he *that* good an actor? Or maybe he was a true sociopath who didn't care that what he was doing was wrong, so he was quite easily able to act this way?

I looked at Jimmy. Could *he* be a triple killer? Sipping his brandy, expressing his love for Svetlana? Or was that just a diversionary tactic?

"Where was everyone when Tanya was killed?" asked Tom directly. "I want to understand what's going on, so could you please all help me?"

"Okay, Tom," said Bud gently. "We're all here except Julie. So let's talk it through. Who was where when Tanya was killed?"

"When *was* she killed?" asked Ian.

It was a very telling question.

Octet

I FELT BEST PLACED TO get the ball rolling. "Having seen her body, and her injuries, it's obvious to me that Tanya was killed when she was inside the ladies' room, which I believe is when you and I were standing near the window wall talking, Tom. You told me you thought she'd gone to the ladies' a little before that, right?"

Tom nodded. "So if we were there, where was everyone else?"

"I was in the men's room with Clemence," said Bud.

"Yes, I saw you go there," I replied. "Did you leave him at all before you eventually carried him out of there?"

Bud shook his head and looked at his shoes. He was annoyed with himself. "No. I stayed with him the whole time, so I didn't see what was going on out here. He wasn't in good shape. He was delirious, though it took me a few moments to work that out. He kept telling me that Miss Shirley wanted to kill him. I tried to get him to explain, but he couldn't. He looked scared, said she was going to kill him, he knew it. He didn't seem to realize it was she who was dead. It was then that I worked out what was going on, and shortly after that, he began swaying, and I had my hands full, quite literally. I managed to get him onto the floor. Then I called for help. All of that couldn't have taken more than . . . ten minutes?"

"How long before we started talking did Tanya go to the washroom?" I asked Tom.

He shrugged helplessly, and his voice was anguished. "I don't know. I was at the dessert table, and I didn't even notice she wasn't beside me until you asked me where she was. I guessed she must have gone in there, because there wasn't anywhere else to go. She might have been gone for five minutes before we started to talk. I wish . . . I wish I'd noticed."

"Did *anyone* see when Tanya went to the ladies'?" I asked.

Everyone shook their heads.

"Did anyone see anybody else go in there?"

"I didn't even see Julie go in there, and she must have done, because she's the one who found the body," said Art.

"I'm pretty sure I was either helping Svetlana sort out rearranging the food, or else eating it," said Ian.

"I did that too," said Jimmy. "The three of us did it together."

"I remember that when Tom and I moved away from the dessert table, you were heading back to the bar, Ian," I said.

Ian blushed. "I don't know. I might have done, though it would only have been for a moment. I don't recall doing it, and I know I ate some of the white chocolate bread pudding at the table. Remember?" He appealed to Jimmy and Svetlana.

Svetlana made a face that signified concentration. "No, I not remember where you are," she said dismissively.

Carl looked puzzled. "I have no idea where I was, or what I was doing, or which particular ten minutes you're talking about. I could have been anywhere."

"Hardly 'anywhere,'" replied Art. "I was getting some fresh water, behind the bar, flushing out the jugs and letting the water run cold, and you weren't there. So where were you?"

Carl said grudgingly, "I was looking for that egg again. Yes, while that poor girl was being killed I was hunting for a damned egg, because it's worth a fortune and, *yes*, because I could do with the money. I did find this." He pulled something out of his pocket. "Not that it's got anything to do with anything, but I found it over there, right where Clemence is lying now. So I was over there, past the far partition, just outside the men's room, hunting about."

"What is it?" asked Bud, holding out his hand for the object Carl had found.

I was curious. "Is it part of the handle from the urn?"

Bud was looking at something that Carl had placed in his palm. I moved closer and took a look myself. It was a small ball bearing.

"Where'd it come from?" I asked Bud.

Holding it in his hand, Bud looked up at the ceiling. He walked to the elevator cylinder, then around it. He moved toward Miss Shirley's body, peered at the partition, then at the privacy screen outside the men's room, along the bottom of which lay Clemence, who was still breathing, but looking pretty sweaty.

"I can't see *anything* here that it might have come from," Bud said finally. "I'll ask Julie if she has any ideas when she's finished in there—she seems to know the lay of the land in this room," he added. "Cait, I wonder, would you mind checking on her? She seems to have been in there for quite a while."

I nodded. "Sure. Is there something we can be doing for Clemence, Bud? It feels so wrong to just leave him lying there."

"Maybe we can keep him a little cooler with some damp cloths, but there's nothing else we *can* do for him, Cait. He's slipped into a comatose state, and the only hope for him is insulin. If they can treat him in time, they might well be able to save him. Tell you what, you check on Julie, I'll get some cloths for Clemence. Okay?"

I managed a weak smile as I rounded the screen and pushed open the door to the men's room. At least, I tried to, but it wouldn't move.

"Does this door stick?" I poked my head around the screen to ask Bud.

"It hasn't been. Can't you get it open?" he replied.

"Only a little bit. There seems to be something heavy against it." My heart sank as I said the words. "Oh, Bud—no!"

Bud joined me, and we both pushed the door, firmly but slowly. It opened enough for me to see Julie Pool's protruding legs, her back wedged against the door.

When we finally managed to shove our way in, it was clear from the outset that Julie was dead. Bud checked for a pulse. He shook his head. "She's gone too."

"Bud, what the hell is going on here? We were all *together*. No one left that room other than Julie. How did she die, do you think? More of Clemence's insulin?"

True, Julie was covered in blood, but she'd been covered in blood when she left us. We agreed that we'd already moved her, so we might as well take the chance to check her body for signs of an injury. There were no visible marks on the parts of her body we could see, not even pinpricks. There was no obvious cause of death. Her head wasn't cracked open, as though she'd slipped or fallen. In fact, it looked as though she'd sat down with her back against the door of her own accord, or had gradually slid down it. Her little evening purse was perched on the counter, her lipstick lying next to it, still open. Her dead lips showed me she'd just applied a fresh coat.

"It might be poison," I said. There didn't seem to be any alternative. "But how would she have ingested it?" I considered the lipstick as a possible means of poisoning for less than a split second—it seemed to be a ridiculously unreliable way to kill someone.

"I saw her drink water she poured from a jug that a few of us have been sharing," said Bud. The thought that several people might have drunk poisoned water was alarming.

"Do you feel okay?" I asked, panicking.

"I feel fine," replied Bud, sounding as reassuring as possible. He looked at his watch. "It's almost 11:00 AM. We've all, somehow, got to get through the next couple of hours alive. I say we all sit in there looking at each other, and don't leave until the cops arrive. You okay with that?"

It seemed the only thing to do. I nodded. "Before we go back in, there's something you must know," I said. "I went back in to get a good look at what had happened to Tanya, and I found a gun. It was poking out of her purse."

"A *gun*?" Bud was incredulous.

"Yes, a handgun. Revolver style. Silver, with a dark grip. But I don't know what sort, exactly. I'm not a weapons expert after all, I'm a criminal psychologist. But I know how you feel. I was surprised too."

"How could Tanya have got it into the place? There was that metal detector thing at the entrance to the elevator."

"I know. That was my thought exactly. I have no idea how she got it in here, but I dumped her purse on our table, and it's there right now, hidden in her purse. I wrapped it in a napkin, in case it's got prints on it. Though shooting someone is the one method our killer hasn't used so far."

"Oh, Cait. This is all such a mess—you've disturbed a crime scene." Bud sounded exasperated. I blushed. "Look, we'd better get back in and break the bad news. Don't let that gun out of your sight again, now that you've moved it. That's not something we want the killer getting their hands on."

"No one's going to go scrabbling about in a dead woman's purse, Bud, so don't panic. But you're right, I'll hang onto Tanya's purse from now on. Just so you know, I'm going to have to take myself off to one side, or somewhere, sometime soon. I need a bit of peace and quiet to 'do my thing,' okay?"

We reentered the main room.

"What's going on?" asked Art. "Where's Julie? How's she doing?"

Bud squeezed my hand as he said, "I'm sorry to tell you that Julie is dead."

Gasps. A groan from Svetlana.

Bud continued, "I don't know how it happened. There are no signs of trauma. And we were all in here the entire time she was in there. But she is, quite definitely, dead. I suggest we all stay exactly where we are until the authorities arrive—though I do want to tend to Clemence to try to keep him a little cooler than he is. Everyone remain seated, and let's all keep calm."

Calm? Right!

Refrain

BUD WAS BEHIND THE BAR with Ian, getting some cloths to cool Clemence. I decided to ask the rest of the group a few questions.

"Did Julie eat or drink anything between the time she found Tanya and when she went to the washroom?"

"Art gave her a glass of water," tittle-tattled Carl.

"Jimmy brought over some banana that he'd sliced up for her," added Art defensively.

That seemed like an odd thing to do. "Did she eat it?" I thought I'd better get the facts straight.

Jimmy looked around and pointed at a plate. "Looks like she might have eaten one or two slices," he said, sounding disappointed. "Ian gave her a brandy," he added in a hopeful tone. "He gave one to Tom as well."

"I feel fine," said Tom.

"Poison?" hissed Svetlana from across the room, catching the meaning of my questions and their responses. Her voice carried wonderfully well, as one would expect from a woman who'd more or less grown up on the stage. "I not eat. I not drink. I not move," she added with determination.

Carl piped up, "Ian could be Miss Shirley's grandson. He's been very quick to point out that he's got a reason for his prints being on the saber that killed her, as well as the corkscrew that killed Tanya. He could have poisoned Julie too, with that brandy, and he might even have pushed Jack on purpose, just so's he'd hit his head. It could be Ian."

At the mention of his name, Ian's head popped up from behind the bar like a meerkat. Bud followed likewise.

"I didn't kill anyone," bleated Ian, "and I think I've mentioned that my mom and dad are alive and well and living in Seattle. I have a sister too. My grandparents live in Bellingham. *All four of them.* I am *not* Miss Shirley's grandson." He sounded frightened and looked it too. He seemed to be appealing to Bud more than to the rest of us. Then his expression brightened. "Look, I can prove it. I've got photos from my gran's eightieth birthday on my phone." He pulled a shiny, black rectangle from his pants pocket and began to slide his finger across its screen, showing it to Bud. "Look? See? That's Gran—my dad's mom. There's my dad with me and my sister. Look—there's my granddad with my father. My dad's the image of his father. Right?"

Bud looked right at me. "There's certainly a family resemblance," he said, "though your grandfather might have been the man who impregnated Miss Shirley."

"Oh, come on, that's gross," said Ian, wrinkling his nose. "Besides, he and my gran have been married forever. Since they were, like, twenty or something. Besides, my dad is sixty. He's too old to be Miss Shirley's son." He looked relieved that he'd finally managed to think of something that might convince us that he wasn't related to the poor woman who was sitting in our midst covered with a tablecloth. "I mean, I can't prove that I'm not related to Miss Shirley, not here, now, but I could if I could speak to my dad." He nodded and put away his phone. "I'll be able to prove it to the cops." He looked more certain of himself as he shoved out his chin toward Carl and repeated himself with confidence. "Yes, I'll be able to prove it to the cops."

"What about the banana Jimmy gave to Julie?" spat Carl. "Who gives a woman who's just found a dead body a banana? Unless you want to poison them."

Jimmy stood. "Carl, I know you're frightened, we all are. But you can't just point the finger of blame at everyone in turn. I gave her the banana because she was clearly in shock, and she'd just thrown up. One of the things you have to be able to do in the theater is look after folks in a high state of emotion. Often they've vomited because of nerves, or tension, and bananas are a good source of sugar, starch, and potassium. Given we don't have access to much of anything else, I thought that would be good for her. Get some stuff into her system that she needed. I did *not* poison her. I am not Miss Shirley's grandson. I know I had a less than traditional upbringing, but Joe, my father, would be in his late fifties by now if he'd lived. No, I didn't know my grandparents, but we were in California, and they were all in Texas. For all my bohemian upbringing, my parents both came from cattle-ranching stock in Texas. My aunt, who lived here in Vegas, is dead now. But, like Ian, I am sure I can prove to the cops when they get here that there's no way I could be related to Miss Shirley. I have no idea why *anyone* would want Tanya, or Julie, dead, so I don't know how to defend myself against that." He looked confused for a moment, then shrugged. "I *wish* I was in line to inherit all this," he added, "then I'd be able to offer Svetlana a very comfortable life surrounded by pretty things forever. She might want me, and she wouldn't need to do what she does in order to have pretty things."

"I love to sing here," said Svetlana defensively.

Jimmy sighed. "You know what I mean. It can't go on forever. You'll have to stop one day."

"Yes, the orchestra can only play so loud, you know," said Carl spitefully. "You have noticed that they play louder and louder these days when you try to hit those notes, right?"

"I am star," shouted Svetlana. "I am Diva Kharlamova. Is enough for audience. I sing with passion." She stood and pulled her wrinkled wrap about herself, setting her chin high, her eyes glittering. I thought she was about to launch into an aria on the spot. Instead, she looked around, retreated into herself, and sat down with a thump. Clearly terror had beaten out pride.

"Maybe you killed them all," said Carl, pointing at Svetlana. "You Russians will do anything. Russians! Who knows, maybe one of those bendy acrobats from the show in the theater is hiding up in the ceiling, dropping down to kill us all off one by one. And if not one of the ones from the Tsar! there's enough of them around Vegas, what with all the Cirque shows that are running. I bet they could wriggle out of a vent somewhere. Maybe that's where the ball bearing that I found came from. Has anyone checked the vents?"

Bud sighed. "It's impossible, Carl," he replied heavily. "Look up, man—the vents are about six inches wide and run in a ring around the entire ceiling. A person wouldn't have to be just bendy, they'd have to be snake shaped as well. Even the vents in the bathrooms are tiny, the same size. You're being completely unreasonable, Carl."

"I wouldn't put anything past Russians!" Carl was getting red around his now-open collar. "God knows why Dad went along with Miss Shirley when she said she wanted a Russian-themed casino. He hated the Russians, and with good cause. They all but obliterated the Armenian population. In fact, that's why his family came to the States—to escape certain death. But there she was, swooning over tsarist antiques and Romanoff décor. She didn't even get the irony that the hotel block is modeled on a style of architecture that was built in Moscow by prisoners. The Seven Sisters? Stalinist trash."

"You not speak like this," shouted Svetlana, holding the sides of her chair as she spoke as though her life depended upon it. "You know nothing! I live there. I am child there. I am woman there. You? You are in America. I am in Moscow. Is easy for you. You know nothing. You do not know what I do to get good parts. You not know how girls in opera are treated by men with high rank in Communist Party. Opera house is built with places just for men to be with girls. Is same in London and Paris, yes, but in Moscow is no choice for girls. Now I sing in casino, and some people say is bad, but then? Then is worse. Much worse. I sing. I work. I have no food, I have no money, no pretty things. Men give me these things. Men. *I hate men.* Big hands, horrible medals on chests, smell of vodka, tobacco. Since I leave Russia I sing private concerts for good people, famous people. Then? I sing in places I am told, at times I am told. I do what I am told, or I not get parts. You do not know. You live here. People say Russia bad now—ha! You see then! You rich boy, you not know what is like to have nothing! Maybe you kill everyone, because you want everything."

Carl was shuffling in his seat, looking very uncomfortable. Clearly he hadn't expected such an onslaught. *Such is the psychology of suspicion . . . defend and accuse.*

Svetlana would have been on her feet were she not in fear for her life. As it was, she remained seated, but waved her arms for effect. "Here? Tsar! Casino is good, is beautiful. Russian people not all bad, not always. Now are good people there, but bad people too. In old times is same. But they had pretty things then, for some. When I am young, no pretty things. Is gray, ugly, full of men with power. Woman not have power, woman only have sex. Is terrible place to grow up. But do not tell me all Russia is bad. Tsar! is best of Russian history. Miss Shirley do good. We talk about Saint Basil's, House of Fabergé, the Great Catherine, beautiful Metro stations for shops downstairs is clever, pretty dolls in shops, shops with furs, good music, ballet, in theater. She is clever—she knows people want these things. Me. She brings *me*. Miss Shirley is clever woman."

"I might not have grown up there," said Carl defensively, "but my dad told me what his parents told him. I guess you'd know more about it than me because you were there through some pretty tough times. But growing up in Vegas, in the sixties, was a weird thing to do too. The city was changing all the time, we moved around a lot, because Dad was always trying to make things better for us. I missed him. He put me in a good school back east, but I just wanted to do my thing with cars. I didn't want to disappoint him. Mom said we had to honor his wishes, because he made the money." Carl looked up and seemed to realize for the first time that he was sharing some very private thoughts with a room full of comparative strangers.

"I guess what I'm trying to say is that all I ever really wanted was a proper home with a couple of cars to fix up in the garage. That's it.

I—I don't really want all this, Art. You're right, it's not me. I wouldn't have killed anyone to get it."

"What about the money, Carl? You'd like that," said Art quietly.

Carl nodded. "Yeah, sure I'd like the money. But killing for it? That's not me, Art. You've known me all my life. You must know that about me. Like I know *you* couldn't have done any of this. It's not in your heart to kill."

"Oh, I've killed alright," replied Art. Svetlana gripped her chair. "I've killed many people. Maybe hundreds. In war. It's not an easy thing to live with, but you tell yourself it's you or them. And unlike Miss Shirley's stepbrothers who didn't make it back from 'Nam, I did manage to make it through the Six-Day War. It happened when I was living out there. I volunteered. Caught up in events bigger than I could really comprehend. It's where I met Stephen Feldblum, the guy who became my CFO—we were assigned to man the same tank. He saved my life. Twice." He looked grim. "It changes you, killing. As the person here who's done all this must know by now."

"Could Clemence have killed Miss Shirley?" asked Carl sharply, looking toward Bud, who was still kneeling over the ailing man, mopping his face. "Maybe he did, and he's hidden his own insulin because he feels guilty."

I made a decision and spoke up. "Clemence didn't hide his own insulin. Someone stole it from him and pumped it into Jack Bullock. That's why Jack died. He was poisoned with a massive overdose of insulin." My words hung in the air.

"Oh thank God," said Carl. "Oh! I didn't mean . . . oh, you all know what I meant. I thought he was dead because he'd hit his head after Art and I had been fighting. I thought *we* were responsible. So, although someone killed him, well . . ."

"It's alright, Carl, we know what you mean," said Art quietly, "and I feel the same way. How dreadful is that? Though, if what you say is true, Cait, it means that someone here, one of us, has killed four people tonight. Today. I don't know what to call this time now. It's all so—weird. Unreal."

"Are you saying that because someone gave Jack all of Clemence's insulin, that's why *he* hasn't got any now?" Ian sounded horrified.

I nodded.

"And Clemence might die because of that?" he continued. "That's harsh. *Cold.* He's a lovely old guy. I didn't really have much to do with him before all of this, but I saw him here often with Miss Shirley. They were like an old couple, you know? They could sit quietly with each other and not talk, but not be uncomfortable."

"Tanya and I were like that," said Tom sadly. "We were very comfortable with each other."

"Maybe *you* just wanted Tanya dead, Tom, and you did all the rest to cover it up, confuse everything," said Carl.

"Carl, stop it!" Art's tone was flat. He sounded exhausted. "Just *stop*. We're all in the same boat. We're all sitting here looking right at a killer, and we don't know which one of us it is. I—I can't believe it's not showing on the person's face. It must."

Those were my thoughts exactly, but I couldn't easily cast anyone in the room in the role of a cold-blooded killer. I had to try harder.

"I'm just moving over here for a few moments," I said, standing and picking up my chair. Svetlana looked alarmed as I approached her.

"Go away," she barked. "I not know you. *You* might be killer. You and him. Together." She nodded toward Bud. "Maybe people pay you to kill us all."

I smiled as brightly as I could. "Yes, that's right, Svetlana, I'm a Welsh Canadian assassin, sent to kill a whole group of people I've cunningly trapped in a private dining room in Las Vegas, using as wide a variety of methods as possible."

"We wouldn't be trapped at all if Miss Shirley hadn't changed those damned codes," said Carl. He was right, of course, and he made a very good point.

"We all die here," wailed Svetlana. "I know this. We all die in this room. Is hot. Is full of dead bodies. Smell very bad. Why someone kill us all?"

"No one can kill any one of us if we just sit here, watching each other, and wait for the cops to arrive," said Carl. Desperation haunted his eyes, and the veins in his neck were twitching.

"Well, while you lot all stare each other out, I'm going to sit here and try to work out who's doing all this," I said angrily.

Looking concerned, Bud asked, "Should you explain what that means, exactly?"

"You're right," I admitted. "I'm going to undertake something called 'wakeful dreaming,' folks. It means I'm going to sit here quietly and have a very deep, free-flowing think through what's been going on here. Outwardly, I'll just look as though I'm napping. It really would be most useful if I could have quiet, because noises around me can creep into my subconscious and influence what I'm seeing, in my mind's eye. I hope that'll be okay?"

"I sit here. I not speak," said Svetlana grumpily.

The men all nodded. I didn't think it would be too tough for them to force themselves to not talk to someone who might be a multiple murderer.

I pulled Tanya's purse under my arm, checked inside it for the gun, which was still there—*thank goodness!*—and plopped myself onto my chair, far enough away from Svetlana that she didn't have a heart attack. I couldn't hope to achieve anything unless I was calm. I shut my eyes and breathed deeply and slowly, forcing my pulse to stop racing. Wakeful dreaming only works if you can let your mind float free. I knew I was safe because Bud was in the room, and I was certain he'd keep an eye on me. I hugged Tanya's nasty pleather purse to my side, tried to ignore the stench in the room, the heat of the air, and the sobbing I knew was coming from Tom, and set my mind to work . . .

Die Tote Stadt

I PICTURED THE SCENE AS it was when I emerged from the ladies' washroom for the first time ... and let my mind wander. Unlike recollection, wakeful dreaming cannot be controlled. It's rather like having a row of buckets full of paint available to you, but you're blindfolded, so you pick up whatever you can reach and throw it about, allowing it to land where it will. When you open your eyes you hope you've created something that's been worth the effort. For someone who prefers to be in control, like me, it's a bit of a scary ride.

The first person I see in my foray into the unknown isn't one of the victims, nor even someone from our group. It is my mother, as she had been when I was about ten, I suppose. She wafts across the sky, which I can see because the top of the egg has opened, and sings like a bell, wearing a stained dress made of pink silk handkerchiefs. She trills laughter at me as she pirouettes, her dress altering from a pink ball gown to one of glittering red. A host of little shards of glass begin to fall on my head, so I duck and run for cover under a giant table covered with a massive white tablecloth. The air is thick and unbreathable, so I stick my head out from beneath the leaden covering to get some more oxygen. Carl is sitting on the floor, cross-legged, reciting his ten times table. He has only one arm, and he is looking at me wailing, "Mommy, Mommy ... where's Daddy gone?"

As I look at him, he jumps to his feet, screams, and runs off to the men's room, which now has swinging saloon-type doors. Peering out from beneath the table, I try to see what has frightened Carl. Now Miss Shirley appears, toting two guns, and shoots Clemence through the heart. His chest explodes, but he smiles at his attacker and waves with his large white handkerchief, which is now covered with thousands of glittering red spots that once again begin to fall and hit me—veering into my den to spear me with their tiny points.

As the table above me dissolves, I can see that the egg has opened up to become long halls with amber-clad walls bedecked with golden-edged mirrors. I run as fast as I can, though I hardly move. The golden surrounds of the mirrors splinter, becoming tiny little gold sabers, which follow me, flying through the air like guided missiles. A door appears next to me, and I run through it, slamming it shut behind me. I smell soap. It is a fresh, clean smell, and my nose seeks out its source. I find myself peering into a bowl containing hundreds of dead fish, ripped open, smiling and staring back at me. Beside them sits one teaspoon of glistening caviar, red, not black. Each bead becomes a blade, and, once again, I run from the attack.

The door by which I entered the space has been replaced with an elevator, but although I press the button again and again, nothing happens. Without warning, a giant Chinese vase crashes at my feet. Tanya appears, sweeping up the shards and whistling. *What is the tune? Ah yes, it's "Kalinka."* As she gathers the pieces of porcelain in an apron that she is wearing, she wilts and cries, "So heavy, so sharp!"

Svetlana sweeps in riding a giant, heaving piano keyboard as though it's a bird, the black and white keys flapping like scale-playing wings. She's wearing a flowing black cape and a white dress, cawing and laughing, waving a flag bearing the red-and-gold Tsar! Casino logo above her head in one hand, a magnificently wrought silver cake slicer of massive proportions in her other. She doesn't seem to need to hold on to the bucking piano keys. The sound of the piano is hurting my ears, I thrash at it, trying to make it stop. I notice that Jimmy is running along the ground beneath the Diva, throwing money into the air, trying to attract her attention.

Miss Shirley reappears, dressed as Mary Poppins, with a crocodile of children following her two by two. But they aren't children, they are all the people who sat down to eat dinner together—Ian, Bud, and myself included. We're all wearing little suits with giant shoulder pads. We look as though we're in a black-and-white movie. Clemence isn't part of the crocodile. He's straggling along by himself, holding what I know is a battered brass trumpet, even though it's hidden inside a red leather case. His eyes are bandaged and he's crying, tears streaming down his face from beneath the white bindings. "Can I join in?" he calls. He has the voice of a small child.

Miss Shirley turns, now she's become a very curvaceous, alluring Marilyn Monroe, and she throws him a giant slice of white chocolate bread pudding.

Clemence rips off his blindfold but his eyes have disappeared. "My eyes!" he calls, then he falls to the ground and begins to search for the pudding, but he is squashed by a huge ball bearing that rolls over him, cracking him like a nut. The ball bearing having passed, all the children gather about him and put him back together again. They dance off, shooting popguns they've taken from their pockets into the air.

Everything goes black. I smell Bud. I smell oil. I smell alcohol. I smell soap. I smell a gun that's been fired. I know I am inside a woman's purse. I feel the satin lining and try to climb up, but it's slippery, so I keep sliding back down.

"La Gazza Ladra," shouts Svetlana in the dark.

"The Silken Ladder," replies Jimmy. Then he whispers in my ear, "Othello knew the truth about reputation. A handkerchief killed Desdemona. La Gazza Ladra must not kill Madame." He is gone.

Now I am inside a hospital room. Miss Shirley, Jack Bullock, Tanya Willis, and Julie Pool are lying side by side in four beds. Each has a plastic tube in their arm. The tubes are connected to huge syringes, which are actually champagne bottles. Clemence runs through the room wielding a silver sword, severing the plastic tubes as he goes. He's still crying, "My eyes!" but now his voice is my grandmother's voice.

Bud steps into the room and begins to wave a metal detector wand over me. I beep constantly. It is alarming. "What do we 'ave here now then, missus?" he says in a cockney accent. He pulls a huge gun from the tiny evening purse I have under my arm. "Can't be 'aving this sort of thing available for all the baddies to get their 'ands on, now can we? Best give it to me, missus. I'm a copper, I am, I knows just what to do with it." He holds the gun aloft, shoots it into the air, and millions of shards of pottery fall from what is now the enclosed glass roof of the egg. The bullet ricochets around the glass, cracking every pane. As the glass falls away I can see a giant mushroom cloud on the horizon.

"Great sight, eh?" says Tom to my right. He is in full chef whites, wearing a necklace of corkscrews. "It's all for love, you know?" he says sadly.

"No, it's not, it's hate," says a snake with Jack Bullock's face, slithering out of an air vent in the floor.

"Follow your nose," calls Julie Pool as she falls from the sky, applying lipstick.

"Follow your heart," shouts Bud, no longer a cockney copper, but now dressed in a vicar's garb.

"Listen to me," shouts my sister. "Listen to me!" I turn to look at her as she bounces around me in circles, like a kangaroo. "Remember Mum as Adele in *Die Fledermaus*? Remember the story—revenge, borrowed clothes, masks, one person is two things? Remember what I told you about *La Gazza Ladra* and the magpie? It's all music, Cait. Trust me, I'm your sister." Then she hops away.

"Are you alright, Cait?"

I thought for a moment that I was still in a semitrance, but it was the real Bud gently touching my real shoulder.

I opened my eyes. "Yes, I'm fine."

"You're sweating," he said, sounding concerned. "Do you want a drink, or don't you trust the water?"

"I trust the water, Bud, and I'd love some." I pressed my fingers against my eyes. I couldn't possibly have any makeup left on them, so it hardly mattered if I rubbed them raw.

Bud returned with a glass of water, which I gulped down.

"Anything?" he asked.

"A lot," I replied, "but I still need to check a few things to make sure I'm not making connections where none exist."

Bud bent very close to me, and I thought he was going to kiss me. Instead he whispered, "What can I do to help?" Then he gave me a quick peck.

"Keep everyone where they are while I have a swift poke about? And I need you to do your own bit of recollection, please."

"Sure," he replied, standing to his full height.

"You hum," observed Svetlana. "Not bad voice." She was addressing me.

"Well, I'm Welsh, you see, Svetlana, and we Welsh do love our music so. Which I believe, on this occasion, might be very useful."

"How is useful?" she barked.

"Well, for one thing, I know the alternative name for *La Gazza Ladra*. My sister once told me. And, luckily for me, as it turns out, your laugh is just like Adele's in *Die Fledermaus*."

Svetlana looked horrified. And that was just for starters.

Third Intermezzo

"I TOLD YOU SHE WAS just like Rain Man," said Jimmy angrily. "Goes off on one and wakes up making wild accusations."

Art looked puzzled. "What accusations? I didn't hear her make any accusations." He looked around bewildered. "What did I miss? Anyone?"

Carl shrugged. "Load of nonsense if you ask me."

"We'll see if it's nonsense," I replied. "Bud's going to make sure everyone stays exactly where they are while I check out a few things, right?"

Svetlana looked petrified. Only her eyes moved, darting to the table where she'd been sitting before she'd adopted her defensive position against the outer wall. "Is not good here now. Too hot. I move to table," she said, with what was clearly forced bravado.

"You can stay where you are, if you prefer," said Jimmy. "It's hot here at the table too." His eyes widened as he spoke, and Svetlana threw him a coquettish smile.

"Very good. I stay," she said. "You are good man, Jimmy."

I suspected she hadn't paid him too many compliments over the years, and I could see a spark of delight, and maybe hope, in Jimmy's eyes as he smiled reassuringly in her direction.

I now had a pretty good idea of what was going on, but I had to be sure. "I have to do a few things and ask a few questions, and I hope everyone answers me honestly," I said in my most professorial tones.

Ian looked taken aback, Art and Carl shrugged, Svetlana threw me a triumphant look, Jimmy sighed, and Tom didn't seem to be taking notice of anything much.

"Tom?" I called. His tear-stained face finally turned toward me.

"Uh huh?" He was exhausted, physically and emotionally.

"Did you, at any point this evening, carry Tanya's purse?"

"What is it with you and Tanya's purse?" asked Tom. It seemed I'd just deposited the final straw upon this particular camel's back. "I'm sick of it. She's dead. Right, I get it. One day I'll love again. I get it. You all look at me and don't know what to say. I get that too. Why are you going on and on about her purse?"

"Because there's a gun in it," I said.

Svetlana paled. "Gun? She has gun? Why she has gun? Where is gun now?"

"I have it, here." I patted Tanya's purse on my shoulder.

"Why would Tanya have a gun?" asked Tom, stunned.

"*How* would she get one in here? That's the question," said Carl.

"Yes, we all endured the metal detector," said Art. "Wretched thing goes off every time I go through it." He noticed the alarmed looks around the room. "New hip," he added, by way of explanation.

"If Tanya had a gun, which I don't believe for one minute by the way, why didn't she shoot whoever killed her?" Tom had asked a very good question.

"Yeah, why didn't she?" Ian sounded well and truly puzzled. "I would have." As soon as he'd spoken, he blushed.

Bud gave me a look that communicated, "What are you getting at?"

I bent and pecked him on the cheek. "Stick close to Tom, Bud. This is all going to be very tough for him when I get going. I'm not sure how he'll react when he finds out who killed Tanya, and why."

"Okay. Done. Though I'm not sure how I'll react, either," said Bud, thereby confirming to me he didn't know what had been going on.

The tension in the room was as thick as the air, which was now becoming fetid.

"Before I get going, I'm just going to see if there's any pudding left. Now where's that big old silver cake slicer gone . . . ?"

The faces in the room told me I'd done something inappropriate. I didn't care—I had to take care of first things first.

Cavatina

UPON FURTHER INVESTIGATION I SAW there was no bread pudding remaining, so I picked up a tangerine and ripped off its delicate skin. At least the aroma was fresher than our surroundings. I tried to look as casual as I could while I was doing it, though I felt anything but calm. Once I knew the answers to a few more questions, I'd be able to put the whole thing together to my own satisfaction—if the answers were the ones I expected. I'd need Bud's help.

As I munched and enjoyed the sharpness of the citrus, I managed to speak to Bud without dribbling. "I'll stay here, because I don't want to mess up the washrooms more than I have already, but I could do with a few things, and your help, please, Bud."

"He not leave us," shouted Svetlana. It seemed she'd decided that Bud was her guardian.

I noticed that Jimmy looked disappointed.

"I can watch over you," the young man said tenderly, looking over at the woman for whom he clearly had very deep feelings.

I watched intently, savoring the fruit, as Svetlana made an assessment of the situation. She looked more serious, contemplative, and older than she'd appeared since we arrived. I thought I caught a glimpse of the girl who'd navigated the wilds of the USSR with nothing but a voice to allow her to clamber from abject poverty to a jet-setting life of glamor and adulation.

I noticed her finally settling her shoulders. She'd made a decision. "Is good. Jimmy look after me. Jimmy is good young man. I not young now. I need young man's blood so I am full of passion."

Her comments put me in mind of a blood-sucking vampire

feasting on an unsuspecting youth, but the expression on Jimmy's face, as he lit up from inside, told me that even if she were about to sally forth on a relationship for her own reasons, he'd be a willing victim. An accomplice, even. *Yes, accomplices.*

I turned to Bud. "See, it's okay—Svetlana says you may leave." I winked and I even managed to draw a faint, wry smile from Art.

"What do you need me to do, Cait?" Endearingly, Bud stood to attention.

"I need Julie's purse from the men's room counter, please."

Bud knew I was finished for a moment, so he took a look around the room, letting everyone know he'd be as good as with them while he was away, and made off to the men's room.

I addressed the rest of the room's occupants. "I'm also going to need Miss Shirley's purse, the red crystal Tsar! purse we saw earlier. I don't know where it's got to in all the confusion. I know that we found it on the floor, thanks to Svetlana's eagle eye, and that Julie put it on the bar at one point, but I rather seem to have lost track of it after that . . ." I looked around the room with a dithery expression and scratched my head. "It's okay, you can all stay where you are, but I really need it, so I'm going to poke about a bit."

I did just that. I didn't talk, and none of the other people in the room seemed ready to speak either.

"Here's Julie's purse," said Bud, emerging from the washroom. "Where do you want it?"

There wasn't anyone sitting at the bar, so I said, "On the bar for now, please, Bud."

"I need to see how Clemence is doing," Bud replied as he deposited the purse, and he did just that. Luckily it meant that everyone's attention turned to that side of the room.

While all eyes looked toward Bud and poor Clemence, I lifted the tablecloth surrounding the dessert table. Nothing. I checked under the table at which Art, Carl, and Ian now sat. Nothing. I gave

Svetlana a sideways glance as I passed her, then lifted the cloth surrounding the table where Jimmy was seated.

"Ah, there it is!" I reached down and pulled the glittering red purse from the floor beneath Jimmy's table. "It's right beside Svetlana's purse, on the floor."

Jimmy reddened a little. "I didn't know it was there. It must have been there before I sat down. Besides—it's just a purse. I mean, I know it's Miss Shirley's, but still, it's just a purse."

"Just a purse" didn't come close. It was quite something, and I could see why it would have cost many thousands of dollars to create. While it was true that the entire construction was a metal box, hinged so it could open like a clamshell, the corners were rounded so that the crystals didn't cut into the hand of the person carrying it, and it was surprisingly lightweight. A metal box covered in precious crystals should, surely, weigh more than that? Still, it felt bulky in my small hand. Miss Shirley had been a smaller woman than me, so her hands must have found it difficult to grasp. I wondered if there was a carrying strap inside, so I opened it to take a look. The clasp unhooked easily, but there was no strap, no decorative chain hidden deep in the folds of gold silk-satin that lined the inside. There was a lipstick, a couple of credit cards, and a key card rattling around in the expansive interior. That was it. But there was also a smell. A smell that I recalled had made Julie Pool wrinkle her nose when she'd opened the purse to retrieve the photograph of Clemence, Miss Shirley, and her children. Even though I'd wiped my hands with a damp napkin, I still caught the sharp notes of tangerine as I sniffed the interior of Miss Shirley's purse.

"She smells for killer," said Svetlana.

I allowed myself a very significant arch of my eyebrow. "You're not wrong."

Svetlana looked surprised. As did everyone else.

I placed Miss Shirley's purse on the bar, next to Julie's, which I picked up. I was disappointed by what I saw inside it. A credit card, a parking pass, a security badge on a lariat, a thin wad of cash.

"I left the lipstick where it was, on the counter," said Bud. "That's okay, right?"

I nodded. "Yes, that's fine. The lipstick's already told me all it can."

Bud made an almost comical face that told me he had no idea what I was talking about. It was the sort of face he often makes when trying to communicate with his gloriously affectionate black Labrador, Marty. *I hope he loves me as much as he loves Marty.*

"Could I get a glass of water, please?" asked Jimmy in a small boy's voice. I was surprised he hadn't raised his hand.

"There's a jug on the table," said Carl dismissively. "Though you won't catch me drinking from it."

"Exactly," replied Jimmy. "I thought I'd just wash out this glass and pour some water from the tap right into it?" He held a used glass toward me, then Bud, clearly indicating he thought we both had some say in the matter.

"There's any number of clean glasses behind the bar," said Ian, speaking to Jimmy as though he were a very stupid little boy.

"I'm sure there are," replied Jimmy testily. "But this one will do just fine, thanks." He stood and made his way toward the end of the bar nearest the dessert table. He'd only walked a few steps when he tripped and fell, coming down with a thump, grabbing onto a bar stool as he collapsed.

Svetlana leapt to her feet, leaving her precious chair for an instant. "Jimmy!"

Jimmy looked up from his prone position. "Stay where you are, Svetlana, I'm fine. I can clear all this up."

"Broke your precious glass?" asked Ian, somewhat spitefully I thought. "I'll get you another." He rose from his seat and made toward the end of the bar that was free from broken glass.

"I'll get one," said Jimmy forcefully. "I—I don't want you

touching anything else I drink from, thanks. Not that I don't trust you . . . I just want to do it myself."

Ian gave Jimmy a wide-eyed, dismissive look. "Suit yourself." He returned to his seat.

"Hey, come on, boys," said Art, which struck me as ironic, given the playground animosity that had sparked between him and Carl all night.

Jimmy bent to pick up the larger pieces of glass.

"Be careful, Jimmy," I called. "I cut myself on that broken urn earlier on. That glass will be even sharper. Use a napkin to wrap it. But don't put it in the bin behind the bar yet."

I turned to Bud. "I'm going to need the broken urn out here on the floor, please. Could you fetch the cloth we wrapped it in so I can open it up and take another look at it?"

"If you promise to be more careful with it this time, yes," replied Bud, sighing.

When Bud went behind the bar to retrieve the shards of the broken urn, Jimmy was already there, dithering about with broken glass wrapped in a napkin. "Not sure where to put it, if not in this bin," he said.

"There's a special glass bin under the counter, at the back," said Ian in a bored tone. "Since it's glass, that would be a great place for it, right?"

Jimmy looked annoyed. "Yes, that seems sensible."

As Jimmy's broken glass tinkled into the glass bin, the broken shards of the urn in the cloth that Bud had retrieved and laid gently on the carpet made quite a different, hollow sound.

Jimmy returned to his seat with a fresh glass full of water. "Svetlana, would you like one too?" he asked. Somewhat belatedly, I thought. "I'm sure you would," he added firmly.

Svetlana looked uncertain for a moment, then nodded with more than appropriate excitement. "Yes. Is good idea," she replied.

While Jimmy repeated the process of getting a glass of water, I said to Bud, "Could you, please, and without disturbing anything too much, check the men's washroom for a couple of small, white plastic bottles?"

"Small?" Bud's eyebrows raised in query.

I indicated something around an inch and a half with my fingers. "About this big. There might be only one, or there might be two. They might not be together."

"Sure," replied Bud. "Is this my last foray into there?"

"I hope so," I replied.

As Bud departed for the washroom, I turned to Art and Carl. "Would you two agree that there was no way for a gun to get past the metal detectors in Tanya's purse? I mean, is it a reliable metal detector?"

"I've already said that my hip always sets it off," said Art.

"I mean for smaller objects," I replied. "Your cigar holder, for example, Carl. That's metal. Does that set off the alarms?"

"Yes," replied Carl. "Every time. It's annoying."

"But necessary," added Art.

"Why so?" I asked. "Why is there a metal detector in use at that point?" I'd been wondering about that, and just couldn't come up with a reasonable answer.

"I can answer that one," said Ian sounding confident, for once. I noticed that Art had also been about to speak but seemed happy to defer to the youthful barman.

"Go on, then," said Carl. "I think it's dumb, so why is it there?"

Ian preened. "You know you get off the escalator from the casino floor in the Babushka Bar, then get into the elevator to go to the Romanoff Room or come here?" We all nodded. "And you know it's a pretty small elevator?" Again, we agreed.

"Is very small, like tiny room," said Svetlana. She was right—I wasn't quite her size, but I'd found myself to be in pretty close quarters with Bud as we'd ridden up in it. It could only hold three people, or maybe four very slim ones, at a time.

Ian continued in a conspiratorial tone. "Earlier this year, just after the Super Bowl, some guy didn't like being so close to another one and a fight broke out. Right inside it, if you can believe that." I found it difficult to picture, but I allowed him to continue. "When they fell out of the elevator, onto the floor of the Romanoff Room, one of the guys pulled a knife and stabbed the other one. It was a terrible night. Paramedics, cops. Took forever, and shut the restaurant down. So then they brought in the metal detector disguised in the archway."

Art nodded. "Ian's right. You can put signs about weapons not being allowed in casinos above every entrance, but if someone's carrying something they shouldn't be, you can't stop them. You can't have metal detectors at every entrance, not to the casino, nor to the hotel. Not even to every bar or public space. But you *can* install them in certain spots. Miss Shirley and I decided it'd be a good idea to ensure everyone's safety in at least the Romanoff Room, and here. It means there doesn't need to be such a heavy security presence in the restaurant itself, and none at all in here."

"The guy at the elevator entrance, in the Cossack outfit?" Art nodded in response to my question. "He's a very large man. I noticed that when we came up. I'm guessing there are many other security guards, also dressed as Cossacks, for him to call upon if anyone's found carrying, and not prepared to give up, their weapon?" Again, Art nodded. *One problem solved.*

"Thanks for that, Ian, Art. That's useful to know. By the way, how many of the men who accompany the Cossack Parade at midnight each night are real security guards? I know they're supposed to look as though they are guarding that fake block of Russian amber, but are any of them real?"

"That's not fake amber," said Art. "And all the guards are real. They're doing a real security job."

"Is real?" called Svetlana, astonished. "Real amber? I think is plastic!"

"Real amber," asserted Art. "The Russians pulled it out of the ocean about fifty years ago. Miss Shirley said it would be a good draw. I think most people come along for the dancing. As you mentioned earlier, Cait, it's a fun event, and it's designed to get people into the casino for midnight. As you know by now, here in Vegas midnight means there's still a whole lot of the night to go, and drinking might be involved. That's why the parade ends at the escalators up to Babushka Bar. Our Miss Shirley was pretty sharp."

I agreed that she had been, but I was surprised that all the fake guards were, in fact, real ones. It made my theory even more likely to be true.

Bud reappeared from behind the men's room privacy screen. He looked down at Clemence with grave concern. He bent low, I guessed to check if the poor man was still breathing. His expression when he stood told me that Clemence still had a chance.

"I found this," said Bud, holding up what was obviously Clemence's medication pouch. It did, indeed, look like a fancy, child's red leather pencil case. "Found it on the floor of one of the stalls," he said. "And there was this too. Found it floating in the bowl. I can't be sure, but someone might have tried to flush it. Whatever, it was still there." He held a small, opaque white plastic bottle between two pads of toilet paper. "Pilocarpine," he said, reading from the label.

"That's right," I said. "That would be a bottle of Clemence's eyedrops. He mentioned they were in that bag where his insulin was kept, along with his pills. I believe he has glaucoma. It's not unusual for those who suffer from diabetes. When Clemence told me he'd been diagnosed as a diabetic not so very long ago, I could see, from his collar, that he'd lost a dramatic amount of weight. Given his age, previous size, and race, I wouldn't be surprised if he's suffered from high blood glucose levels for years, but never had it investigated. That's why the disease is so dangerous—there aren't really uncomfortable symptoms, maybe for decades. Glaucoma is one associated problem. When Clemence came out of the men's room earlier on, his pupils were contracted to pinpricks. It's how my grandmother used to look when she'd used her glaucoma drops. I suspect that the drops, the use of his large handkerchief, the diabetes—they're all linked. And that stuff? Lethal."

"Oh, come on, it won't do worse than give you the trots," laughed Ian.

I sighed. "Please don't tell me you're one of those barmen who thinks that a tiny amount from a bottle of eyedrops is a good way to get revenge on an annoying customer?"

Ian blushed. "Not me. And I don't know anyone who's done it. But it is spoken of. You know, if someone's real annoying, or real fussy . . . it's the sort of thing we whisper to each other and laugh about. But, no, I've never seen anyone do it."

"Good," I replied in my professorial voice, "because it's very dangerous. There's absolutely no evidence that dosing someone with eyedrops will give them diarrhea, but there *are* many cases on the books proving that it's killed. It can cause bronchial spasm, which suffocates a person, or it can cause tachycardia, leading to the heart stopping completely. So don't think about doing it. In fact, if you could spread the fact, rather than the fiction, you might end up saving someone's life one day." Ian looked suitably chastised.

I nodded. "Clemence's eyedrops look to be the culprit in Julie's death. Agree, Bud?"

"No petechial hemorrhages in her eyes that I could see, so suffocation is unlikely. Though I'm no medic. But heart failure? Maybe."

I continued, "We can't ask Clemence how many bottles he carried with him. He had two insulin pens, because he thought he might mess up with one due to his less-than-steady hands. I believe it's likely he also had two bottles of eyedrops with him—unsteady hands can also make it difficult to drop liquid where it's needed, right into the eye, so he might have wasted quite a bit and carried a backup in case he ran out. Is that one empty, Bud?"

"It's funny you should mention needing a backup, Cait, because I *think* this is empty, but it's tough to tell, unless you can hear the liquid through this thick plastic. I'm not convinced that Clemence's hearing would be up to that, so if I were him, I'd carry a backup, I can tell you that much. I'm going to put this on the bar, near the purses."

"Good place for it—you can add the ball bearing you've got in your pocket," I said.

Bud pulled it out, eventually getting it to stop rolling about on the granite bar top. "I'd almost forgotten about that," he said.

"I hadn't," I replied.

Cabaletta

I WALKED TO THE BROKEN urn and picked up a couple of the larger shards that now lay scattered upon the tablecloth in which Bud had wrapped them earlier on. As I'd thought, they were quite thick. I moved to the unbroken urn, which still sat on top of the end partition. It was as light as a feather. One heavy, one light. *Yes.*

As I walked to the bar, Bud said, "Done with it already? How about I clear that away again? We don't want any sharp objects littering up the place, eh?"

I could tell he meant he didn't want any potential weapons ready to hand, but I wasn't sure why moving the pot away would help when we were surrounded by an array of knives on the dessert table, a gun in the purse on my shoulder, and any number of blunt objects in the shape of bottles of booze. *Maybe he wants to help—I should let him.*

"Thanks, Bud. That would be great."

As he gathered up the cloth and headed behind the bar, I gave my attention to Svetlana. "Is there any chance I could have a look in your purse, please, Svetlana?" I made my inquiry sound as friendly as possible.

"You like purses, yes?" she asked curiously.

"I do happen to like purses, but that's not why I'm asking to look inside yours. Would you mind?"

Svetlana looked toward Jimmy, who said, "It's still here, under this table where Svetlana left it. If it's alright with her, and I'm sure it will be, I can pass it to you."

Svetlana nodded. There'd been a significant shift in power in the relationship between Svetlana and Jimmy, and I was pretty sure I knew why. I wanted to confirm what I thought and the purse might start me off on that road.

I took the purse from Jimmy. A large gold-leather pouch, it matched the Russian diva's dress very well. It was made of the softest leather, and I could feel its lumpy contents. I opened the clasp at the top, peered inside, and said, "Would you mind if I emptied the contents onto the table here?"

"Is good," replied Svetlana imperiously.

A lipstick—the shade she was wearing; a key card—slimy and sticky; a couple of tissues—*Yuk! One is used*; a miniature can of hairspray. That was it.

"Thanks, Svetlana," I said politely as I put everything back into the purse. "Nice purse. Lots of room in it."

Svetlana took her refilled purse from me and set it on her lap, placing the narrow chain around her wrist.

"Is for evening. Not big, not small." She beamed.

"I know what you mean," I said. "We women don't really need a huge purse just to go to dinner, right?" Svetlana shrugged. "I mean, what do we really need at dinnertime? Though it was very handy that you had some chocolates in there, Svetlana—thanks for sharing them."

"I always have chocolate," she smiled. "I like sweet things."

"And pretty things. Let's not forget pretty things, Svetlana."

"Is not bad," she pouted.

"That depends," I replied, heading for the bar once more.

I raised my voice and looked around at everyone in the room. "I know that some of you think I've become fixated on evening purses," I began, "and maybe you have a point. But, you see, I had to work out exactly how the gun I found got into the dining room, and hidden in a purse seems the most likely explanation. You gentlemen are all wearing well-tailored suits that wouldn't be likely to accommodate a gun. I've worked through the possibility that Ian might have brought up a gun before any of us arrived, or that he might even have been working with someone in the kitchens who placed a gun on the dessert table, which, of course, came up through the floor, rather than going via any metal detectors. In fact, it's laden with metal objects of all sorts, so it would be an ideal way to smuggle a gun into the room."

All eyes turned to Ian, who fidgeted. Tom, suddenly alert, glared at him, and I could see that Bud was ready to act, but he stayed where he was, on guard, within just inches of the grief-stricken young man who'd been mentally absent for most of the time since Tanya's body had been discovered. I needed to address what he was feeling, in the open.

"Tom, please keep calm. I know that you're experiencing enormous anger about Tanya's death. I daresay you want nothing less than revenge on the person who killed her. When Clemence mentioned 'an eye for an eye' regarding Miss Shirley's death, he referred to a quote that harks back to one of man's most natural instincts—to avenge the death of a loved one. That's what you're feeling, Tom—a *natural* feeling, so allow yourself to experience it, but stop yourself from acting upon it. A vicious circle of revenge and retribution is just that, a circle. It goes around and around, hurting the people it's supposed to help. I see it so often with victims' families. They stand in front of the cameras on the steps of a courthouse somewhere and say that the sentence given to the killer of a loved one is, or isn't, 'fair.' Whatever their words might be, what it shows is that they have made up their mind about what would be 'fair.' When it comes to murder, there's no such thing. Fairness doesn't exist, so raw, unfettered anger sets in."

Bud was nodding and keeping a close eye on Tom. Ian looked uncomfortable when he spoke. "I can't prove it, but I really, honestly, have no idea where the gun came from. If it came up on that table, which it could have done, I didn't know it was there, and it wasn't being sent for me. I don't have anything to do with the food. It's the servers who do that. If they'd been able to get back in here, they would have attended to the dessert. If they were coming, that is. Unless we were going to serve ourselves? See! I don't even know that." It seemed that Ian was claiming ignorance and therefore innocence.

"Does anyone know if servers were expected here again?" I asked. I thought that Julie would have known, but I couldn't imagine anyone else would be sure.

Though it shouldn't have, it surprised me when Tom spoke. "I've been in the kitchen many times when Miss Shirley, or Art, was hosting dinners here. It's normal practice for the guests to serve themselves to dessert, but for at least one server to arrive to offer assistance with fetching and carrying and, of course, clearing the tables. This room has two dedicated servers when it operates. One does the last part, clearing up; the other goes back into the pool servicing the Romanoff Room."

"So it would have been likely that one server was about to make their way up here from the kitchen, to attend to the dessert table," I said. "I don't believe the gun came into the room on the table. You see, it's clear from my own recollections, and from what you've all told me, that Miss Shirley didn't go near the dessert table before the security system kicked in."

"What's that got to do with anything?" asked Carl. "Even if there's someone in the kitchens below who's in on all this, there must be someone in this room, now, who's been doing all the killing."

"Not with a gun," I observed.

Art, who'd been attending to the back and forth between Carl and me, finally sat back in his chair. "You're right, not with a gun."

"They'd give themselves away with a gun," said Carl perceptively. Art looked surprised.

"You're right," I said. "You couldn't shoot a gun in this room and expect no one to hear it, right?" Everyone shook their head. I continued. "So nobody thinks they heard a gun tonight, at any time?"

Again, all heads shook, but now faces were puzzled.

"A gun's real loud," said Art. "I'm sure Bud would agree?"

Bud nodded.

"So why is the gun here, then?" I asked.

Svetlana snorted. "I not know. You do. You play game. Tell us."

"I need to ask Bud to do something for me first, okay, Bud?"

Bud looked at me indulgently. "Sure," he replied. "What can I do now?"

"Come and stand beside me and close your eyes for a moment. Don't worry, Svetlana, Jimmy and I will keep watch over you, and everyone else, right, Jimmy?" The man smiled at me and nodded. Bud stood beside me and squeezed his eyes shut tight.

"Now, Bud, thinking about what I was saying earlier, about how our memory works, I want you to sniff what I'm putting in front of your nose. Tell me what it makes you think of. Not what you can smell, but where that smell takes you, what it conjures in your mind. Okay?"

"I'll do my best." Bud sounded unsure, but I knew my plan would work. I rolled up my sleeve and put the crook of my elbow in front of Bud, close to his nose. I always spray perfume on that spot, so despite the rigors of the night, I knew it would still be there.

Immediately Bud caught the scent, and he smiled broadly. "I'll have to be careful about what I say, so let's go with . . . this smell makes me think of rich dinners, the acrid smoke of extinguished candles, a wet dog running happily along the beach, and feeling warm, safe, and loved." He grinned again. "It's your perfume, Cait. *Coco Chanel.* It's Cait Juice. That's who you are, and what you are, to me. Safety, and love."

Svetlana smiled, but I knew, at least, that Bud was on track.

"Good job, Bud." I purposely praised him as I might have done a pet. *It's a thing we do. It's funny, to us.*

"Don't open your eyes. Now try this." I placed Miss Shirley's large glittering purse, wide open, under his nose. His nose wrinkled.

"I know that smell . . ."

"Don't tell us what it is, tell us where it takes you," I repeated.

"I'm with my father. We're at the river, fishing. No, no, we're at the lake. That's right. This smell, it's to do with the lake . . ." He sniffed some more.

"There is lake in purse?" asked Svetlana.

"Shush, Svetlana, let Bud concentrate," said Art.

"It's not the lake. I mean, it's *at* the lake, but it's not *of* the lake. We're behind the cabin, near the lake, and my father has lined up some old tin cans so I can shoot them down with his BB gun—that's it! This is gun oil. But it's not real gun oil, it's BB gun oil, which is a bit different. The cabin was where I first learned about guns, and my dad and I shot our BB guns together for years after that, even when I was in the service. Great way to keep your eye in without having to go to the range or shoot deadly bullets. Can I open my eyes now?" he asked politely.

"Yes, by all means."

Blinking a little, Bud said, "What was I smelling?" I showed him, and he looked puzzled. "Really? The inside of Miss Shirley's purse?"

I nodded. "The ball bearing? It's from this." I pulled the gun from Tanya's purse. It was still wrapped in its napkin. I carried it to Bud and let the folds fall open.

Bud sounded totally professional as he spoke. "Smith and Wesson M&P—that's Military and Police—R8 revolver. Uses a CO_2 cartridge and .177 caliber BBs—so .177 caliber ball bearings."

"Do you think this would have sounded like a gun if it discharged, or like something else?"

"The pop!" exclaimed Bud.

"Pop, pop? What pop?" asked Svetlana.

"Everyone close your eyes a moment, please," I said quietly.

"No, no, I not do this," replied Svetlana. "Is not safe."

It seemed pointless to push the woman, so I relented.

"Okay, just all think back to the seconds before the security system kicked in. Do any of you remember hearing anything?"

Art and Carl shook their heads. "Nothing until the loud noise of the metal collar thing coming down from the ceiling," replied Art.

"I agree," said Carl.

"You weren't in the room that whole time, were you, Carl?" I asked as gently as I could.

Carl spluttered, "I was. I don't know what you mean."

"Carl, I realize it might be a little embarrassing, but admitting that you had to rush to the men's room is rather less serious than being accused of murder, surely?"

"What?" He looked frightened.

"Oh, come on now, Carl," I said quietly. "You were near the men's room when the lights came up, but when we restaged those moments you plopped yourself in your seat. It can't be that awful to admit you had to go, surely?" Men's waterworks can make them feel very unmanly at times, especially when they reach a certain age, so I wanted to tread softly.

"I'd drunk quite a bit of water," said Carl, red-faced. "It was an urgent call of nature."

"There you go," I replied, smiling. "Perfectly natural. And it explains why you assumed a different position in our little recon-struction. No problem." I stopped then, because I realized I was probably overcompensating for his awkwardness on the topic.

"I might have heard something . . ." said Ian.

"Any idea what?" I wasn't hopeful.

"I'm not sure," he replied with obvious uncertainty. *What a surprise.*

"I didn't hear a thing," muttered Tom.

"You're sure, Tom? Nothing at all?"

Tom looked annoyed. "Why pick on me? I didn't hear *anything*. To be honest, and I know this sounds awful now, I was thinking about those dolls they sell in the Tsar! store downstairs—the ones that nest inside each other, you know? *Babushkas*, I think they're called. I wondered if I could get a set made up that looked like Tanya. For our one-year anniversary. There's a guy who makes them to order."

"Is called *matryoshka*. Is correct name. Babushka is grandmother, not correct," said Svetlana to Tom impatiently. "Not pretty things. And at time you talk of, I hear ... I hear nothing," said Svetlana to me, sounding disappointed. "I think I listen to song on music system." *That figures.*

Jimmy nodded. "I remember it was one of Svetlana's arias that was playing, so I think I was attending to that as well," he said. *That also figures.*

"Bud?" I knew he'd be useful.

"There was a pop, and a dull crack, then the collar started to descend, then the lights went out."

"Thanks, Bud. That's interesting. You see, this tells me why the gun was in the room, and it tells me who fired it. And there's one more thing you should know—"

I admit it, I paused for effect.

"What?" asked Svetlana, agog.

"Having ruled out every other possibility, I have concluded that the only person who could have brought that gun into this room was Miss Shirley herself, which explains why she carried such a large purse that didn't match, or even complement, her dress."

"Miss Shirley?" It was Art who expressed everyone's astonishment.

"Yes, Miss Shirley."

Grand Cadenza

CARL'S TONE WAS DISMISSIVE WHEN he said, "Rubbish. Why would Miss Shirley bring a gun here?"

"To shoot the urn," I replied.

"I not understand," said Svetlana plaintively.

"That's because she's talking a load of rubbish," said Carl.

Bud stepped in. He's seen me unravel complex puzzles before. "You know what, everyone? We're going to be out of here before too long, so why don't we give Cait a chance to tell us what she thinks has happened here tonight, last night, whatever you want to call this time we've all been together, before everything else kicks off, eh?"

"We're not going anywhere anyway," said Art.

"I want to know who killed Tanya," said Tom.

"Go ahead," said Jimmy.

"I can't wait to get out of here, but I guess you might as well talk till they all arrive," said Ian, his voice cracking with exhaustion.

"You said something about the urn?" Bud gave me a chance to speak, so I took it.

"Yes, thanks, Bud. The urn. I'll get to that in a moment, because it's almost where the whole thing started. One of the most puzzling aspects about Miss Shirley's death was how the murderer planned to get away with it. I'm sure you'll all agree that, even if we'd been able to release the lockdown immediately, we'd all have been subjected to interrogation by the police about her killing. It would have been clear from the outset that the murderer was among us."

There was general agreement in the room.

"Well, I believe that the real killer planned to get away with

Miss Shirley's murder by pinning it on another member of our group. And I'm afraid to say that was you, Ian."

Ian was suddenly wide awake and fully alert. "Me? What do you mean, me? I didn't do it. I didn't kill anyone. How could anyone think it was me?"

"Your fingerprints are on the saber," said Art.

"I know, but you all saw me use it to open the bottles of champagne," bleated Ian. "And why would I kill her? I liked her."

"How often do you think you've been at Miss Shirley's house in the past year?" I asked quietly.

Ian sighed. "I don't know—a lot? Why? What's that got to do with anything?"

Art spoke. "Were you really just there to be her private barman, or was there more to it?"

"What?" Ian exploded.

"And there you have it," I said. "The killer knew you were often at Miss Shirley's home. The killer knew she took a 'special' interest in you, and the killer planned to use how that might look to the outside world against you. A lovers' spat? A jealous young man cast aside by his rich, older lover? That's what the killer counted on as suggesting possible cause. Because it would be your word against the entire Vegas rumor mill. You might not have been able to convince people you weren't lovers or that you didn't have a reason to kill her. You were her favorite, invited to her home on numerous occasions. You were the one wielding the sword, so your fingerprints are on it. You were it—the fall guy."

Ian's face conveyed as much terror as if he'd been in front of a jury. "But we weren't lovers! She's . . . well, you know, she was a lovely woman, but she's . . . old. I know I don't have a girlfriend, but that's because—well, just because I don't happen to have one right now. You have to believe me. Anyway, Miss Shirley wasn't over her husband's death. She was always talking about him."

"Did you kill Tanya?" said Tom, leaping to his feet, ready to grab Ian, who cowered in his chair.

"Tom! Sit!" Bud's voice was powerful enough to make Tom draw back from the edge of his anger. Bud moved even closer to Tom, putting his arm around the young man's shoulders. "Tom, this is going to be tough for you. You've got to let her finish. She's already said she believes that Ian was set up by the real killer. So let's just allow her to talk us through the whole thing, right?"

Tom's chin puckered as he nodded silently.

"Go on, Cait," said Bud. "I'll stay here with Tom."

Ian looked relieved, as did a few others in the room. "So who set me up?" asked Ian bluntly. "And how did they think they'd get away with it?"

"All they needed were a few things to work together in their favor. Your fingerprints, the fact that Miss Shirley had a long-standing reputation as a man eater—"

"Don't say that!" said Art. "She was a good wife to Carl's father."

Carl agreed. "To be fair, she was."

I continued. "Carl, your father's will stated that she had to outlive him by one year *and* remain single for that year to inherit his shares. Why do you think your father made her not remarrying a condition of her inheritance?"

Carl shrugged. "I don't know. I always thought that was strange, but Dad did love her a lot—maybe he just wanted her to be his for a bit longer. You know, after he'd gone."

I shook my head. "I think it's a reflection of how well your father knew Miss Shirley. Remember what Clemence told us about her? She wasn't that good at picking men, was she? Pregnant by a married man at seventeen. Married a much older man, then a handsome singer who, by the sounds of it, was glad to take her money. She knocked around with men who helped her through tough times, finally marrying a guy who ran a successful business into the ground. It seems to me that the only stable relationship, a relationship between equals, that Miss Shirley ever had was with your dad. When she was young and poor, she turned to older men with money. As soon as she had a successful business, the chain of diners, she sold up and gave everything to a dashing young man. Your dad knew her, loved her, but could see that she might, once again, be drawn to someone who didn't have her best interests at heart, but simply saw her as a source of income. What was to stop her, desperately unhappy in her grief at the loss of your father, from hooking up with a totally unsuitable man who'd run through her money and maybe even undermine the entire Tsar! Organization?"

Art shifted uncomfortably in his seat. "I really don't think you should be speaking about Miss Shirley this way. It's not fair, and it's not right."

"I'm sorry, Art. I don't mean to hurt you. I've seen a vision of Miss Shirley take shape that shows me she was a woman of great compassion. Accepting and nurturing Clemence when going about as a mixed-race pair wasn't exactly popular illustrates that. I'm not implying that Miss Shirley was going to fritter away what was legally her husband's estate, but the prosecution could say what I've just said about Ian in court, and it could carry enough weight to allow the fingers to point at him as her lover. For the record—not that we're on it, but you know what I mean—I don't believe that Miss Shirley would have acted that way at all. I think that, like many young people, she made some bad decisions, but that her marriage to Carl's father would have allowed her to see, from the inside, how a good relationship can be. Let's be fair, she didn't have a useful model from her own family life to refer to when she was growing up, did she? No father in the picture, except a stepfather who built a new family with her mother, a family that squeezed her out. At least, leaving home so young, that must have been how she felt."

"So I would have been done for her murder?" said Ian, still red in the face and looking horrified.

"Never know what a jury will do," said Art.

"They love their forensics these days," said Jimmy, "and they would have had your prints to help them with that. But what about the real killer's prints?"

"Good question, Jimmy," I replied. "I believe it would have been easy enough for the killer to simply pick up the saber with a napkin and use it. This shashka is designed to be held by the elaborately decorated pommel—it has no D-shaped guard through which you'd have to thread your hand. It's made for both slashing and spearing. So you'd just have to hold a napkin, hold the sword, ram it in. Bud and I had a conversation earlier on about the practical ability of anyone in the room to deliver the fatal strike, and we both agreed it was within anyone's capability, except, maybe, Clemence's."

"So, if it wasn't Clemence, and it wasn't Ian, who was it? There aren't many of us left," said Tom. "And I know it wasn't me."

"You *would* say that," snapped Carl.

"Carl, please. Enough," said Bud sternly. "Cait . . ."

"Right, let's start at what I believe was the beginning. Julie told us that the process of getting the security system installed proved problematic for Miss Shirley, and that she'd said to Julie that she'd show the installation company that she was the boss. Julie thought that meant Miss Shirley wouldn't pay their invoices on time. I think it gave Miss Shirley an idea. Clemence told me that Miss Shirley, and Carl's father, used to enjoy practical jokes. I believe that this evening was supposed to be part of such a joke, but played at the expense of the security-system installation company. Tom, you told me about Miss Shirley owning a gun range, and also said it was common gossip that she was an excellent shot. I believe that Miss Shirley's plan, all along, was to bring the BB gun into the dining room and shoot at the urn on the partition to set off the alarm, around midnight. The Cossack Parade with the precious block of amber takes place then in the casino below us, and calls for the attendance of most of the security guards."

"You've got a point," said Art. "This room going into lockdown right then would cause chaos at that hour, with few responders available. Miss Shirley liked to keep people on their toes, and she'd not been very pleased recently with our head of security who'd recommended the installation company that messed up. She was angry with them, with him, and with herself for trusting them all. The alarm going off right then would have tested him to his limits."

"Exactly," I continued. "Earlier on tonight, Julie mentioned that the keypad numbers were big enough to allow Miss Shirley to use them with her arthritic hands. I think that arthritis made her less of a crack shot than she used to be, so she missed the body of the urn and just managed to clip the handle. That was enough to make the system kick in in any case."

"The urn," said Carl, "was worth a fortune. It's one of a pair." He sounded horrified.

"Was pretty," said Svetlana quietly, and sadly.

"Miss Shirley planned more carefully than that, Carl—don't panic. You haven't lost a valuable part of your inheritance. Clemence told me Miss Shirley once had a vase made just so she could break it and give her husband a fright. I believe she did the same with the urn. I should have noticed that it was really too thick and heavy for Sèvres when Bud and I were clearing away the broken pieces, but I was distracted by our conversation at the time. Upon examining those pieces again, and checking the other urn, it's quite clear that the one that's broken is a fake. I have no idea where the original might be, but I'm guessing it's somewhere safe."

Art chuckled. "Sounds just like her," he said.

"In order to accommodate the gun, she needed a large metal purse that would hide it in more ways than one when she walked through the metal detector at the entry to the elevator. After all, the security guards were unlikely to ask the owner herself to open her purse when it set off the metal detector. Also, Bud mentioned that Clemence said something interesting when he was delirious. Apparently Clemence shouted that Miss Shirley was trying to kill him. Although he was napping opposite his old friend when she took her shot, I wouldn't be surprised if some aspect of her actions seeped through into his subconscious. He interpreted her pulling a gun out of her purse and shooting it as an attempt on his life."

"But why did she change the codes?" asked Art.

"I have to admit this is supposition, but, of course, she didn't know she was going to be killed. All she thought she was doing by changing the codes was inconveniencing the installation company. As Julie told us when the codes she used didn't work, the control pad recorded the fact that the Tsar! security office had also made their three attempts to free the system. It would have been at that point, I suppose, that they'd have called the installation company to come to attend to it. I believe that Miss Shirley wanted there to be as big a stink as possible. By changing the codes without telling anyone, she'd have been the only one able to unlock the system. Maybe she had plans for us to all be enjoying white chocolate bread pudding, cheese, fruit, and champagne in here, while a lot of people were stressing out about the security system out there. The killer was as surprised as the rest of us that we couldn't get out of here."

"How you know this?" asked Svetlana snippily.

"Because a part of their plan was for the cops to get right in here, find Miss Shirley and the saber, hold us all, and have the finger of suspicion point at Ian as quickly as possible. The real killer collected the evidence of Miss Shirley's plan—the gun—from the scene. And I believe they were planning to plant the gun behind the bar, where it could be inferred that Ian had hidden it. But we didn't get out. The killer was stuck, we were all stuck."

"And then?" Carl wasn't looking very convinced that my ideas held water.

"Becoming trapped in this room wasn't the only surprise for the killer. Clemence's bombshell about Miss Shirley having twins was not something they'd expected."

"None of us expected that," said Art. "None of us had any idea that Miss Shirley had any children at all."

"I think you're wrong about that, Art," I replied. "Clemence certainly knew, and maybe Miss Shirley had told her late husband, but there was one other person here who knew too. At least, they knew a *part* of the story. I believe that the killer knew they were Miss Shirley's grandchild. They knew their father was her son, but didn't know that she'd had twins."

"That means it's one of you two," shouted Tom, glowering at Ian and Jimmy. "You are the only two who could be her grandson."

"I didn't say grandson, I said grandchild," I replied.

"But there isn't anyone here who could be Miss Shirley's grand-*daughter*," said Art.

"I know," I replied. "You're right."

"Tanya could have been her granddaughter," said Jimmy, keen to defend himself. "You thought it was her at one point, right? I heard you talking to Tom about it."

"Clearly Cait was wrong," said Tom. "Whoever killed Miss Shirley and Jack Bullock also killed Tanya and Julie. That just leaves us."

Tom was trembling with rage. I knew I had to address his suspicions before he acted.

"I'm sorry, Tom, I know this will be difficult for you, but that's an incorrect supposition. I believe it *was* Tanya who killed Miss Shirley *and* Jack Bullock. Before you start shouting, let me explain why I believe that. A great deal hinges on Tanya's father committing suicide. You told me she cleared out his house after he died. You also told me that her general attitude, and specifically her attitude toward Miss Shirley, changed shortly after that. I believe she found something that told her that Miss Shirley was her father's mother. I can't be sure, but I'm going to bet on it being a version of the photo that Miss Shirley carried with her, but a version that showed only Miss Shirley holding one baby. It's the sort of thing a mother might pass on with a child they've surrendered. Tanya commented, when she saw the photograph, that Clemence was standing holding '*another*' baby, not 'the other' baby. It was as though she wasn't surprised by the idea of Miss Shirley having *one* child, but by the fact she'd had *two*. Tom?"

Tom raised his head a little and seemed to pay attention to me. "Whatever you say, I won't believe that she did it."

Bud stepped in. "Tom, Cait knows what she's talking about. Listen."

"Tom, you told me yourself that Tanya's father had been protected by Miss Shirley on several occasions. Then there was Miss Shirley's very useful introduction of a scholarship for a place at university just when Tanya needed it. I believe that Miss Shirley had traced Tanya's father and knew he was her son. I believe that she supported him as best she could, by various means, over the years. Finally, when she knew she couldn't help him anymore—when she decided to stop enabling his gambling habit—she switched her support directly to her granddaughter. Tanya's father was a mess, you said as much, Tom. He'd followed a path that led him from disaster to disaster, and Tanya had been abandoned by her own mother at a very impressionable age."

Although I'd mentioned my suspicions about Tanya to Tom earlier on, this was the first time that Art and Carl were considering her as a suspect. They looked interested, but puzzled.

"But she was just a girl," said Art. "If she did it, and I'm not saying she did, Tom, what would have set her on such a path?"

I continued, "Tonight we have seen several types of grief displayed in this very room: Clemence's response to Miss Shirley's death—a woman I believe he has loved deeply since he first met her, Julie's reactions to her husband's demise, and Tom grappling with the loss of Tanya. Grief takes many different forms. As does the response to abandonment. Losing someone you love, whether they have died, or because they have left, or been taken away from you, is much the same thing. The human psyche has to make sense of that loss. There's a well-known, though some would say questionable, concept of various 'stages of grief.' The idea addresses the fact that grief is something that needs to be 'dealt with,' psychologically speaking. Now is not the time for a discussion about whether I agree with one theory or another, but the fact is the theories exist because they need to. There's a similar situation when it comes to abandonment—it's just that it's not so well recognized. Tanya's mother walked away from her. Her father killed himself. She was abandoned twice."

I took a breath and knew that what I was about to say wouldn't carry much weight with every person in the room. "Clemence mentioned that when he was twenty-one years old, he thought he was a grown man. Maybe only those in this room over a certain age can understand how very young we are when we're in our twenties. We think we know all the answers then. It's not until we're a good deal older that we realize we don't even know all the questions. At Tanya's age a person cannot comprehend what life still has to throw at one. Her mother left when she was a teen—a *choice* to leave her behind. Her father killed himself when she was just twenty-four—another person *choosing* to leave her. I'm sure she saw Miss Shirley's choice to hand over her babies, either to the authorities or to families directly, as another abandonment. In fact, she used the very word 'abandoned' when she referred to Miss Shirley's placement of her babies."

I could see people nod as they, too, recalled how Tanya had acted earlier on. "I believe Tanya had no idea about her grandmother's identity until her father died. When her father's suicide pushed her to a depth of despair she didn't know how to handle, she heaped all her grief and anger, accumulated over years of feeling abandoned, alone, different, and, finally, betrayed by her father, onto Miss Shirley. The woman she'd just discovered to be a blood relative. If Miss Shirley had not given up her father as a baby, he'd have had a very different life, and I believe that, in her grief, Tanya blamed Miss Shirley for the way his whole life turned out. Maybe even for him taking his own life. Tanya must have loved her father very much. She was still checking in on him regularly, despite juggling her own life with you, Tom, and a demanding career. That's why it was she who discovered his body. Her anger toward Miss Shirley brewed up over the past few weeks. And let's not forget that this young woman, who didn't have a sure sense of herself in company, was publicly embarrassed when Ian sliced the cork from a champagne bottle and drenched her on a very important evening, her anniversary dinner with Tom. Becoming the center of attention in such a negative way probably had a great impact on her. She put the two sets of hatred together, planning Miss Shirley's death and your downfall, Ian."

Ian seemed to sag as I addressed him. "It must have been Tanya who originally suggested the saber be used to open the bottles of Dom Pérignon tonight. You've only performed the trick once before here in Vegas, you said, Ian, and Miss Shirley wasn't around that night. Tanya was in this room, alone with Miss Shirley, the day before her birthday party, and she could have told Miss Shirley about the trick then, which was why it was Miss Shirley who asked you to 'perform' for us tonight."

"I don't believe any of it," said Tom simply.

I knew that Tom wouldn't budge in his belief that his girlfriend was innocent unless I could give him more to think about. "I think Tanya knew about the gun, the urn, and Miss Shirley's practical joke on the security company, and I believe she told Miss Shirley about Ian's trick with the champagne bottles so he'd, helpfully, cover her planned murder weapon with his fingerprints. Tanya knew exactly when each thing would happen, and, therefore, she knew when the security system would kick in and the lights would go out. When it all happened, she picked up a napkin, then the saber, ran it into Miss Shirley's back, continued around between the tables and the window wall, and rejoined Tom at the bar. Tom? You said Tanya tried to convince you that she was closer to Miss Shirley than she really was when the lights went out?"

Tom didn't look up, but he nodded heavily.

I continued, "That was because she wanted to deflect focus from the fact that she was closer to the other end of the bar, making her return route to you quicker. I can't say that the head with a flat hairdo that I saw flash in front of the windows was definitely Tanya's, but it could have been. Also, someone who smelled of soap passed by me in the darkness."

I looked at the people in the room, who were all rapt, but still puzzled. "Hey, look at us," I said, trying to encourage everyone to at least participate in some active thinking. "I know we all look a pretty sorry state now, and I bet none of us smell too good either, like this room. Given the general way that people presented themselves for dinner, I'm going to suggest that everyone here wears a cologne, an aftershave, or a perfume."

There seemed to be at least a slight acknowledgment by everyone present that this was the case.

"Maybe yours is pretty light, Ian, because of your job?" I asked.

"Yeah, they don't like us to wear anything that's overpowering, because it's off-putting for the people we serve—you're right," replied Ian.

"I'm guessing you're wearing something tonight you don't usually wear, Tom, right?"

Tom's voice was heavy. "Anniversary present from Tanya. She gave it to me the night Ian sprayed her with champagne."

"But I'm guessing you didn't give her perfume as a gift, right?"

Tom shook his head. "Didn't like perfume. She said it was stupid. She didn't care much for finery, or show."

"I know," I replied as tenderly as I could manage, recalling the girl who'd looked thrown together, rather than put together. "Everyone in this room presented themselves for tonight's special dinner in a manner of dress that suggests to me we all wore some sort of fragrance, except Ian—who smelled of spilled champagne—and Tanya. Did she always use the same soap, Tom? Just a plain, light, fresh fragrance?"

Tom sighed. "I don't know. I guess."

I didn't believe I was going to win Tom over to my theory anytime soon, so I just pushed ahead. "Tanya had motive, opportunity, physical capability, and access to the weapon. She had time to pick up the saber, kill Miss Shirley, and return to her spot at the bar before the lights came up, but she *didn't* have a chance to retrieve the gun. Her plan was to wait until the lights came up and there was a general hubbub of activity around Miss Shirley's body to retrieve the gun—and that's what she did."

I knew I had to allow my audience a moment to digest that idea. I did, pausing before I said, "When the lights first came on I saw Miss Shirley's purse on the floor beside her chair. Having shot at the urn she'd replaced the gun in her purse, which fell to the floor when she was killed. During the general confusion that followed the discovery of the body, Tanya took her chance to grab the gun out of Miss Shirley's purse, but the pink silk handkerchief in which Miss Shirley had wrapped the gun to protect the lining of her purse fell to the floor in the process. It has gun oil stains on it. The lining of the purse does not, it just smells of the oil. I didn't see the handkerchief at all until I peeped under the tablecloth-shroud."

"Even if that's all true," said Carl, "why would Tanya kill Jack? And how did she do it?"

I felt completely exhausted, but I knew I had to press on. "I honestly believe her original plan was just to kill Miss Shirley and let Ian take the fall. It hadn't occurred to her that she would have been the inheritor of more than half this business empire. But a few things happened tonight that showed Tanya that was the case. Julie told us that Miss Shirley had referred to a letter she'd written pertaining to her will. Next, there was the information that Miss Shirley had gone to Los Angeles with twin baby boys and returned without them. Finally, there was the acknowledgment that Jack Bullock, originally from LA, was a man of the right age to be Miss Shirley's son, who she encouraged to be close to her, giving him an opportunity to have a successful career as a lawyer. Tanya was a very bright girl. And she wasn't the only one in the room at that time thinking that Jack Bullock might be Miss Shirley's son, right?"

Both Art and Carl blushed like naughty schoolboys. I'd seen their sideways glances at Jack at the time. "Tanya had already killed for revenge—why not inherit the prize as well, even if she hadn't planned it that way to start with? I don't believe that Tanya was a bad person, through and through, Tom. But you said yourself she found it difficult to mix with others, and that she yearned for what she thought of as a 'normal' life; something she'd never had. A part of that psychopathy is for the person experiencing it to have their own rules, to decide that the society shunning them has no ability to decide right from wrong for them. She saw killing Miss Shirley as her way to avenge her father's sad life and tragic death. No more, no less. Having taken that step, she decided to kill Jack in order to achieve a newfound dream of great wealth and power. Clemence didn't make it any secret that he was a diabetic, and Tanya used her wits and knowledge to devise a plan. She was close to Clemence's seat and could have easily lifted his little bag from his jacket on the back of his chair and injected Jack with the drug during the melee. She was acting on impulse, on adrenaline. She bore no animosity toward Clemence, she just wanted his drugs. Her big purse was certainly large enough to accommodate both the gun and Clemence's medication bag."

"But she's dead," said Tom flatly.

"And she couldn't have killed *herself* the way she died," added Ian.

Finale

"WHO KILL TANYA?" ASKED SVETLANA quietly, still looking frightened.

I felt my shoulders droop. "In a way, both Bud and I have to take some responsibility for that, and I hope you'll forgive us for it, Tom."

Tom's head shot up. "What do you mean?"

Bud looked aghast.

"I don't believe Julie was really asleep when you and I were talking, Bud. She could easily have overheard us, and then she saw how Tom reacted when I mentioned my suspicions about Tanya to him. We all saw how distraught Julie became after her husband's death. She and Jack had a very deep, powerful relationship. Think about what she told us about herself—she gave up a moneyed family, a gilded future, and a life of luxury to follow Jack Bullock to Vegas, to be with him. 'Her prince,' she called him. That takes courage. I know they worked in very different worlds, but I believe they both derived enormous strength from their relationship."

As I looked at the faces in the room, my gaze dwelled on Bud's. I wondered what I'd do if I suspected someone of doing him harm.

I pressed on. "Julie picked up the corkscrew and followed Tanya into the ladies' room fully intending to at least threaten her, or maybe do her some sort of harm. Julie struck me as someone who respected the law, though her attitude toward me when we first met suggested she had a capacity for spite, maybe even cruelty. Maybe she intended to kill Tanya, but I think it's more likely that Julie would have enjoyed seeing her husband's murderer accused in public, brought to justice by society. Maybe things got out of hand. Having overheard our conversation, Bud, I think Julie drew her own conclusions, and she believed, quite rightly, that Tanya had killed her husband. Julie was a lithe woman who worked out regularly—I could tell that when I noticed her toned and well-developed legs. Maybe there was a struggle. Whatever happened fueled her rage. Julie would have easily had the strength to kill Tanya. Although we probably all thought of it as a reaction to finding Tanya's corpse, what we really saw was how Julie's body reacted to having killed—her vomiting and subsequent uncontrollable shaking were equally violent. So I believe Julie Pool killed Tanya."

"So who killed Julie?" asked Jimmy. "And why?"

"When I found Tanya's body, her purse was on the floor beside her. Clemence mentioned he had insulin pens, eyedrops, and pills in his little red leather bag. When Bud found that red leather bag in the men's room, where it definitely had not been during our earlier search, and the floating empty bottle of eyedrops, I knew what had happened. It might well be that Julie had seen her suspicions confirmed when Tanya's purse fell from her shoulder in the ladies' room and Clemence's stolen bag fell out. Tanya's purse had scattered some of its contents onto the floor when I found it. After she killed Tanya, Julie took the little bag, hid it in her own evening purse, and then went to the men's room where she drank the eyedrops, intending her own death. Remember how she spoke to you before she went there, Art?"

Art shook his head. "No, I don't recall—oh yes, she said I'd been fun to work with. Is that what you mean?"

I nodded. "Those comments, and her remark that she was 'as good as dead' herself were very final, don't you think? Her acceptance that there'd be a future where you and Carl could bicker away? She seemed very calm at that moment. And then, of course, there was the lipstick."

"Yes, I don't know what you mean about that," said Bud.

I allowed myself a half-smile. "There was a point earlier on when I looked at myself in the mirror and saw what a mess I'd become, but, because of the circumstances, it felt wrong to find my purse and reapply lipstick. It just seemed too frivolous. When we found Julie in the washroom, she'd already applied fresh lipstick—not something, under normal circumstances, a woman who's just lost her husband would do. Not unless she was thinking about her final, defiant act—stepping away from this life to be with her dead husband. She killed herself. It's that simple, and that dreadful."

"Nothing simple," said Svetlana.

Art and Carl agreed.

Ian raised his hand. I smiled. "Yes, Ian?"

"So, let me get this straight . . . Miss Shirley planned to annoy the security company, Tanya killed her and tried to set me up, then Tanya killed Jack because she thought he might be Miss Shirley's son, then Julie killed Tanya, then Julie killed herself. Is that right?"

I nodded.

"Wow," was all Ian could manage. Then he added, "So Clemence lying over there nearly dead is just, what, collateral damage?"

"Sadly, yes," I replied, looking over at the poor man, who was still breathing, at least.

"I still can't believe it of Tanya," said Tom, but with much less venom than before.

"No one alive here is killer?" asked Svetlana.

"No, there is no killer in the room. You're safe," replied Jimmy.

It was as though a weight lifted from each pair of shoulders in the room. Every face bore a thoughtful expression.

"What about the missing golden egg?" asked Carl. "How does that fit in?"

I smiled. "It doesn't."

"But it must. It's gone," he replied.

"You're right," I agreed, "but before I address that, I'd just like to get myself a glass of water." Bud moved as though to get one for me. "Thanks, Bud, but I'd rather get it myself. I haven't ventured back there yet, and you know how much I like to get behind a good bar."

I walked around the end of the bar, turned on the tap, and let the water run. Feigning surprise, I picked up the priceless golden egg that lay at my feet, held it aloft, and said, "Oh, look—here's the egg! I wonder who searched back here and couldn't find it. It must have been flung across the room during the fight. Anyway, it's not damaged, so I'll just put it here on the counter with all these purses. No harm done." I drank my water, then walked to the dessert table, where I kicked the end of the silver cake slicer that was poking out from beneath the tablecloth. "Oh dear, look, this has fallen on the floor. This shouldn't be used again. It's been on the carpet very close to where Jimmy fell earlier on, so there might be little pieces of glass on it. I'll put it back on the table, but don't use it."

I hoped that I managed to be so casual about my discoveries that no one would catch on to what I was up to. The next comment to be uttered suggested I had been successful.

"Why would anyone use it?" asked Ian. "There's nothing left to eat. Besides, with the stench in here, who'd want to?"

I threw Jimmy a meaningful glance as I said, "Jimmy, given your earlier comments, and Svetlana's obvious lack of terror now, it might be a good time for you two to have a little chat?"

Both Jimmy's and Svetlana's expressions brightened, and he turned toward Svetlana, looking apprehensive. The Diva's expression suggested he'd receive an agreeable welcome. Art, Carl, and Ian looked somewhat embarrassed. Tom was still in a world of his own, and Bud was looking rather surprised.

"I'll come with you for moral support," I said brightly, and I all but pushed Jimmy across the room. When we arrived at Svetlana's side, I crouched to speak to her as quietly as possible, and motioned that Jimmy should bend in too.

"Svetlana, I know you took Miss Shirley's glittering red purse—twice—and I know you lifted the egg when no one was looking. It might be only a 'little one,' but it's worth a fortune. And I know you nabbed the cake slicer too. 'No more *La Gazza Ladra*,' that's what you said to Svetlana, right, Jimmy?"

Jimmy nodded. His eyes betrayed his anxiety.

"I know that the translation of the title is *The Silken Ladder*, but as I mentioned I also know the alternative name for that opera. It's *The Thieving Magpie*, isn't it?" I knew I was right.

Again Jimmy nodded. This time his entire demeanor expressed defeat.

I pressed on. "Luckily for me, my sister, the opera buff, has mentioned that to me in the past, so I was finally able to make sense of your reference. Svetlana, I do realize that kleptomania is a very real condition. It's not something you can always control. I daresay in your specific case, it's driven by your challenging upbringing and further fueled by your love of pretty things, both of which are deeply ingrained as part of how you judge your self-worth. You need to get treatment, Svetlana. Soon. *Now*. A reputation is a very valuable, and fragile, thing. Rumors can run through a place like this very quickly. Jimmy, you might not be prepared to be Svetlana's assistant anymore, but will you help her with this, at least?"

Jimmy nodded eagerly. "Of course I will. Even if she doesn't want my affection, she'll always have my loyalty. And thank you, thank you so much for giving me that little heads up before. It gave me a chance to drop the cake slicer when I 'fell,' and to hide the egg behind the bar. No one need know, right?"

"They won't know from me," I replied. "But this needs to be addressed, by a professional. It won't just go away or stop. You understand that, Svetlana, right?"

Svetlana Kharlamova, world-renowned diva and an undoubted thief, pursed her mouth like a pouting child, dropped her eyes, and slowly nodded her agreement.

"Thank you," she said. I didn't get the idea she said it that often. "You very kind. Jimmy very kind. Miss Shirley very kind. She know. She not speak. I not bad. I work with doctor, I promise. Jimmy helps. Jimmy very good man. Very handsome man." She looked up at Jimmy and smiled an almost girlish smile. "We talk alone now?" she said to me.

I stood upright, groaning. "Yes, you talk alone now," I said as I walked away. I wondered if they would make a go of it.

Returning to the remainder of our group, which now consisted of just Carl, Art, Ian, Tom, and Bud, I said, "They should be here soon. How do you think we should play this? Do you want to explain it all to the cops, Bud, or do you want me to do it?"

"I'm happy to make the introductions, but I think it should fall to you to explain the details, Cait, and I'll back you up," said Bud.

The men nodded their agreement.

"Hell of a night," Art said, then added, "though it's the afternoon now. I don't even know what day it is. I'm going to sleep for a week after this."

"You're not wrong," said Ian. "I should have been on duty downstairs in Babushka Bar at ten this morning. Could you square it so I get a couple of shifts off?" he asked Art.

"Sure," replied both Art and Carl.

"How are you doing, Tom?" asked Bud, his arm draped across Tom's shoulders. "Alright?"

Tom looked dazed. "No, not alright. Totally and utterly not alright. I know that what you said makes a sort of sense, Cait, in that it's a logical explanation of all the facts. But I didn't think Tanya had it in her. To kill. Nor Julie, for that matter. I must be a terrible judge of character, I guess. Mom says I'm only good with ingredients, not people. I guess she's right. I just can't—"

Bud hugged Tom. "Hey, come on. Don't beat yourself up about it. We all make mistakes about people. It's easily done."

"So who do you think gets Miss Shirley's shares?" asked Carl. "I guess it'll be me, with Tanya and Jack out of the way."

"Oh, don't be too quick to think that," replied Art.

"Why not?" asked Carl.

I smiled. "I think Art's referring to the fact that we might have all been very wrong to think that Jack Bullock was Miss Shirley's son. Yes, I'm convinced that Tanya's father was one of her sons, but who's to say who the other boy became? The way Miss Shirley treated Jack Bullock might just have been one of the things she did out of the kindness of her heart. I suspect she helped people along as some sort of overcompensation for having given up her babies, but we don't *know* that Jack was her son. Tanya's father's twin could be living any sort of life anywhere in the world. We don't know. Maybe Miss Shirley put some information in that letter she mentioned."

"But there *was* no letter," said Carl sharply.

"How do we know there's no letter?" I asked.

"Because Miss Shirley never gave a letter to Julie Pool," snapped Carl.

By way of a response to Carl's point, I asked Art, "Who's your lawyer?"

Art looked puzzled. "I don't know how that's got anything to do with all this, but Julius Feldblum in Saint Petersburg is my guy. In Florida, not Russia, of course. He's Stephen Feldblum's brother. Heck of a family that one. Four brothers—an accountant, a lawyer, and two doctors. Their mother was one proud woman. Why?"

"Julie Pool thought that Miss Shirley would have given her that letter, and I think everyone agreed with that assumption. But Julie was employed by the Tsar! Organization, not Miss Shirley directly. It's more than possible that Miss Shirley had her own lawyer, to whom she would have entrusted the letter."

"I don't understand. Why did Miss Shirley go through her will with Julie and not her own lawyer if she had one?" asked Carl.

I smiled. "It strikes me, from what I've learned about her, that Miss Shirley knew the true value of a dollar. Why pay for expensive external help by the hour when you already have people who can do the job on salary?"

Art grinned. "Just like Miss Shirley. She'd pay for a guy to hold on to a letter for her, but use the free legal help at her disposal whenever she could. Ian being on call as a barman at her house? She might have met him when she hired in outside help, but once he was on salary here, he was free to her. Same with this restaurant. Saved her a mint on catering at her home. Yep, certainly knew the value of a dollar," mused Art.

Bud had left Tom's side and was next to me. "I've checked on Clemence, and he seems stable. I'm taking comfort from the fact that I know paramedics have saved people who've slipped into a coma like this and been that way in their home for a day or so before being discovered. Let's hope they can do the same for him."

I nodded. "How's Tom?"

"It's going to take some time for him to get over all of this." He looked around, then whispered, "What on earth was all that stuff about the egg? You're a hopeless liar, Cait Morgan."

"I'll tell you when we're alone, but for now just let it go? No need to make a big deal of it when we're running through the case with the police, okay?"

Bud was just about to answer when a sound like a jet engine came from the ceiling above us.

"It's the air-conditioning!" called Ian, closing his eyes with relief.

"Won't be long now," said Carl with the excitement of a small child.

"Thank heavens," said Bud. "We're nearly done."

It Ain't Over Till . . .

AN INSTANT AFTER THE AIR-CONDITIONING kicked in, a woman's voice began to sing over the loudspeaker system.

Svetlana beamed. "Is me," she said. "I have very good voice. Is short piece for encores. 'O Mio Babbino Caro.' From *Gianni Schicchi*. Puccini. People think is from *Madame Butterfly*. Is not."

I knew the tune well, and my sister had talked to me about that particular opera years ago, when she'd first heard it. "That's the opera with all the fuss about a will, right?" I asked.

Svetlana nodded absently. "Is beautiful aria. Very good for me."

"An aria entitled 'Oh My Beloved Father,' from an opera about a contested inheritance? Very apt," I observed.

A loud metallic shudder signaled that the collar surrounding the elevator was about to move. I was very grateful. Bud and I had been up and about for twenty-six straight hours, and I was beginning to flag.

As soon as the aria finished, Art led a little round of applause, nodding at the Diva, who allowed herself a gracious smile.

Jimmy clasped her hand to his chest. "Magnificent, Madame," he said.

The Diva looked at him with real tenderness in her eyes. "Please. I Svetlana for you now. I Svetlana for my Jimmy forever, I think." She nuzzled against him. It was a sight that gave me pause. Love is a very strange, powerful emotion, as is the need to not be alone.

As our applause died away and we watched the painfully slow progress of the metal cylinder as it rose, Bud grabbed my hand and said, "You never asked me why I brought my good suit to Vegas."

For once, I didn't quite know what to say. "It's a very nice suit, and I assumed we'd be celebrating your birthday somewhere fancy," I replied weakly. "Though I think a trip to the dry cleaner's might be in order after all of this."

He smiled. "You're right. I look far from my best. Though I guess we could all do with a wash and brushup. But I don't think that's going to happen right away. Of course, our first priority is to see that Clemence gets the treatment he so badly needs, as soon as possible. And then? I guess it'll be quite some time before the cops are done with all of us, though if you tell them what you've told us, I think things might go a little faster."

We all nodded our agreement.

"So that means I have to do this now." Bud rose from his seat, then dropped to one knee in front of me, taking my hands in his. Svetlana gushed, everyone smiled. My eyes began to fill up with tears. We all knew what was happening.

Bud looked serious as he spoke. "Just over a year ago I asked you to marry me, Cait Morgan, and you said no."

"It was one year, two weeks, and three days ago, to be precise," I said. "Not that I've been counting. I just happen to remember, that's all." I couldn't help but grin as I spoke.

"Well, it's been a very unusual one year, two weeks, and three days, Professor Morgan, and I've enjoyed every moment we've shared. Even those when our lives have been in danger, or we've been trying to save the lives of others. I have respected your wishes to wait for a year. I love you, Cait Morgan. Will you marry me? I haven't chosen a ring, I know you'd want to do that yourself, with me"—*he knows me so well*—"but I want you to marry me, Cait. Now. Here in Vegas. As soon as we're done with the cops. We can get refreshed and run off to one of those little chapels they have all over the place."

"No," shouted Art excitedly. "Do it here, in the Tsar! wedding chapel, on us. We'll all come. We can be your witnesses. Maybe Madame Kharlamova will even sing for you . . ."

"Yes, yes, I sing at wedding," Svetlana clapped her hands like a happy child.

I didn't respond to anyone but Bud. He deserved that much.

I looked into the eyes of the man I'd first respected, and now loved. "Oh, my darling Bud, yes, I *will* marry you. But not here in Vegas. Not now. Could we wait a little? Please?"

Bud looked delighted, then crestfallen. "Oh, I'm so pleased, Cait. But why wait? There's no one back in Canada we really want to be with us, right? We could be married by the time we fly back—" He paused. "I wonder if we'll make our flight in the morning? That hadn't occurred to me—oh well, we'll just have to get home some way. So that's even better, we could honeymoon here. Please, Cait?"

I squeezed his hands. "Bud, there's nothing I want more than to be your wife." I managed to stop myself saying 'Mrs. Anderson,' though I couldn't help but think of the late, lamented Jan. "But I promised my sister, Siân, she could be at my wedding. With Mum and Dad gone, she's the only family I have. We both thought it would never happen, but she's been on at me for months to let her be with us when we marry."

In the now-silent room, I could almost hear Bud smile. "Pretty confident I was going to ask you, eh?"

I nodded, a tear beginning to slide down my cheek. "It's what I've been hoping for."

"Your sister means a lot to you, doesn't she?"

I nodded.

"Right then, but she'll have to come to Canada from Australia— we're not going there. Maybe we will one day, but not for our wedding. And I don't want to wait forever, either." He smiled. "As soon as possible, please?"

I nodded. "How about Wales, between Christmas and New Year?"

"Wales?"

I nodded. "If we go east and Siân goes west, it's sort of half-way . . . There's a wonderful place I know and love just outside Swansea. A fantasy building on a spur of land that juts into the sea. It's wild and magnificent. I believe they rent it out for weddings . . ."

"You've thought this through, haven't you?" Bud grinned.

"Just a bit." I indulged in what I trusted was an impish grin. "I've never thought of myself as a romantic, but it would be a wonderful place to get married."

"Tell you what, you two," piped up Art. "If we can't host your wedding, I insist you have the ring on us—there's a great jewelry store downstairs. We'll move you to a suite until we fly you back to Vancouver on the Tsar! jet, whenever works for you."

Bud looked at me but spoke to Art. "Thanks, Art. We'll take you up on all of that, and I will take this woman to Wales to marry her. Three months, Cait Morgan. Right?"

"Yes, Bud Anderson," I replied, every fiber of my body tingling. "Three months."

I hardly noticed the first cop emerge from the elevator. The man I loved had proposed to me. I felt as light as air, and I knew the adventure of our life together was just beginning.

Bud held me and kissed me. After that delight, I felt my face crease into a broad grin, and I hummed the wedding march from Wagner's *Lohengrin* to myself.

WATCH FOR CAIT MORGAN'S
NEXT MYSTERIOUS ADVENTURE, IN
The Corpse with the Sapphire Eyes.

Un (1)

GENERALLY SPEAKING, I BELIEVE THAT when life gives you lemons, you should make yourself a large gin and tonic. Or a lemon mousse. Okay, preferably both.

However, there didn't seem to be a silver lining to the apocalyptic weather system that had turned the cliff-top castle in Wales where I was due to marry Bud Anderson in two days' time into a creepy and uncomfortable place to be. Gale-force winds had quickly blown away all my romantic notions about Gothic Revival architecture.

As we shivered in the drafty Bridal Boudoir of Castell Llwyd, my sister, Siân, tried to comfort me, but my mood had become as gloomy as the skies. "Buck up, sis. The storm will blow itself out by Monday. It didn't stop you and Bud getting here from Canada, or me from Australia, so it could be worse. We're all here, safe. Though why you chose this place to get married, I'll never know. It's like something out of a Vincent Price movie."

"Why here?" I moaned. "Because I allowed myself to believe I could celebrate the start of my new life in a fairytale castle. For once, just once, I wanted to be a giddy, giggly romantic and wallow in luxury. I suppose it serves me right for trying to do something just a bit impractical for a change."

"Come on, sis," said Siân gently, rubbing my back as though I were a sick child. "It'll be alright. And at least it can't get any worse. Now, show me your wedding dress. I can't wait to see it."

As if on cue, there was a knock at the door. I perked up immediately at the sound of Bud's voice. "Cait, can I come in?" His tone was urgent.

I pulled open the heavy oak door, smiling expectantly.

As soon as Bud started talking, my nerves were set on edge—he was using his calming voice. "Now, don't panic, Cait. And don't get cross. You don't need to do anything. Mrs. Jones, the cook, has everything under control. Besides, he's dead anyway, so there's no real rush. Don't panic. Right? This death will *not* spoil our wedding on Monday. I promise."

"What do you mean? *Who's* dead?"

Regardless of whatever reaction he might have hoped for, I felt that panicking was an entirely appropriate response to Bud's statement. Siân seemed to be in agreement as she rushed to my side.

Immediately reflecting my own undoubted look of horror, Bud scooped me up in his arms and gave me an almost suffocating hug. "Oh, Cait, I wouldn't have had this happen for the world. But it'll all be sorted out without too much fuss, I know it will." Over my shoulder he said, "Hello again, Siân. I'm glad you're here. You can help me keep her calm."

Despite the fact that he was speaking of me as though I were a child in need of a good talking to, Bud's warmth against me was innately comforting. *Hugging's underrated.* But while I would have liked nothing more than to linger in his embrace, I knew that wasn't realistic.

"Okay, okay, you can let me go now!" I snapped a little, and I hadn't meant to, but I didn't need cuddling. I needed information. "Both of you can stop worrying. I'm perfectly calm, for a woman whose wedding weekend is about to be thrown into chaos by a death at the venue, in any case. So, what's happened, Bud? Please, just tell me."

Bud drew back, held onto my hands, and sighed as he spoke.

"The choirmaster fell down the servants' staircase and he's ... well, he's broken his neck, Cait. He's dead. But, like I said, it'll all be sorted out before we know it. For once, this isn't our problem. It's not pleasant, I won't pretend it is, and I'm very sorry for the guy, but this terrible accident won't impact our wedding. I won't let it." His tone was measured and sounded almost matter-of-fact.

"What choirmaster, Bud? When? How?" was all I could muster as I leaned against the creaking door. I felt my eyeballs throb inside my eyelids as I closed them, wishing away Bud's low-key announcement of a cadaver on the premises.

Acknowledgments

AS IS ALWAYS THE CASE, many people have helped me bring this book to fruition. My mum and my sister were my first readers, my husband has been more patient and supportive than you can imagine (though he did enjoy doing the research with me!), and my dogs have either sat quietly at my feet or allowed me an excuse to run around the garden throwing sticks as I plot and plan.

To Arthur and Jean Sauber and Stephen Feldblum—I know that you're nothing like the characters who now bear your names, but I'm so happy that I can acknowledge our friendship in this way. Three cruise buddies forever on the page. Happy reading!

Special thanks go to Lyle Tolhurst, divisional manager at the Eiffel Tower Restaurant at Paris Las Vegas, for allowing me to gain such valuable and fascinating insights into life in a fine-dining restaurant that is an elevator ride away from a casino. To Mon Ami Gabi at Paris Las Vegas, for serving food that has inspired the dishes in this book, especially the white chocolate bread pudding. Terry Lynch, the executive chef, and all the management, servers, and kitchen staff are so good at what they do, they made it tough for me to put together only a single meal fit for Miss Shirley—but I hope she'd approve. I found the excellent archives of the *Las Vegas Sun* to be a valuable resource—thanks to Brian Greenspun and the entire team.

To every member of the TouchWood team, each of whom plays their unique role in allowing Cait to have her adventures, and to Frances Thorsen, my tireless editor.

Last, but far from least, my thanks to you for choosing to spend some time with Cait Morgan—as well as to all the printers, distributors, librarians, booksellers, bloggers, and reviewers who might have helped you find, and get your hands on, this book. Without all of you, Cait would be simply a figment of my imagination; because of all of you, she lives, breathes, eats, drinks, solves murders, and has a wonderful time doing it all. Thank you, on behalf of Cait Morgan.

Welsh Canadian mystery author CATHY ACE is the creator of the Cait Morgan Mysteries, which include *The Corpse with the Silver Tongue, The Corpse with the Golden Nose, The Corpse with the Emerald Thumb,* and *The Corpse with the Platinum Hair.* Born, raised, and educated in Wales, Cathy enjoyed a successful career in marketing and training across Europe, before immigrating to Vancouver, Canada, where she taught on MBA and undergraduate marketing programs at various universities. Her eclectic tastes in art, music, food, and drink have been developed during her decades of extensive travel, which she continues whenever possible. Now a full-time author, Cathy's short stories have appeared in multiple anthologies, as well as on BBC Radio 4. She and her husband are keen gardeners, who enjoy being helped out around their acreage by their green-pawed Labradors. Cathy's website can be found at cathyace.com.